The One I Need

The Rolling Hills Series

Book 2

Chelle Sloan

This is a work of fiction. Names, places, characters, and events are fictitious events in every regard. Any similarities to actual events and persons, living or dead, are coincidental. Any trademarks, service marks, product names, or named features are assumed to be the property of their respective owners and are used only for reference. There is no implied endorsement if any of these terms are used.

Cover Design: Kari March Designs

Cover model: Michael Croft

Cover photographer: Katie Cadwallader Photography

Editing: Kiezha Smith Ferrell, Librum Artis Editorial Services

Proofreading: Michele Ficht

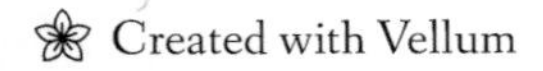

To Georgia

My first author friend. We've come so far since Salvation Society. Thanks for liking me an adequate amount.

Chapter 1
Oliver

My head is spinning and pounding at the same time, and it has nothing to do with the loud music playing at this wedding reception or the obnoxious amount of liquor I've consumed.

Okay, the spinning is because of the booze. But the pounding? That's because my best friend Wes is a fucking idiot. I'm hammered out of my damn mind and even I see that. And I'm seeing three of everything right now.

"It's *your* future that's going to be alone and miserable."

Wes shoots a glare to our friend Simon, who isn't backing down to Wes's insane logic. "But her future is what I'm trying to save!"

"Is she not a part of your future?"

Wes snaps a look to Shane, our friend who usually keeps his mouth shut. Hell, Simon and I both are now staring at the normally broody one of the bunch, surprised he chimed in.

"What did you say?" Wes asks.

Shane leans his elbows on the table. "I said, before this fight, was Betsy not part of *your* future?"

"Of course she was."

"Then why can't you be part of hers?"

Damn...I can actually feel my brain explode with the truth bomb Shane just dropped.

I look over to Wes, who still hasn't said anything.

Is he really this dense? He has to be. He has this amazing woman who came into his life when he least expected it, fell in love with him, loves his kids like they are her own, and yet because he can't get out of his own way, he's going to fuck everything up.

Does he not realize people would kill for that kind of partner? That it's what some of us look for our entire lives? That some of us—*me*—are starting to think that it's just not in the cards? Is he really going to throw that away?

"She loves you, Wes," I say. I think I interrupted him, but I don't give a shit. "She loves the kids. She's the kind of woman you hope to fall in love with one day. I don't know what's going on in your head but don't push that away. Some of us look for this kind of love our entire lives. You have it. And now look at it."

I nod to the dance floor where Betsy is dancing with one of Wes's former Nashville Fury teammates. It's a slower song—a wedding staple, if you ask me. Everyone who's here with a date is on the dance floor.

Which means that's my cue for another trip to the bar.

I love weddings. I'm the best wedding date there is if I do say so myself. I like to dance and have fun. I will lead any conga line. Need a dancing partner for the great-grandmother? I'm your guy. Need someone to hype the newlyweds up? I'm here for it.

And when it comes to catching the garters? No one is better than me. Most guys run away from it. Not me. I'll grab that thing every fucking time and celebrate like I just caught a foul ball at a Tennessee Arrows game.

The old wives' tale is that when you catch it, you're next. Bullshit. It's all bullshit. I've caught seventeen of them. Yet here I am, still alone.

"Jack and Coke."

I don't know why I needed to say it. I've been to the bar so many times tonight this man knows my drink by now. He sets it in front of me, and I turn around to watch the couples on the dance floor.

I should be out there. I thought Shannon, the girl I was seeing as of today, was going to turn into something special. Yes, it was stupid to say what I said. And I apologized. Apparently she's never said or done anything stupid before, like proposing marriage during sex.

Whatever. That just means she wasn't the one. The woman who I'm supposed to be with is out there somewhere. One day I'll find her.

Hopefully. Maybe. Possibly.

"Jack and Coke. Make it a double."

I look to my left and nearly lose my footing. And not because of the six Jack and Cokes I've had tonight. It's because of the woman standing next to me.

She's that damn gorgeous.

Her fiery red hair is sleek and smooth, running down past her shoulders. The gold dress she's wearing is fitted and catching every one of her mouthwatering curves. And a woman who drinks Jack and Coke? Now that's my type.

And because I'm so drunk, I'm seeing two of her.

Double the pleasure, double the fun.

"Do you want to dance?"

She turns to look at me, and even in my drunkenness I can tell she doesn't know if I was talking to her.

"Excuse me?"

I nod over to the dance floor. "I asked if you'd like to dance?"

"Do you always ask strangers to dance?"

"Only the beautiful ones."

She rolls her eyes. "Now that's a line if I've ever heard one."

I shake my head. "Not a line."

"Really?"

"Really."

"Well, sorry," she says as she takes her drink from the bartender. "I don't dance."

"What do you mean you don't dance? Who doesn't dance?"

"Me," she says before taking a sip. "Sorry to ruin your night."

She turns back to the bar, but I don't let that stop me. I'm persistent, if nothing else. It's part of my charm. At least I like to think so.

"I'm Oliver."

I extend my hand to her, because that's what drunk me feels like is the right thing to do at the moment. For a second I think she's just going to walk away. She looks down at my hand and then back up to me. I'm about to pull it back and crack a joke to make it a little less awkward when her hand meets mine. I don't know if it's the booze or what, but I swear I think I was just electrocuted.

"Nice to meet you Oliver. I'm Izzy. How about another drink?"

Chapter 2
Izzy

WHAT THE HELL AM I DOING?

Why am I asking this guy if he wants a drink? Why am I still holding onto his hand? None of this makes sense.

Then again, I didn't expect a tall, blond, god-like man with a voice that makes me tremble to be standing in front of me.

I had one rule for myself when I agreed to come to this wedding tonight—get in and get out as fast as possible. It's nothing against the bride or groom. I love Whitley and Jake. They've been nothing but nice to me in the three or so years that I've known them. It's just on general principle; I'm against weddings in all forms.

I had a plan. Show up. Say hello. Get just tipsy enough to tolerate the festivities but not drunk enough where I wouldn't be able to drive myself back to my apartment in downtown Nashville. Leave during the first ballad of the night when no one would notice me exiting. Get some greasy fast food and a chocolate shake on the way home so I have snacks for when I watch some early seasons of Forensic Files.

It was going to be the perfect exit. That was until I realized that because of the venue being an old barn in the middle of a field, golf carts are taking guests back and forth to their cars, which are parked at the neighboring hotel. And the carts don't start for another half hour.

I was mad about that. Now? Well, now it doesn't seem so bad. Because if this guy keeps smiling at me with that adorable smirk, I'm not leaving for a very long time.

"Love to," he says, letting go of my hand to signal the bartender. "And a round of shots."

I should say no to the shots if I have any wish to drive home tonight, but I can't seem to find the words to protest. It's like every time this man opens his mouth, his voice puts me into a trance. I can tell from his cadence he's a little drunk, but that doesn't hinder the immediate effect his voice has on me. It's why I even responded to him in the first place. It's deeper than I thought, based on his outward appearance. Which I know is a shitty thing to do, to judge a book by its cover and all, but it's human nature. And if you say you don't do it, you're a liar.

His long, honey blond hair is the perfect length to run your hands through while also giving off the vibe that he's a surfer boy. His lean, yet filled frame only adds to that assumption. His hazel eyes seem kind and sincere. And that's based on the fact that this dress practically dares men to look at my cleavage, but not once have his eyes wandered. Which is more than I can say for the single football players I was sitting with earlier.

On the outside, everything about this man screams golden boy. That's why I'm thrown by him. This man did *not* strike me as the kind who would make your pussy clench just by the sound of his voice. But here I am, clenched as fuck.

Maybe that's why I asked him for a drink. Because I could listen to this man talk to me all night long.

I could also listen to him growl into my ear. You know, if he'd be up for that.

"Bride or groom?"

I jump a little, not realizing how much I had drifted off into fantasy land. I guess that's what happens when you let your imagination venture into naughty thoughts about being called a good girl.

"Um, neither?"

He gives me a confused look as the bartender places the round of drinks and shots in front of us. We each hold up our tiny plastic glasses, filled with what I'm assuming is whiskey, and slam them back. The booze stings only for a second, which tells me that I'm more than halfway to drunkville. I wish I would have gotten a hotel tonight. No way am I going to be able to drive now.

"So how do you not know the bride *or* groom?" Oliver asks. "Wait! Are you a wedding crasher? I've always wanted to meet one of you."

"I am." I go along with his question, because why not? He seems fun, and this sure as hell beats sitting at the table with the horny football players. "I'm a venture capitalist from New Hampshire."

"Impressive," he says as he leans against the bar on his elbow. "Though I was hoping you ran an emerging maple syrup conglomerate in Vermont."

"And I was hoping you were a pimp from Oakland."

Our smiles grow as we realize we each played into the bit from one of the best comedies of all time, and then we both burst into laughter. And I'm not just talking about polite chuckles; I'm talking hunched over, might pee myself laughter. The bartender is looking at us like we're crazy, which only makes us laugh harder. I'm about to fall over, so I quickly stumble back to my table, which isn't far from the bar. Oliver follows me and we both plop into the chairs, each of us needing deep breaths to get ourselves under control.

"I don't know the last time I laughed that hard," I admit as I wipe another tear from my cheek. And it's true. I laugh often with my best friend, and boss, Hazel, and her husband Knox. I laugh at the comedians I follow on social media, especially that hot as fuck young guy who has abs I want to lick.

But laughing with a man? This is new. Usually I'm laughing at men due to their audacity.

"Marry me."

My whole body freezes at the sound of those two words. Two words that I've vowed to never hear again. Two words that send me to an immediate state of panic.

I stare at him, because he has to be joking. Right? No one says those words after meeting someone fifteen minutes prior. Yes, that's it. I try not to laugh, because Oliver has such a serious face right now, but I can't hold it in. I feel it starting to bubble in my stomach. Wow, he's really playing into this. His face is completely flat, but his eyes haven't left mine, like he's searching for an answer in them. The more I sit in silence, the more I feel like I'm keeping him waiting for an answer.

This guy is freaking hilarious.

"Izzy? Will you marry me?"

That's it. I can't hold it in any longer. If I had a drink I'd be spitting it out at the ridiculousness of his question.

"You're fucking hilarious!" I slam the table between howls. My other hand wraps around my stomach because it's starting to hurt. Holy shit I haven't laughed like this in a long time. "Marry you? Sure. I bet the officiant from earlier is still here. Maybe Whitley and Jake won't mind that we just take over their reception and have one of our own. And, you know what, how about after this we head upstairs and start trying for the baby?"

My laughter is about to turn into a roar when I realize Oliver isn't laughing. Not even a little bit. He actually looks like I ran over his dog. He'd probably have one of those cute Yorkies.

"Shit, were you serious?" I ask, suddenly sobering up.

He shakes his head and lets out a forced chuckle. "No...of course I wasn't. Totally kidding."

His lips might have just said those words, but I don't think he means them.

"Hey," I say as I reach over for his hand. "I'm sorry I laughed. I just...well, I wasn't expecting that."

He shrugs, giving my hand a squeeze back. "And you shouldn't have." He chuckles under his breath, like he's telling himself a joke. "That might have set a new world record for fastest proposal. And definitely a personal best."

"A personal best? Do you propose often?"

He quickly stands up and holds out his hand for me. "How about another drink?"

I don't call him out for the clear deflection. If I did, I'd be the pot calling the kettle black. No one deflects better than me.

My eyes signal to the two barely touched Jack and Cokes on the table. "We still have drinks."

He shrugs. "And?"

I like his style. "And nothing. Let's go."

~

"Who are they?"

I point to the two elderly ladies on the dance floor, who I decided about an hour ago I want to be when I grow up.

"That's Daisy and Doris Abernathy," Oliver says. He's been giving me a rundown of the wedding attendees since I only know a few people here. Most of the guests are from Oliver's hometown of Rolling Hills, which is where the bride and groom also reside. I've never lived in a small town, so it's fascinating to hear Oliver talk about all these people and their life stories. Especially these two. If I wasn't looking at them right now with my two eyeballs I'd never believe women like this existed.

"They are Rolling Hills royalty and about to celebrate their ninety-ninth birthdays. They go to The Joint, our local bar, every day, and have exactly two beers out of the mason jars that only they can drink out of. They've never been married, have lived together their entire lives, but make sure that everywhere they go, they're the life of the party."

Life of the party indeed. These two baddies are in the middle of the dance floor, walkers and all, grinding on two of the Fury football players. They are giving a whole new meaning to making their knees touch their elbows.

"Fucking legends." I fall back against the seat cushion of one of the patio chairs. About an hour ago, Oliver and I decided it was time for fresh air. That and the bartender cut us off. But that didn't stop us. I stole two bottles of champagne while the bartender was distracted, and Oliver snagged a tray of shots before we made our getaway.

This patio is absolute perfection. It's the ideal setup for people watching—one of my favorite pastimes. The renovated barn where the reception is being held is modern rustic in every way. But one wall is entirely glass, letting guests sit outside, away from the crowd, while still getting to take in the festivities. Or in our case, giving me a perfect view inside while Mr. Popularity tells me about the guests.

"You want to be Daisy and Doris?"

I look over to Oliver, who's seated across from me. His arms are resting on the arms of the chair, an empty bottle of champagne in front of him on the table. His tie is undone, and the top button of his white dress shirt is unbuttoned. Every time I take him in I have to force myself not to lick my lips.

"Hell yeah. Never married? Living their best lives? Sounds fucking awesome."

"You never want to get married?"

Here we go. The marriage talk. This is one of many reasons why I avoid weddings. It never fails that when you're a single person attending a wedding, someone asks you when it's your turn. Or why you don't want to get married. Or if you're going to try and catch the bouquet because you're next.

Fuck that shit.

"I don't," I say strongly.

"Can I ask why?"

"You can," I say as I take a sip of my champagne. "But it can be wrapped up in a few words. Not for me."

"Really?" he says, sitting forward and resting his elbows on his knees. Which is impressive. I know he's drunk, but he's acting very sober. It's like his super power.

"Really," I say. "Really, really. Love isn't real. Marriage is a scam. It was probably invented by men to lock down women or some shit."

"How can you think it's a scam?" he says. "It's sooo beautiful."

Aw, there's the drunkenness.

"You want to get married?" I'm starting to think now with all this wedding talk that his proposal earlier might have been for real.

"Yup," he says with an exaggerated pop at the end. "Married. Kids. The whole shebang."

I hold up my nearly empty bottle. "Well, good luck to you my friend. Make sure to invite me to that one. I promise I won't steal your booze."

"You aren't going to crash it?"

"I mean, I could," I say. "But would that be any fun, crashing a wedding of someone you know?"

"True," he says. "You never answered my question from earlier."

I take a sip and sloppily wipe the remnants away with the back of my hand. "Which question? Because if it's the one about me marrying you, I think you should know your answer by now."

He chuckles under his breath. "Not that one. The question about if you knew the bride or groom?"

"Oh," I say, realizing through the bottles of champagne, and multiple, multiple shots of whiskey, that neither of us have shared much detail about each other. I usually do that by design. Tonight it's just been because our conversation has flowed from the second we met. "Hazel, one of the bridesmaids, is my best friend. She's also my boss. I met Whitley and Jake through her when we moved here from California."

"Ah yes, the billionaire dating app mogul who snagged our favorite local mechanic," Oliver says knowingly.

"That's the one," I say as I stand up. Well, I try. The second my butt leaves the seat, I start stumbling, nearly falling over myself. Somehow, even though Oliver is just as drunk as I am, he stands and catches me. I fall into him, and my hands grip his forearms for balance.

Holy shit... I didn't know you could feel veins in forearms.

I knew Oliver was likely one of those sneaky built types. The guys who never skip the gym but their bodies are discreet about it.

I love it when I'm right.

"Sorry," I say, trying to right myself.

"No need to apologize," he says. We stare at each other for a few seconds. At least, I think it's only a few seconds. I have no concept of time right now. Between Oliver's voice, his closeness, and the cologne I'm now breathing in, I can't think straight. It's probably how I don't realize that I'm slowly starting to sway to the love song that is currently playing.

"I thought you said you didn't like to dance?"

I slide my hands from up his biceps and across his shoulders before my hands are looped around his neck. Oliver follows suit, gently placing his hands at the small of my back.

"No." I shake my head as he starts slowly moving with me to the words of the song. "I said I don't dance. I never said I didn't like to dance."

"Is there a difference?"

If this were any other person, I'd deflect. I'd change the subject for fear of letting one single iota of vulnerability slip out. That's what I do. And it has always served me well. But when I look up at Oliver, for some reason I can't pull that bullshit. His hazel eyes are looking at me with such sincerity I don't think I could actually lie to him.

Or maybe it's the champagne. Either way, my defenses are as down as maybe they've ever been.

"I don't like dancing in front of people," I whisper as I look down, unable to look Oliver in the eye right now. "I hate feeling like everyone in the room is staring at me."

Fuck, I just said that, didn't I? I've never said that out loud before. Not in thirteen years.

I begin to pull away, because I can't bear to look at Oliver right now. Stupid champagne making me all vulnerable and shit. But just as I'm about to step back, Oliver's grip stops me and pulls me closer. His fingers gently touch my chin, lifting it up so I have to look him in the eye.

"It's just me," he says, "just you and me."

We start dancing again, though I can't tell what song is playing. All I know is that I don't know the last time I felt like this. I can't even pinpoint the exact feeling. And it only has a little something to do with the firm expanse of his chest under my chin as we sway to a beat all our own. I haven't felt this good, or free, in a very long time. Between the alcohol, the laughter, the conversation, and, well, Oliver, I don't know what could make this night better.

"Izzy?"

That. Oliver whispering my name in my ear in his perfect baritone is what makes this night better.

"Yeah?"

"Want to get out of here?"

And have Oliver whisper more things into my ear? Preferably while we're naked? Hell yes. Perfect night.

"Your place or mine?"

His eyes go from kind to heated in an instant.

Oh, I like where this is going...

"I have a room at the hotel."

I tip up my chin just enough to place a gentle kiss on his chin, his stubble already giving me fantastically dirty fantasies. "Then what are we waiting for?"

Chapter 3
Oliver

I CONSIDER MYSELF A PATIENT GUY. HELL, I TEACH FIRST graders. I'm the king of patience.

But if this goddamn door doesn't open in the next thirty seconds I'm going to lose my shit.

I insert the card into the door again, begging the green light to flash so I can open the door and do everything that my body is screaming at me to do with, and to, Izzy. But no...fucking red dots flash every time.

"There a problem?"

Izzy words against my ear send a shot straight to my dick. Fuck, this woman is going to be the death of me. She knows exactly what she's doing. In her heels, Izzy is nearly as tall as me, putting her at the perfect height to nibble and kiss at the curve of my neck while whispering into my ear. The feel of her lips is sending chills down my spine and blocking all function to my brain. Combine that with the alcohol, and I can barely function.

I certainly can't get a key card to work.

"The door won't open."

"Here," she says, stepping around me and taking the card from my hand. "I got this."

"Oh, do you now?"

"It's just a key."

It's cute she thinks two can't play this game. As she goes to insert the card, I press up against her from behind, resting my hands on either side of the door frame. My hips are against her ass, pinning her against the door, leaving no question in her mind how hard I am right now. She starts grinding into me as her neck falls back against my shoulder. I look down at her and let out a groan. I can't help it. This woman is every fantasy every man has ever had.

I release one of my hands from the door frame and start tracing my fingers up her arm. She lets out a soft moan as my finger drops slightly to trace over her peaked nipple. The gold dress isn't hiding anything, which is fucking hot as hell. Her breathing is heavy as I continue my journey across her chest, across her collar bone, before gently placing my hand around her neck.

"You sure about that? Seems like you're having a little trouble concentrating."

I grab on to her a little tighter as my lips make my way to her neck. From the second I saw her at that bar, I wondered if she tasted as good as she looked. So far it's better than I imagined. And I'm just getting started.

"Open the door," I say in a low tone. "Unless you want the other guests to see how I'm about to eat your pussy."

I don't look to see if she has any success opening the door. I'm too focused on the curve of her neck and how I can't wait to kiss every inch of her creamy skin. It's why I don't see anyone walk behind me.

"Excuse me! That's my room!"

We both jump back as we hear the voice of the man to our

left. He's wearing a suit and tie, but I don't remember him from the wedding. And I think I would have, considering he's old enough to be my father but has a girl on his arm that looks barely old enough to drink.

"I'm sorry," I say, moving Izzy and I away from the door. *Oh! That's why the card wasn't working!*

"Just move," the asshole says as he pushes past us. "And I don't want you two keeping us up tonight."

"Don't worry. We will," Izzy says. "You'll know because my screams will be real, unlike hers."

The man shoots daggers at Izzy before pushing into his room, pulling the girl inside with him. Somehow, Izzy and I both hold in our laughter until the door slams shut.

"You had the wrong room!" she yells, playfully smacking me on the chest.

"Obviously," I say, pulling her back into me. "I was a bit distracted by a certain someone."

Her hands slide up and around my neck, her fingernails working the nape of my neck. "I'm good at distracting."

"Yes, you are."

"Want to know what else I'm good at?"

"Of course."

She doesn't say anything, instead letting her hand travel down the front of me until she's stroking my cock through my pants. "I'd rather show you."

"Funny. I was thinking the same thing."

Our eyes are locked on each other. Neither of us move. There has been tension and fire building between us all night. But right now? It's about to fucking explode.

"Open the door, Izzy. Now."

I see her swallow, but she does as I ask. She inserts the key card into the scanner and the door immediately opens.

Finally.

I pull her into the room and slam the door shut. Before either of us can get our bearings, I'm lifting her up and pinning her against the door. I hear her dress rip as she wraps both legs around my waist. Fuck, I didn't realize that sound was so fucking hot. Then again, everything about this woman is scorching, so why would that be any different?

Our mouths collide in a frenzy of lips and tongues. Somehow, we resisted kissing until now. I wanted to do it in the elevator. I wanted to in the hall when I was teasing the hell out of her. If I'm honest, I wanted to kiss her the second I laid eyes on her. But I resisted, knowing that as soon as I started, I wouldn't be able to stop.

And I was right. I'm going to kiss this woman, and every part of her, all damn night.

"Oliver." My name comes out of her mouth in a breathy moan as I pull down the front of her dress. I knew she couldn't have been wearing a bra; the back of her dress was so low it should have been illegal, but the sight of her gorgeous tits spilling out is enough to make me come on demand.

"Fuck," I growl before I bring one of her breasts to my mouth, sucking it like it's going to keep me alive. Her hands are now clawing at my back, and I know if I didn't have my jacket and shirt on right now she'd be leaving marks.

She will. I'll make sure of that.

I keep my mouth on her as I walk us over to the bed. Thankfully this room isn't big, so it only takes me a few steps to get there. I lower Izzy down on her back, and as much as I want to follow and continue exploring every inch of her, I decide to stand up and take this in for a second.

Her dress is a torn mess. There's a hint of light coming from the window, allowing me to see her red hair in stark contrast to the white linens. I keep my eyes fixed on her as I kick off my shoes and undo the rest of my tie, tossing it to the side. I take off my jacket and start to undo the buttons of my shirt when I see her prop herself onto her elbows.

"I was going to do that," she says.

I undo the last button, but don't take it off. "Were you now?"

She nods as she sits up, her legs now off the bed. "I was. I had lots of things planned."

"Oh really," I say, walking between her legs so she has no choice but to spread them. "Care to tell me about any of them?"

She shakes her head, but not before looking at my dick and licking her lips. "I'd rather show you."

Fuck...I can picture her mouth around me. Her pretty manicured nails stroking me in tandem with her beautiful mouth. And as much as I want that—and believe me, I do—I want something more. Because I have a feeling this is going to be my only night with this woman, and I'm not leaving with any damn regrets.

"Interesting that you say that," I say, tipping her chin back up to look at me. "I had some ideas too."

"Care to tell me?"

I lean down, pressing the softest kiss I can on her lips before gently backing away. "I'm going to eat your pussy until you can't see straight. I'm going to make you forget your name. But that's *after* I fuck you."

I crash our lips together, sucking any response she had out of her mouth. That's the final match needed for the embers between us to go up in flames.

We're all lips and hands as we frantically work to strip each other. I find the zipper of her dress and yank it down as she works the shirt off my shoulders. I stand her up, just enough so I can push the dress to the floor. It's then I realize she isn't wearing any panties either.

Fuck, this woman...

"Turn around."

She does as I ask, and she even goes as far as to read my mind, crawling into bed on all fours. I can't take my eyes off her as I grab a condom out of my wallet before kicking my pants to the side. I just about have the condom rolled on when she looks over her shoulder, giving me a seductive look that I'll remember for the rest of my life.

"What's taking you so long?"

If my cock wasn't rock hard before, those words do the trick. It takes me two steps to get to the bed, where I immediately drape myself over her back, letting my lips come just inches from her ear.

"Remember when you told those neighbors you were going to keep them up tonight?"

She nods, a slight purr coming from her mouth.

"Make sure you let them know how good I'm fucking you."

I sit back up on my knees and position myself as I slam into her. This isn't like me. Usually I'm the king of foreplay. My rule is I don't come until she does twice. And she will, eventually.

But I need to fuck this woman more than I need to breathe.

I slide right in as I grip her hips, pounding into her like we're on a timer. Which we are. I know this is a one-night thing. I might not have ever had a one-night stand before, but I know this is one. This is the culmination of the right people, at the right time, doing exactly what feels right.

And holy shit does this feel right.

I give her ass a smack, which sends her back into an arch as she screams my name. Her hair drapes across her back, begging me to take it in my hands. I crawl my fingers up her spine, which makes her already tight pussy clench around my dick before I wrap her red locks around my hand, giving it a pull. Fuck, I want to do so many things to this woman. But not yet.

"This is going to be fast," I growl in her ear. "Because I want your thighs around my ears and your hands tangled in my hair. But I can't do that until you come for me."

"Yes, please," she moans.

I release her hair but let my hand wrap around her front, playing with her clit as I continue to thrust into her. That does the trick, as I feel her start to throb around me.

"Let go, Izzy. Fucking let go."

She screams and falls into the pillow as I feel her orgasm clench around me. The feeling sends me right over the edge. I slowly work us both down from our orgasms as I collapse on top of her.

Holy...shit...

"I think you killed me," she mumbles into the pillow.

I laugh and give her a quick kiss on her cheek before I roll off her and head to the bathroom to dispose of the condom.

That was fucking intense...

I've always been a relationship guy. Yes, I love sex. And I mean I fucking *love* sex. But I always thought it was better with a person you loved.

I was very...very...wrong.

I head back to the bed and see that Izzy hasn't moved. Her cheeks are as red as her hair, which looks thoroughly fucked.

"You okay?" I ask as I slip back into bed.

She shakes her head. "I can't move."

"That's too bad," I say, gently rolling her over to her back.

She seems dazed, and a bit confused, as I take a pillow and put it under her ass. "What are you doing?"

I press a soft kiss on the inside of her thigh before I position myself exactly where I've wanted to be all night.

"I told you I wanted your thighs as earmuffs. So lay back, Red. It's going to be a long night."

Chapter 4
Izzy

THERE IS NOT A SINGLE PART OF MY BODY THAT ISN'T IN some sort of pain.

I haven't even opened my eyes, but I know they already hurt. I woke up because my head is pounding from the amount of alcohol I drank last night.

The other parts of me? Well, I wouldn't call that pain. That's better classified under the sore category. A sore I will take every day of the week and twice on Sunday.

I roll onto my stomach and stretch as much as my body will let me. I feel myself smiling as I remember when I was in this exact position last night. Oliver was on top of me, his weight feeling so good as he worked me into one of my *many* orgasms of the night. Or was that one technically this morning? I'm honestly not sure. After the third orgasm I lost all sense of time. Hell, at one point I forgot my name, address, and what city I was in.

Just as I start to open my eyes, I feel his fingers tracing circles on the small of my back, sending a thousand shivers up my spine.

"Don't even think about it," I say into my pillow.

"Think about what?"

"You know exactly what I'm talking about." I roll over so I'm now facing him. I didn't think he could be any more gorgeous than he was last night. But here he is, looking all morning sexy and shit. His hair, which is lighter with the sun coming in from the window, is a mess. His scruff is perfect. And his already deep voice is an octave lower. I don't think I have another round in me, but I don't know if I'm going to be able to resist if he starts in.

"You mean this?" He rolls me back over and starts slowly kissing me. Methodically. Like he's trying to savor every moment.

Shit, this might be more potent than last night. And that's saying something.

Intense. Insane. Life changing. Those are the first things that come to mind when last night plays over in my mind. I knew Oliver was going to be fun, but I didn't think he was going to potentially ruin me for other men.

But this kiss? This is soft. Sweet. So sweet he's making me wonder if he's the same man who said the most filthy things I've ever heard just hours ago.

"Something like that," I say as he pulls back, resting his head on his elbow. His other hand is gently tracing lines on my body that feel too good.

"Well, don't worry. As much as I want to—and believe me, I really, really, want to—I'm afraid the night has caught up to me."

"Oh thank God," I say in relief.

He laughs. That sexy, deep laugh of his. "I don't think I've ever laughed at a woman relieved to not have sex with me."

"In my defense, it's not that I *don't* want to have sex with you. It's just I don't know if I can."

"I'll take that as a compliment."

"You should. And I don't give those out lightly."

He snuggles into my side, holding me even tighter. "I'm flattered."

I chuckle as I look down at Oliver, who looks so damn relaxed right now. His fingers are still gently caressing me, and his face is now resting on my stomach. I don't even think about it as I start lightly combing my fingers through his hair.

This is bad. This is so fucking bad.

I don't do mornings like this. I don't do mornings at all. If I sleep with a guy, I make sure I'm gone, or that he's gone, before the sun comes up. There's no morning cuddles or pillow talk. There's no breakfast in bed or the awkward conversation about calling each other again.

That's why this is so fucking bad. 'Cause not only am I not itching to get out of here, but I'm more relaxed than I've been in years. Maybe it's because I've been fucked better than I ever have in my life. Maybe it's because this bedding is some of the softest I've ever slept on.

Or maybe it's the man who's now holding on to me like I'm his favorite stuffed animal.

I knew I was attracted to him last night. I became more so after the time we spent together. Even through the booze I remember that. But this version of Oliver? The sweet and gentle one? He might be the most dangerous.

And one I need to stay far away from.

"Can I see you again?"

I almost don't hear him, his words coming out so faint. But I know exactly what he said. And it's the worst thing he could have asked.

Because Oliver is a relationship kind of guy. And I am most definitely not that kind of girl.

I knew from the moment we started talking that Oliver

wasn't the kind of guy who did hookups. That theory was confirmed when we had our discussions about marriage. It did throw me for a bit when he asked me back to his room. The porn-star level sex also raised a few doubts. But now in the morning light it's confirmed, Oliver is a one-woman kind of man. And I'm a no-man kind of woman.

Oliver sits up and looks down at me, his eyes so caring and wishful. I hate that I'm about to take that spark of hope away. But I have to be up front with him. I have many flaws, but leading someone on is not one of them. If anything I'm too honest. But I think it's better to be honest than to lie or string along. That's how people get hurt.

"Oliver," I say as I sit up, making sure my front is covered with the sheet. Yes, I know he's seen, and licked, every inch of me, but I need this extra layer of armor. "Last night was great."

"Here it comes," he says as he dramatically falls back onto the bed, his forearm covering his eyes.

His thick...veiny...forearm.

Focus Elizabeth. Don't let the arm porn distract you.

"If you knew it was coming, then why did you ask?"

He brings his arm down and looks up at me. "I had to shoot my shot."

"I appreciate that," I say. "But I don't lead on, especially with guys I like."

He pops back up to his elbow with the energy of a golden retriever who just got told he was getting a treat. "So you're saying you like me?"

"Easy there, skippy. Yes, I like you. And it's because I like you that I can't see you again."

He raises an eyebrow. "That's a new way of saying 'it's not you, it's me.'"

"But it is," I continue. "I could see you again. Maybe sober this time. I'm sure we'd have a lovely time, laugh as much as we did last night, and end it with another round of phenomenal sex."

"I'm failing to see a problem in what you just said."

I let out a sigh. "The problem is that I can never give you what you want."

"How do you know what I want?"

I tilt my head. Is he really going to make me say it? "You're a relationship guy Oliver."

"Says who?"

Really? He's going to continue this game? "Oliver...You asked me to marry you last night. You said that marriage was your end game. You cuddle. You're a relationship guy if I ever saw one."

He lets out a defeated sigh. "And I'm guessing as you say all of this, and since you called marriage a scam, that you aren't looking for one?"

I shake my head. "I'm not built for the long term. I'm sorry."

He nods his head as he reaches for my hand. I'm so shocked by the motion, I don't fight him. Instead I take in the feel of our fingers laced together, knowing this will likely be the last time I feel this. "Thank you for being honest."

"You're welcome. And I'm sorry. I am."

He shakes his head. "Don't be. Never apologize for who you are."

I push down the emotions that are trying to bubble to the surface. This isn't the first time I've had this conversation. It's never easy. Hell, I had one guy who cried. Like full on ugly tears.

But with Oliver? I don't know, but I almost wish I didn't have to have this conversation. I haven't had a serious relationship since I was eighteen years old. And that's by design. If you're not in a relationship, you can't get hurt. No one else can have a say in your happiness. No one can control you.

And for the past sixteen years, that has served me just fine. But, if I ever were looking for a relationship, Oliver wouldn't be a bad option. A man who's sweet and caring in the streets but a freak in the sheets? That wouldn't be bad at all...

But I'm not looking for a relationship. Not now. Not in a month. Not in a year. So as much as I'll miss not having a second turn with this man, it's the price I'm willing to pay.

I hear a buzzing coming from somewhere. At first it's faint, but as it continues, I feel like it's getting louder and louder.

"I think that's one of our phones," I say.

"Probably mine," he says.

He rolls out of bed, naked in all his glory. I never had a chance to really look at his ass, but I can't help staring as he walks over to where his pants ended up last night. Fuck, that's a nice ass. Too bad he's not a friends-with-benefits kinda guy. We really could have had some fun.

Especially if he fucks like that without booze.

"Shit, I have to go," he says, bending over and picking up his pants.

"Everything okay?"

"Yeah," he says as he begins to get dressed. "I'm being summoned for a grand gesture."

"A grand gesture?"

"Yup," he says, walking over to grab his shirt, which was nowhere near his pants. "My friend Wes really fucked things over with his girl, Betsy, a week ago. I'm guessing he's pulled his head out of his ass and needs all hands on deck."

Wow, I didn't realize this was a common thing. I had heard about grand gestures when it came to relationships, and up until a few years ago, I thought they were just something written about in movies and books.

Then I witnessed one when Knox stepped up for Hazel. Was I moved by it? Of course. I might have a black heart, but I do know that love can exist for others. But I thought Knox's grand gesture was just something that happened in the moment. That it wasn't a common thing.

Apparently I was wrong.

Knowing that it's time to make my exit, I scooch to the side of the bed, swinging my legs over the side.

"Where are you going?"

I look over to Oliver, who's walking over to me as he buttons his shirt. "If you're going, I'll go too."

"No," he says, standing in front of me. "You don't have to rush out."

"I know, but I can."

I try to stand but Oliver blocks me. "Stay. Take a shower. Order room service. If I can't ever take you on a proper date, let me do this for you."

I swallow the lump that is suddenly in my throat. Damn, this man is really pushing my beliefs...

"Thank you," I say.

He leans in and softly kisses my cheek. "No, Izzy. Thank you. Maybe I'll see you around someday."

Oliver doesn't say anything as he finishes getting dressed. He gives me a small wave as he walks out the door.

And out of my life.

Chapter 5
Oliver

I STEP INTO THE ELEVATOR, PRESS THE BUTTON FOR THE first floor, and fall against the wall. I know it sounds corny, but with every floor we go down, my spirits go right with it.

I knew last night was going to be a one-time thing. I knew it when I asked her to come to my room, and I knew it when I asked to see her again this morning. I knew the answer before it even came out of my mouth. Yet, I still asked.

Part of me had to know. I had to hear the words from her mouth, because if I didn't, I'd spend hours and days wondering if she would have said yes if I had only asked.

Well, now I know. And yes, I might not have that regret, but that doesn't make me feel any better in the present.

The elevator dings and the door slowly opens to the lobby. I'm not even one foot out the door before I see Shane, who suddenly has his hands in my shirt and is dragging me down the hall.

"What the fuck, man?"

I stumble as he is now in an all-out sprint, still holding on to me.

"Where the fuck have you been?"

"In my room," I say, wondering why he's so mad. "I came as soon as I got your message."

He lets go, but my feet don't stop, causing me to stumble a bit as I get my bearings. "We've been trying to get a hold of you all morning. Why weren't you picking up your phone?"

"I did. I came down as soon as I heard it."

"Check again. You'll see about thirty missed calls and fifty unread texts."

I do as he says, and yup, he's right. Hell, were we that in our own world that I didn't hear any of these through the morning?

"Sorry, man," I say. "What do you need me to do?"

He leans in and smells me. "I really need you to take a shower so you don't smell like booze and sex. But we don't have time for that."

I tilt my head down to try and take a whiff. Yup. I stink. I also can still smell her perfume on me, so I choose to focus on that instead.

"Sorry. What do you want me to do?"

"Here," he says, shoving a piece of poster board into my hands. "Just hold this and don't move until Betsy comes by."

I look down at the poster board to see an arrow pointing to my right. I look that way and see the automatic door, which is opening and closing as guests file out. Just outside the door, holding another sign, is Shane.

Oh my gosh, are we holding signs like in *Love Actually,* except instead of words it's arrows pointing to where Wes is waiting for Betsy? How damn romantic. I hold back a tear, so proud of Wes for coming up with this on his own. Usually this is something he'd call me for. I'm the romantic of the group. Back in high school, I'm the one my friends turned to when they needed to buy a thoughtful gift. When we were older, I was the one Wes called when he proposed to his now ex-wife.

I'm still pissed I wasted an epic proposal on her gold-digging ass.

But Wes did this all on his own. Then again, he could have called me, based on the dozens of mixed texts and calls. Normally I'd feel bad about that. But knowing who I was with, and what I was likely doing when I missed those calls, I don't feel bad at all.

My smile turns sour real quick, knowing that I'm never going to see Izzy again. I mean, it's possible I could. Rolling Hills isn't far from where she lives in Nashville, and she does have friends who either live, or work, in Rolling Hills. I don't think it's out of the realm of possibility that I'll see her again. But last night's interaction was a one-time-only performance.

And what a performance it was.

I know I can be intense when the lights go out. And for some, it's not their cup of tea. Actually, for most it's not, or so I've been told by my *many* ex-girlfriends. But somehow I had a feeling with Izzy I could be exactly the man I am. And for every minute I spent with her, I let that man take over.

It was fucking glorious.

The feel of her skin as I kissed every inch of her. The way her back arched when I pulled her hair. The sound of her ass being smacked echoing the room. Fuck, it's enough to make me march back upstairs, lock the door, and make her forget everything she said to me.

But I know that can't happen. For starters, I know when no means no. And second, I know that if I had her again, if she would have said yes to seeing me again, that she'd only seep further into my veins. Right now, I think I can detox. But after another hit? I know I'd be a goner.

Fuck, why does this happen to me? Only I can meet a woman who laughs at my jokes, drinks Jack Daniels like water, is fucking sexy as hell, and lets me be the real me, only for her to end things before they can begin.

I thought before the wedding that it was never going to be my turn. After last night, I'm really starting to believe it.

"Oliver? Are you okay?"

I shake my head as I hear Betsy's voice. Shit, I didn't even see her come toward me. I also forgot for a second what I was doing here. Oh yeah, helping my best friend get his girl back because they're in love. Blah...

"You're lucky I like you."

"Okay..."

Shit, I shouldn't be talking to Betsy like this. She's great. Wes is great. I can't be fucking up their reunion just because I'm in a piss-ass mood.

I nod toward the door, seeing out of the corner of my eye that Shane is ready with his sign. Betsy follows my eyes, but does as I signal for her to do. I follow behind her, curious myself as to what's going on. I stop as she talks to Shane for a second before continuing on to our friend Amelia, who has the next sign.

"Wes think of all this?" I ask Shane.

"Mostly," he says. Amelia gives a smile and nod to Betsy, who turns left out of our viewing. The two of us start walking toward Amelia, wanting to see what happens next.

"Look who's alive," Amelia says. "We thought we lost you."

"I'm here."

Neither of us say anything as we watch Betsy walk toward Simon, who drops his arrow, only to hold up another sign.

Just so you know, we're Team Betsy

We chuckle under our breaths, not wanting Betsy to realize we're spying as Simon steps out of the way so she can walk toward Wes. Her Jeep is covered in streamers and balloons. It's reminiscent of what we did for Wes a few months ago when his divorce was finalized. I can tell that Betsy's laughing, which is a good sign. Because as much as I don't believe in soul mates right at this moment, I know those two are meant to be together.

"Well, look who showed up," Simon says as he joins our group. "Where were you this morning?"

"Don't worry about it," I say gruffly.

"Excuse me?" Shane says. "Since when have you ever been the type to not tell us every single detail of every part of your day? Hell, you send a message in the group text when you find a pair of socks you like."

I shrug. "I don't feel like talking about it."

"Bullshit," Simon says. "Something is up, and I'd rather you not let it be pent up for weeks and then you have diarrhea of the mouth. Our work here is done. Let's go back to Rolling Hills and meet at Mona's. I need some waffles in my life."

"I'm out," I say. As much as waffles sound delicious, I can't be around these guys right now. They'll know something is up because I'm a shit liar who doesn't hold back a detail of his life. And right now, I can't talk about this. Though I might get some waffles on the way home and eat them in privacy while I watch *Top Gun* for the five-hundredth time.

"You're out? No, you're not." Simon looks over to Shane and Amelia for help. "Tell him he's not out."

Neither of them say anything, but I don't think telling me to go get waffles is on the top of their priority list. They're looking at each other, but they aren't. It's weird. He's looking down, and she's looking at him, but as soon as he looks up, her eyes shoot to the sky. Again, weird. They're acting like they just saw each other naked. Which obviously didn't happen. Amelia is the mother of our group. She's the one to tell us when we're being idiots, but also comes in from time to time to help us pull off our shenanigans. None of us have ever looked at Amelia in "that" way. So I have no idea what this whole awkward thing is about.

"Sorry, I'm out too," Amelia says. "I need to get home and make sure the kids haven't burned down the house. Plus, I have a shift tonight at the hospital."

"Fine. Play the kid card. Shane? You in?"

He looks at Amelia one more time, who quickly looks away. Okay, I might be depressed and slightly hungover, but this shit is *weird.*

"Nah, I'm good."

"Fuck all of you," Simon says, throwing his arms in the air. "Fine. I'll go to Mona's by myself. And I'm going to take a picture of the waffles and send them all to you and make you jealous."

Simon stomps back toward the hotel, which is why I look that way and see Izzy walking out of the door. She took a T-shirt and a pair of shorts from my luggage, and her red hair is now piled on her head. I try to hold in a laugh as she carefully checks her surroundings, seemingly trying not to be spotted by someone she knows.

She looks over and catches my eye. Fuck. Did I forget in the hour we were apart how beautiful she is? Or is it just seeing her now like this, wearing my clothes, making her even more sexy?

She gives me a soft smile, which hits me straight in the heart. I return the gesture, only for her to give me a small wave before she walks away.

"Who's that?"

I look over to Shane, who's now next to me. I'm guessing Amelia also left, since she's nowhere to be seen.

"My future wife."

I hear him chuckle as he slaps me on the shoulder before he walks away. He's probably thinking this is just another one of my dramatic renditions of another failed relationship. Or since it was just a wedding, an attempt at one. And most of the time, he'd be right.

But not now. Only I know it's the truth.

She's the one who got away.

Chapter 6
Izzy

"Monday you have the morning call with the London office. Tuesday you're packed. You have meetings and calls all day starting at ten..."

I know this Friday huddle with my assistant, Jules, is important. She likes having my calendar set down to the minute and wants to make sure I'm aware of my week coming up so if she needs to move anything around, we have time to do it. I love that about her.

Except right now. Right now I hate it. All I want to do is go home, kick off these heels, take off my bra, and hide from the world for the next forty-eight hours. I want to eat junk food, watch my favorite reality show—that has piping hot scandal right now—and just not speak to anyone.

Maybe then my mood will get better.

Oh, who am I kidding? A few days isn't going to magically fix me.

It's been a week since the wedding. Well, six days, but who's keeping track? Definitely not me. Because I don't do shit like count the days since I last had sex or the last time I genuinely smiled.

And I've tried everything to snap out of this funk. I went to the gym and tried to sweat it out. I nearly broke the spin bike from how hard I was pedaling. I tried to get drunk, figuring I could cure my blues with some sort of fucked-up hair-of-the-dog mentality. I figured liquor got me into this situation, maybe it could get me out. That only gave me a hangover and a worse mood than I had already been in.

Everything I've tried has been for nothing. Stupid Oliver and his stupid smile and his stupid penis. This is all his fault. I think somewhere in between the orgasms and the dirty talk, Oliver put a spell on me. That's the only thing that makes sense.

"Izzy? Do you have any questions?"

I shake my head, which Jules takes as a signal that I don't have any questions, when in fact, I didn't hear a damn word she said.

"Okay, then, I'm going to take off. See you Monday, bright and early."

Bright and early? I want to ask her what that means, but that would signal I wasn't paying attention, and she doesn't need to know that. I flip open our calendar to see that bright and early means *five in the morning* for a call with the London office.

Super...

"Just saw the morning meeting on Monday?"

I look up to see Hazel leaning against the door to my office. "Why do you insist on meeting so early? And why do I need to be on that call? And again, who schedules a call that early?"

She laughs as she takes a seat across from me. "Because we are less than a year from the international launch, and my head of communications needs to be on calls."

"I'd do better at communicating if it was after eight. Or if you just transferred me to London like I've asked a thousand times. Either would be fine."

Hazel smiles, knowing I'm just being difficult. Except the transfer thing. This isn't the first time I've brought that up. "I'll note that for next time."

This is the best part of working for your best friend. No one else would put up with my sarcasm—or my brutal honesty that sometimes comes out quite snarky. But Hazel just rolls with it. Sometimes she encourages it. It's what makes us a good team—I'm the one who will call people out and do what needs to be done for our message and app to work, and she shakes the hands and kisses the babies.

It's also why Left for Love is the most successful dating app in the country. And about to be the most successful in the world.

"Any plans for the weekend?"

"Just a hot date with my couch and my UberEats account."

"Oh," Hazel says. "I was hoping you were going to take the weekend to remove the thorn that's been in your ass all week."

Look at my best friend throwing my signature snark back at me. Good for her. "I don't have a thorn in my ass."

"Could have fooled me. Actually, no. You didn't fool me. You might have been able to convince everyone in the office that you've been fine all week, but I know you too well. So, are you going to finally tell me, or are we going to both pretend something isn't the matter?"

And this is the bad part of working for your best friend. "I'd like to."

"Sorry. Can't do that," she says, kicking off her heels and propping her feet up on my desk. "You've been off since the wedding."

"I told you I didn't want to go."

"I know you did. So when I didn't see you after a certain time of the night, I figured you pulled your classic Irish goodbye and took off. But then I come to find out that not only did you stay, but that you left with a man. And then didn't leave until the next morning, wearing some man's clothes."

I feel my jaw dropping and my eyes popping. How does she know this? I didn't see anyone we knew when I left the next day. Yes, I knew I probably drew attention to myself when I left in oversized gym clothes, wearing my heels, but I thought I was in the clear.

Apparently not.

"Face it, Izzy. You're busted, so you might as well come clean."

I let out a sigh, knowing I can't get away from this conversation. There have been many times over the years where the tables have been turned and I've made her have difficult conversations with me. I knew sooner or later it was going to be my turn.

"Fine," I groan. "Yes, I did try to leave the wedding when I told you I was going to. But the carts weren't running yet to take me back to my car. So I came back inside and went to the bar. That's when I met Oliver."

Hazel's feet fall off my desk, and her eyes bulge out of her head. We've now worked together for the better part of a decade, and this is probably the first time I've ever said a man's government name. Usually if I'm talking about a guy he gets the fun nicknames like "Twinkie Dick" or "Douche Canoe."

"Okay...Oliver," she says as she gathers herself.

"He's just a guy I met at the bar," I say, trying to sound convincing. "He was nice. We laughed and got super drunk together."

Her eyebrows shoot up. "And..."

"And what?"

"Don't 'and what' me. Because no way am I going to believe that you just hung out with this guy and said goodbye at the end of the night."

"What if I did?"

"Then I'd ask who you were, what you did with Izzy, and when are you returning her to planet Earth?"

I laugh under my breath. "Fine. We went back to his room."

This makes her smile. "And?"

Normally I don't mind gloating about my sexcapades with Hazel. And I've had many over the years. Some of them she's accused me of making up because of how wild they've been. But this one I want to keep for myself. I'm also choosing not to read into that at this time.

"And we had a great night."

"That's it?"

I nod. "Yeah. That's it."

Hazel blinks a few times, not expecting that answer from me. I can't even be mad since I don't know who I am right now.

Yup, he was a wizard.

"Okay," Hazel says, clearly trying to think in the moment of what to say to me next. "Sorry, Iz, I'm a bit thrown. Usually I buckle in for fifteen minutes of intimate details of his tongue ability."

I laugh. "I know. And for the record, ten out of ten."

"That's a little better," she says. "Okay. So we have Oliver, who gets a real name, with a ten out of ten tongue that has made you a raging bitch this week. Am I right so far?"

"Yeah. Though I don't think I was a raging bitch. Maybe grumpy twat."

"Same thing," she says. "So, since this is brand new territory, I'm going to ask you a question that I've never asked, and you can't get mad at me. Deal?"

"Fine," I say with a sigh.

"Are you going to see him again?"

"Ha!" I laugh out loud. "This might be bizarro world, but let's not get crazy here."

Hazel's face goes from hopeful to sad in an instant. "I had to ask. In all the time we've worked together, you've never, not once, used a man's real name. Not before a date, and definitely not after. You didn't spill explicit details of sex positions you were put in that I later had to Google with an incognito window. Sorry for thinking that maybe this would be the guy who would finally make you take a chance at love?"

Hazel's always wanted me to be happy. And when we were both single, we were content living out our boss bitch dreams. Then she met Knox, fake dated him, real dated him, and fell in love. Now she's insistent that if I just took a risk like she did, that I'd find love too.

She's hilarious.

"Sorry to disappoint you," I say. "Yes, Oliver is a good guy, and we had a great night together. But we want different things, and I don't want to lead him on."

"Wait," she says. "So he wants to see you again, but you put a stop to it?"

"Yup," I say and start to gather my things. "He's a relationship guy, Hazel. I'm not that kind of girl."

"So you've said."

I shoot her a look. "I've said it because it's true. Now, are we done?"

Hazel nods, knowing that I'm done with this conversation. "I'm sorry I pressed."

"You're fine," I say, walking around my desk to give her a hug. "I know you mean well. I appreciate that. And I'm sorry I've been a bitch all week. I'll be fine after the weekend. I just need some time alone to reset."

She nods. "If you want company, just let me know. I'll

come over, and we can have a wine and popcorn night like we used to."

"Thanks, but I'm good. I really just want to be alone."

"I understand."

She puts back on her shoes as I grab my purse and computer bag and we walk out of my office, flicking the lights off before shutting the door. I wait for her to grab her things out of her office, which is right next to mine, before we head to the elevators.

"You know, I got excited when you said his name," Hazel says as she pushes the down button. "I was starting to think you weren't telling me names before because you never actually knew them."

I laugh. "Oh, I've known them. They just never deserved name recognition."

"But Oliver did?"

A smile tries to push through my mood as I think about Oliver. His smile. His voice. His eyes. His mouth. "Yeah, he did."

We step onto the elevator and ride in silence down to the lobby. I think the part that's bummed me out all week is that Oliver is one of the good ones. Women should be lining up at his door. When he finds that person, she is going to be the most loved and sexually satisfied woman to ever exist.

Sometimes—not often, but sometimes—I wish I was built differently. It definitely hasn't happened since we relocated Left for Love from Los Angeles to Nashville. I doubt it would change if Hazel were to grant my wish and send me to London. But every once in a while I wonder what it would be like if I was built differently. If history wasn't what it was.

Then again, if history was different, I wouldn't be here. I wouldn't be working with Hazel. And I definitely wouldn't be the woman I am today.

And I like her. Even if she's a little alone sometimes.

"Izzy?"

I look over to Hazel, whose car is next to mine. "Yeah?"

"You know you'll still be you if you let your guard down a little."

I nod. "I know."

"Maybe someday?"

I laugh. I don't lie often, but when it comes to getting people to move on about my dating life, I'll do it all day long. "Yeah. Maybe someday."

Chapter 7
Oliver

WHEN PEOPLE FIND OUT THAT I TEACH FIRST GRADE, THE first question they ask is how I do it. More specifically, how I have the patience to do what I do. And most of the time I laugh it off. I love my job. I love working with kids. To me, there's no better grade to teach. They're old enough to start really putting together their own ideas, while still having the innocence you only get once in life.

I love each of these kids as if they were my own. I'd jump in front of a moving vehicle for them. But, and I say this with all the love in my heart, fuck these kids. 'Cause they have been on their bullshit this week, and I can't take much more.

"Mr. Price?"

I do my best to suppress a groan. We have five minutes left in the school week, and I just can't take another question. I usually love their curious minds, but not when I can smell forty-eight hours of freedom.

"Yeah, Bailey?"

"I made you something!"

I mentally hit myself for assuming the worst. "Really? Well, let me see."

She nods her head so hard I think her pigtails are going to come loose. "Here!"

She hands me the piece of paper, and like most projects my kids give me, I have no idea what it is. But that doesn't mean I don't love it all the same.

"What do we have here?"

"It's fun socks!" she says. And as I look closely, it *is* in the shape of a pair of socks. Kind of. "I know your favorite candy is Skittles, so these are socks with Skittles on them!"

I now regret everything I thought bad earlier about these kids. I love them so much.

"Thank you, Bailey. This is awesome." I hold out my knuckles for her to bump them. "Maybe this weekend I can find real socks like this."

Her face goes from excited to shocked. "Really?"

"Of course. These look like the best socks ever."

The bell rings, and Bailey gives me a quick hug as she runs out the door. This is my week off pickup duty, which I've never been more thankful for.

I stand up and stretch, which untucks my pink pastel polo shirt from my khaki pants. I don't bother tucking it back in since I'm now alone. Which is exactly how I plan to spend the weekend.

When I get out of a relationship, I'm usually in the dumps for a few days. But I'm normally able to pick myself up quickly, give myself a pep talk that she just wasn't the one and that I'm not going to find love on my couch binging *Game of Thrones*. And yes, I did get dumped the day of the wedding, but that's not why I've been depressed all week.

It's been because I can't get Izzy out of my head.

I know we only spent one night together. I know she made

it abundantly clear that she wasn't looking for anything serious. My head knows this. My heart just hasn't caught up yet.

"So you are alive?"

I turn back toward the door where Wes is standing. "Yes, I'm alive. Why would you ask that?"

He walks into my class and sits in the chair I normally use for story time. "Probably because you haven't talked to me, or Shane, or Simon for that matter, all week. Amelia said you left her on read. So I had to come in here and make sure nothing happened to you."

I want to roll my eyes at his assumption, but I can't. I'd be doing the same thing if it were any of them. "Sorry. It's just been a weird week." I finish cleaning up the toys at my feet before taking on one of the desks near Wes—who's looking at me like he's waiting for me to say more.

"What?"

"You're not going to elaborate?"

"Elaborate on what?"

He shakes his head as if he's confused. "Okay. I know you look like Oliver. You're dressing like him, and that's his voice. But not elaborating? Not telling your friends every single thought and feeling going through your head? I'm sorry, but you, sir, are not Oliver Price, and I'm going to need whatever alien is in there to leave now."

Now I roll my eyes. "You're hilarious."

"Seriously. You okay? I really am worried."

"Don't be," I say. "I'll be fine. Just a slump. Oh, but I should ask, how are you and Betsy? Everything work out?"

"Yes, everything is fine. But don't divert. I can smell your bullshit from a mile away."

Sometimes it's great having friends that you've known for twenty-plus years. Sometimes it's the worst.

"Just drop it, Wes," I say, standing back up. "I just need the weekend to clear my head. A few days alone will do me some good."

"Nope," he says, popping out of the chair. "You're coming to The Joint tonight, and we're going to fix you up."

I shoot him a look. "Do I have a choice?"

He shakes his head. "Would you give me one if the role was reversed?"

I let out a sigh, knowing he's exactly right. "What time?"

"Seven. And it's our lucky day. Simon's coming, which means he's buying."

"Here we go, boys. Four beers and four shots." We nod and say thanks to Porter, the owner of The Joint and Wes's cousin, as he sets down our drinks. "Whose tab?"

"His," we say in unison, pointing to Simon.

"What the fuck?" We all start laughing, even though he should've known this was coming. "I'm not the only one at this table who makes six figures."

He looks over to Wes, who holds his hands up in surrender. "I did make six figures. Now I'm a high school football coach who pays an ex-wife more than I care to admit, but it's worth it to keep her out of my life."

Simon raises his shot glass. "I'll drink to that. To the Wicked Witch of the Exes being gone and to Betsy staying forever."

"Hear hear!"

We all clink our shot glasses, before giving them a table tap then shooting them back.

Whiskey...

As soon as the liquid hits my throat I'm immediately taken back to last Saturday. I think for the rest of my life I'll associate whiskey with Izzy. Yes, I know that sounds dramatic. And so what if it is? There was something about her that got under my skin, and apparently it's not coming out for a long time.

"Okay, what the hell, dude?" Shane says, slamming his beer bottle on the table. "What the fuck is that look for?"

"What look?" I'm trying to play dumb but clearly my three best friends aren't buying it.

"That one," Shane says. "You had it the morning after the wedding. You have it now a week later. Is this because of Shannon? Because dude, and I say this with love as your best friend, get over it."

"Which one was Shannon?" Wes asks.

"The one he proposed to while they were having sex," Shane says.

"Wait!" Simon interrupts. "I thought I was his best friend?"

Shane shakes his head. "It was a figure of speech. I wasn't assigning anyone best friend roles."

"You better not be," Simon says, sitting back, taking his bottle of beer with him. "Because we all know I'm Oliver's best friend, and you and Wes are best friends."

"You're fucking ridiculous," Shane says before turning back to me. "Now, back to you. Shannon wasn't it, dude. She wasn't the one. You've never been this down in the dumps about a woman before. So what is it?"

I take a sip of my beer to stall for a second, because I'm in a predicament I've never been in. I want to tell my friends about Izzy. I want to tell them about every single part of our night.

Well, not every part.

But for some reason every time I try to open up about her, something in my gut tells me I need to keep this to myself. Which is the problem, because I don't keep *anything* to myself.

I tell my friends everything. They have never *not* known one of my secrets. In fact, I've never had a secret because that requires something to be hush for more than thirty seconds. Not only were they present during my first kiss, which came from playing spin the bottle when we were in seventh grade, but immediately after it was over we had to take a time out from the game so I could debrief them. They were there when I proposed for the very first time. Which I'm glad, because then they were there when she told me no. I tried to get them to come the second time, having a feeling it was going to be a celebration. They did, only this time they were waiting at my car with a case of beer, knowing she was going to say no. After that, I quit inviting them.

"I don't want to talk about it."

Silence falls around the group. The three of them all share a questioning look before turning their attention back to me.

"You," Shane begins. "Oliver Price. The man who gives us play-by-play of what he does at the gym each morning, has nothing to say. Doesn't want to talk about whatever it is that's on his chest?"

I shake my head. "I'm good. But I do appreciate it. I just need a few days to process some things."

Wes nods. "You do whatever you need. Just know we're here for you."

I give Wes a friendly slap on the shoulder when someone catches my eye at the bar.

"I'll go get us another round," I say, not waiting to hear if anyone actually needs a beer. I quickly look around to see if I catch a glimpse of red hair, which I don't. But the next best thing is currently at the bar, waiting on Porter to serve her.

"Hazel?" I ask, though I know it's her. Everyone in this town knows who Hazel Montgomery-Calhoun is. Billionaire CEO. Married to the local mechanic. And most importantly, best friends to Izzy—well, I don't know her last name yet, but I will.

Oh God, even in my head that sounded creepy. All I need is a ball cap and to hide behind plants every time I walk into a room.

"The man of the day," Hazel says with a smile.

"Excuse me?"

She softly laughs. "Nothing. Just a funny coincidence running into you tonight. How are you?"

"Fine, thanks," I say, though I'm confused. I've technically never met Hazel before. Her husband and I are casual friends, but not close. I didn't expect her to know who I was. "I wanted to ask you a question, if you don't mind?"

She smiles. "Let me guess. You're wondering about Izzy?"

"How did you know I was going to ask that?"

"Call it a hunch."

Okay. Now I'm thrown. I didn't know what I was going to say to Hazel when I came over, but I definitely didn't expect this. "I wanted to come over and ask...well, what I meant was... Izzy and I..."

Hazel smiles as my words trail off. "Can I ask you something, Oliver?"

"Of course."

"Did you enjoy the time you spent with Izzy last week?"

I swallow the lump in my throat, because I didn't realize she knew. "I did."

"And did you ask her out?"

"I did."

"And let me guess, she said no?"

"She did."

"And yet here you are, asking me for help, when I'm guessing, knowing Izzy, she was very clear that she didn't want anything more than that night. Correct?"

If I would have known I was walking into the gauntlet I would have taken another shot of whiskey first. "Yes, she did say that. And I respect that. I do. It's just...there was something about her. I've never connected with a person like that. From the moment she first smiled at me, I was mesmerized by her. She's like this mystery box that every time you unwrap a layer, there's another layer beneath it. I feel like that night I just got past the first layer, and I can't imagine what else there is, but I want to know. I want the chance to know. Because I think she's the most fascinating and beautiful woman I've ever met."

Shit, was that too much? I meant every word, but Hazel's not saying anything. Wait...is she crying?

"Hazel?"

She shakes her head and waves me off. "You might not be able to force a horse to drink the water, but you sure as shit can drag them to the stream."

"I'm sorry, what?"

Hazel grabs an abandoned pen and a napkin from the bar and starts furiously writing. It has to be more than a phone number, because she's quickly filling up the entire napkin. "Izzy has been my best friend for more than ten years. And in all that time, she has never once used a man's first name. Yet, Oliver, I know yours. And it's not because of my husband or his friends. And now that I'm seeing you here? And hearing that? Well, I don't believe in coincidences."

She hands me the folded napkin. "What's this?"

"I won't give out her number without permission..."

I shake my head. "And I'd never ask."

This makes her smile. "You're one of the good ones. I can tell. Inside that piece of paper is the way to my girl's heart. She insists there's not a heart there, but I know that's a lie. Do with it what you will."

I open it up to see a list of random things. From a quick glance I see a coffee order, a few musicians, and a list of foods.

"Are you sure?"

Hazel nods and gives me a pat on the arm. "There is no one in the world who deserves to be loved more than Izzy. I knew one day it would just take the right guy to do the job. And Oliver, I have a feeling you're that guy."

"Thank you," I say. "She's someone special."

"Damn right she is."

Hazel takes her drinks and walks back to her booth with Knox. I look down at the paper again before folding it gently and putting it into my wallet for safe keeping.

Holy shit...my mind is spinning. Because yes, I know what Izzy said. She doesn't do relationships. She wasn't in for a long term. I appreciate her honesty.

But I've been in enough relationships to know that what we shared wasn't a byproduct of the right place at the right time. People don't connect like that immediately. People don't share what we shared because of one crazy night.

So I have to try. If she turns me down again then I'll walk away knowing I did everything I could.

Because she's worth the effort.

Chapter 8
Izzy

If someone says they aren't affected, or even worse, say they like Mondays, they are damn dirty liars. Mondays are the green Skittles of the days of the week—there, but no one wants them. They are even worse when they start with a conference call at five in the morning to recap things we talked about in the last meeting and then to plan on what we'd talk about in the next meeting. Somewhere in between two new things were brought up that could have been an email.

Corporate life is just the best sometimes.

"If I ever see a five a.m. call again on my calendar I quit," I say to Hazel as we start gathering our files as the call ends.

"No, you won't," she says. Though, I do see that she lets out a yawn. "You're stuck with me forever."

"Not if you keep pulling this meeting-before-the-sun-is-up bullshit."

Hazel walks over and gives me a side hug. "Fine. Next one will be at six."

I let out a groan but return the hug. "You're lucky I love you."

And I do. Ever since we met thirteen years ago, Hazel and I have been inseparable. I'll never forget the night we met. I mean, I don't think people ever forget the night their lives change forever.

I was drunk as hell, sitting by myself at a dive bar in Los Angeles, trying to figure out what the hell I was going to do with my life. At that point, I'd been in LA for three years and had put myself through school on a fast track while trying to erase my past. I graduated with a marketing degree, but it was going unused, so that meant waiting tables to make ends meet. I couldn't ask my family for help because, for lack of a better term, I was dead to them. Once I left Nebraska and defied their wishes, I might as well have dropped off the face of the Earth.

Then there was my love life. When I left my small hometown, I swore to myself I'd never let a man dictate my future. I'd call out the red flags when I saw them, and I'd never, ever, fall for lines of bullshit again.

Then I did. Because when it comes to men, I'm a fucking idiot.

So there I was. I was drunk, pissed at the world, and was trying to figure out what the hell I was going to do next. The only thing I knew was that I was tired of letting a person who claimed they loved me dictate my life, while simultaneously lying to me on a consistent basis. Nope, I was done with that shit. I was going to find a career where I could excel. That I could control. Love and relationships were contingent on others. Well, I tried that. Zero out of ten. Do not recommend.

Then, somewhere in between my thoughts about love being a farce and wondering if I really could take a Louisville slugger to both headlights, I overheard Hazel and her developer talking about their dating app. I remember thinking it was hilarious that I was hours out of a breakup and swearing off love, and here I was, sitting next to two people who were trying to sell people on the idea love existed.

To this day I still don't know why I said anything. Maybe because I was trying to figure out how to finally use my degree and their project clearly needed a marketing plan. Maybe it was just the right place at the right time.

Whatever it was, the rest is history. I spoke up. I invited myself to their office the next week. Thirteen years later, I'm now the head of communications for a billion-dollar company, and I haven't had a serious relationship since that night.

Everything has worked out according to plan.

"What's the rest of your day like?" Hazel asks as we turn the corner toward our offices.

"No clue, but hopefully time for a nap," I say honestly. "Jules will tell me whenever I need to be somewhere."

"You'd be lost without her."

"Don't I know it?"

"Well, if you have time, come by my office for lunch. We'll order out and debrief from that meeting. And, you know, anything else that might need talking about."

"Okay..." I say, wondering why she phrased it like that. "I doubt anything major is going to happen in the next four hours."

She shrugs before opening her door. "You never know."

I stare at her in confusion as she walks into her office. What the hell is she talking about? But before I can think too far into it, Jules is at my side, iPad in hand.

"How was your meeting?"

"Early," I groan as I open my office door. "What's the rest of the day look like?"

We walk into the office, which triggers the automatic lights. I hear Jules saying something about a meeting with the social media team, but I don't process any of it. Because all I can do is stare at the cup of coffee on my desk, next to a single pale pink flower.

"What in the world?"

I drop the files and my laptop that I was carrying on the edge of my desk before walking over to further inspect. I pick up the flower and smell it. It's sweet and almost looks like one of those flowers drawn on a birthday cake. I put it down and pick up the coffee, which is still hot.

"Did you bring this in?"

She shakes her head. "I didn't. A delivery came about twenty minutes ago for you, so I figured you ordered it to have ready after your meeting."

I pick up the hot beverage to inspect it, when I see a note written on the side of the cup.

I've been thinking about you a latte, so I figured I'd send you this. Have a great day, Red.

I read the note again, which is when I notice the markings on the cup. It's my usual morning latte order, and it's perfect, even down to the three pumps of vanilla and oat milk.

"You didn't see who brought this?"

Jules shakes her head. "He was one of the regular delivery guys. I didn't pay much attention."

I read the note again, bypassing the corny joke and focus on one word:

Red.

Three people have ever called me that in my life. The first was he-who-will-not-be-named. It was all he ever called me in the years we were together. The second was a creepy finance guy we hired years ago who once got a little too handsy with me. After he called me Red and grabbed my ass, I kicked him in the balls so hard he couldn't walk for a day. It could have been longer, but I don't know because Hazel fired him on the spot.

Then there was the third man. He might have only called me that name once, but for some reason, I didn't mind it when it came out of his dirty, delicious mouth. Probably because I was having the best sex of my life. I'll let a nickname slide for a good orgasm.

Did Oliver send this? No. He couldn't have. How would he know my exact, and very specific, order?

"Do you want me to call the service and see who sent it?" Jules asks.

I shake my head. "No, it's okay."

"Are you sure?"

"It's fine," I say, taking a sip of the caffeinated goodness. I should be more annoyed. I mean, I am annoyed. I hate being out of the loop. I hate secrets. I hate feeling like people know things that I don't know.

Yet, as I sit back and enjoy the hot beverage, I can't seem to find it in me to have Jules get to the bottom of it. My tired state must be making me lose my edge.

"If you're sure, I'll go get everything set up for the social team meeting in a half hour."

I nod as she exits the room. I read the message over and over again, knowing in my heart of hearts it has to be Oliver. He's the only one I know who could write a joke *that* corny and it actually makes me laugh.

What's his deal? What's his game? I told him we weren't going to be a good fit. I thought I was clear.

Then again, how can I be mad at anyone who sends me the perfect cup of coffee on a Monday that included a meeting at the asscrack of dawn?

The sound of an email being delivered brings me back to

the present, which in turn makes me look at my inbox. It's overflowing.

Ugh. Fuck Mondays and everything that comes with it.

Except this coffee. It can stay.

TUESDAY

"Jules!"

I know I could use the intercom, but that would require taking my hands off the keyboard, which I clearly do not have time for today.

"Yeah, boss?"

"Late lunch order," I say without looking at her. "And get whatever you want. I have a feeling it's going to be a long day."

"On it."

Today has been nonstop, which Jules warned me about. This is the first fifteen minutes I haven't been on, or in, a meeting today. So in between replying to emails, and doing my actual job, I figured this was as good a time as any to get my midday pick me up and a quick snack. I think I'm hungry. I'm honestly too busy to really know.

"Here we go!"

I look up to see Jules back, carrying my coffee order, and hers.

"How the hell did you get it that fast?" I ask, taking the iced drink from her. Yes. Hot coffee in the morning. Iced coffee in the afternoon. Those are the rules. "Because if that's your super power then I needed to know about this a long time ago."

She laughs. "Actually, I was waiting at the elevator to head downstairs, when the same delivery guy from yesterday was waiting for me with these drinks and a bag of sandwiches."

I narrow my eyes. "Oh really."

"Yeah," she says, pretending to be shocked. Now I know something is up. "Weird, right?"

I snatch the bag from her hand and dump the items onto my desk. The first thing I notice is a flower similar to the one yesterday, only a shade darker. Then there's the food—an assortment of grapes and cheeses and what looks to be a chicken salad sandwich. Which Jules knows is my normal late afternoon meal if I forgot to eat lunch. And of course, there's a note.

Why did the chicken salad sandwich cross the road? To try to get a date with you.

"Oh, for fuck's sake," I say, throwing back my head.

"What?" Jules asks. "Do you want me to take it back?"

I slap her hand as she tries to take the sandwich away from me. "Don't you dare touch it."

Jules slowly walks out of the office back to her desk as I read the note again.

If I wasn't sure yesterday, I'm damn sure now.

I don't know how he's doing it.

And even more importantly, I don't know why I'm not madder about it.

~

WEDNESDAY

"Delivery for Izzy McCall?"

I let out a groan as I look up from my computer and out the glass wall of my office to see a delivery guy standing at Jules's desk, holding a basket wrapped in cellophane. We had made it all day without a delivery or any sort of surprise. I had hoped that Oliver got it through his head after two days of surprises without me reaching out to him that I wasn't going to bite. Granted, I don't have his number, but I'm smart and resourceful. I also have access to an IT department filled with computer geeks who know corners of the internet I didn't know existed.

"What the fuck?"

Jules signs for it and takes it from him just as I get to her desk. "Excuse me! Can I ask who sent you?"

He just shrugs. "I was just told by my boss to deliver this here. But, I think I saw a card."

He walks away and I rip the card that's taped to the wrap.

You know how they say we only use 10 percent of our brains? I think we only use 10 percent of our hearts.

I fight the urge to roll my eyes at the classic *Wedding Crashers* quote. And while I might be able to fight that, I can't fight the smile that's threatening to appear.

"What's in here?"

I turn back to Jules, who is examining the contents of the basket. She sets it down on the desk, which is when the smile finally comes through.

Because Oliver got me a basket filled with popcorn, my favorite movie candy, a pink flower tucked inside, and, of course, a copy of *Wedding Crashers.*

"This man..." I say under my breath. Luckily, Jules doesn't hear me. Or if she did she doesn't react. Which is good, because I really don't know what else there is to say.

Am I still annoyed? Yes. Am I less annoyed than I was on Monday? Yes. Am I going to go home tonight and eat every one of these Sour Patch Kids and watch this movie? Also yes.

I mean, he went to all this trouble, it would be rude of me not to.

~

THURSDAY

I HATE that every time there's any sort of commotion around my office this week I've looked up to see if it's a delivery from Oliver. I've never paid this much attention to who, or how many people, walk past my office every day. I swear this isn't me. It's like his corny charm and hurricane tongue have made me into some sort of pining girl.

I don't pine. I don't wait for men to call me. I don't get giggly when scenes of a movie remind me of them.

Yet, here I am. Pining and giggling. Makes me sick.

I check the clock on my computer to see that it's four forty-five, which means it's technically fifteen minutes from quitting time, though I don't remember the last time I left at five. Hell, most nights I'm lucky if I leave by seven. But you know what, fuck it. I don't have anything that needs done right now and I can't sit here any longer waiting on something that I shouldn't be waiting for to happen.

I power down my computer and grab my bag, closing my door behind me.

"Where are you going?" Jules pops up from behind her desk. "Are you leaving? It's not five!"

"I am, and you're coming with me. No sense in you being here if I'm gone."

Her eyes go wide as she looks at me, toward the elevator, then back to me. "You can't leave yet."

Oh this girl really needs to work on her stealth. "And why is that?"

"Well," she begins. "It's...well...it's not five o'clock."

"I'm aware," I say. "I also know that I'm pretty sure I'm allowed to leave a few minutes early occasionally."

"Of course you are. I didn't mean it like that. I was just saying, well, what I meant was..."

I'm about to tell her to spit out whatever she wants to tell me when the sound of the elevator grabs both of our attentions. Stepping out of it is some sort of delivery person, but I can't see his face because it's covered by an insane amount of pink and white flowers coming from a vase. Flowers that look suspiciously like the ones I've been getting delivered every day this week.

"Delivery for Izzy McCall."

I'm not counting, but there has to be two dozen flowers. The colors range from white to a hot pink and every shade in between. The second I'm handed the vase, my senses are overloaded in the best way with their sweet scent.

I shoot a look to Jules. "I take it you knew about this?"

She looks everywhere but me as she gathers her things. "Don't know what you mean, boss. See you tomorrow!"

I laugh as Jules makes a beeline for the elevator. I set the vase down and grab the card, wondering what this one will say.

Shockingly, it only has two things written on it—a phone number and Oliver's name.

Well played, sir...well played.

Chapter 9
Oliver

I HAVE BEEN KNOWN TO PULL SOME CRAZY SHIT OVER THE years when it comes to women. In my defense, all have been in the name of love. Or at least what I thought was love at the time.

There was the time a girlfriend said she loved a certain band. Not only did I get her two tickets to see said band—floor seats, of course—I arranged a backstage meeting.

She broke up with me the day after the concert.

Another woman I dated sold clothing and jewelry over social media. I was so into her I was her assistant on her live videos. She broke up with me because she said she needed to "grow into her girl boss self" and a relationship would just get in the way. I think she was just mad that I sold more of those weird-looking leggings than she did.

And I know prom-posals are all the rage these days with the kids, but I invented that shit. True story. I don't know of another high school senior back in 2006 taking a girl to a candlelit picnic where you had the words "Go to prom with me?" written on a pizza.

Then there's that whole I've proposed thirty-three times over the course of my life—thirty-four if you count the one from the wedding with Izzy.

So in the grand scheme of things, the gifts and lengths I went to this week probably don't crack the top five of most elaborate things I've ever done, but it does stick out in one major way—it's for a woman I'm not yet dating. Who wants nothing to do with dating me.

I was raised by a single mom who had three sisters. If there was one thing I grew up learning is that when a woman says no, she means it. For my entire life, if I asked a woman out and she declined, I went about my way.

Until Izzy came into my life.

Each day that I sent her a package, the knot in my stomach just kept getting tighter with nerves. Even my first graders were wondering if I was okay. Bailey asked if I needed to "frow up."

Was this the right thing to do? Did I make up how I felt that night? Does she think I'm certifiable with each passing day? Would I have had a chance if I would have just asked her out again like normal, but now because I went balls out so soon I don't have a chance?

I fall back on my couch, bringing a pillow up to cover my face before I scream into it.

I haven't looked at the clock in two minutes, so I'm guessing it's still around six-thirty. She got my delivery two hours ago. I didn't expect a call right away, but I was hoping for at least a text to put me out of my misery.

Or maybe she won't message me at all because she hated everything.

Fuck...what did I do?

My brain starts going a million miles a minute when I hear my phone vibrating on my coffee table. I launch the pillow across the room as I nearly fall off the couch to answer it.

"Hello?"

"Since when do you answer the phone with a hello?"

I look at the screen to see that it's Shane calling me, not the beautiful redhead who has been a part of my every thought for the better part of two weeks.

"Isn't that the appropriate way to answer the phone?"

"Only for a job interview."

"Well excuse me for having manners. What do you need?"

"Sheesh," he says. "Nice talking to you too, asshole. God forbid I call to make sure you're alive."

I groan as I fall back on the couch. I don't know why I'm being an ass to Shane. He's one of my best friends in the world. We're the only two out of the four guys who lived in Rolling Hills for a majority of our adult lives. The only time we didn't was when I was in college and he was serving his time in the Army. Because of that, we have a closeness that we don't have with Wes or Simon. So I get why he's calling to check if I'm still alive. I've been so preoccupied with Project Presents that I kind of forgot that the outside world existed.

"I'm here," I say. "And sorry I was short with you."

"Is everything okay? You haven't been yourself for a few weeks now."

I open my mouth to start talking, but nothing comes out. This happened when they first asked me about what happened the night of the wedding. I thought then that it was because everything was so fresh and I didn't know what I really felt. And maybe I'll tell them after I hear from Izzy. Or should I say if I hear from her. But right now I need to keep this to myself.

"Everything is fine."

Shane doesn't say anything back, which is exactly what I expected. Honestly, if any friends were the ones to check on me, I'm glad it was Shane. He's the only one who won't press me for more information, or double down on the question.

Because that would require more conversation, and Shane Cunningham avoids that more than he avoids relationships. Which is saying something.

It's funny sometimes to think that out of everyone in the group, I'm closest to Shane. Don't get me wrong, I'd take a bullet for each of them. And we all have our functions. When we need the shoulder to cry on, it's Amelia. When you need romantic ideas or advice, I'm your guy. When you need someone to overanalyze something, but in the end give you a solid pro-con list, you go to Wes. Shane's the one who will give you the slap on the head and the "Come to Jesus" talk. And Simon? Well, he's the one we call when we need to hear what we don't want to. Or if we need a body buried. Figuratively, of course.

But when it comes to Shane and me, he's usually the one I go to first for general advice. He knows my history. He knows all the crazy shit I've done when it comes to women. He knows all of the girlfriends and almost girlfriends. He knows about every proposal.

Well, except the last one.

"I still don't believe you're okay, but I'm not about to drive over there and force you to talk," Shane says. "If it's about Shannon, get over it. If it's about someone else, then figure it out. I never thought I'd say this, but I miss your ass texting me every day."

"I knew you loved it when I did that."

"I'll never admit it in public."

I laugh and am about to do the polite thing of asking him how he's doing when I hear the sound of a call coming through. I take the phone away from my ear to see an unknown number.

"I gotta go," I say abruptly. I don't even wait for him to answer before I hang up and accept the call that I hope is Izzy.

"Hello?"

I did my best there to seem cool, calm, and collected. You know, like I hadn't been waiting by the phone for the past two hours. I honestly can't tell you if it worked or not. At least my voice didn't break like it did when I asked out my first girlfriend in sixth grade.

"You play dirty."

Goddamn it...just the sound of her voice does something to me. While it's sexy as hell, and I need to remind myself that we aren't back in that hotel room, it also somehow calms me. That's a weird but at the same time amazing combination.

"I don't like to think of it as playing dirty."

"What would you describe it as?"

"Playing for keeps."

"You're a confident one, Mister...."

"Price," I say. "Oliver Price."

"Nice to meet you Mr. Price. I'm Izzy McCall."

"Nice to officially meet you," I say. What I don't say is that I knew her last name after looking her up last week. In my defense, I was just looking at Left for Love's website for its address. Before I knew it, I was reading her bio and looking through her Instagram. But I didn't follow her. I'm not *that* crazy.

Neither of us say anything for a beat, and as much as I want to, I know I need to let her control this. If she's really closed off to the possibility of a relationship, then her calling me is a huge step. So I can wait. I waited all week. I waited today. What's another few seconds?

"What I was going to say," she continues, "is that you're a confident one, Mr. Price. And honestly, kind of ballsy."

"I felt like I needed to pull out all the stops," I admit.

"Why did you?"

"Excuse me?"

"Why did you?" she repeats. "I mean, I thought we left

things on good terms at the hotel. And I thought I was clear that I don't do relationships. Or date, for that matter. Yet, you went for it one more time. Why?"

I take a breath as I think about exactly what I want to say. This is it. This is the moment that all the presents and deliveries and wishful thinking were leading up to. Yet I can't remember a single speech I rehearsed.

"I know you're not a relationship girl, and I respect that," I begin. "You were right that I'm a relationship guy. Which might make us seem like opposites. But you want to know what we have in common?"

"Good sex and a love of whiskey?"

"Besides that."

"Color me intrigued," she says. I don't know how, but I can tell she's smiling, which gives me all the confidence I need to keep going.

"Us."

"Us?"

"Yeah, us," I say. "Out of all the people at the wedding that night, it was us who ended up at the bar next to each other. We could have walked away then. We could have made casual conversation and went about our nights. But we didn't. I don't know why you didn't, but for me, it was because from the moment I asked you to dance, I knew there was something different about you. And I was right. And call me crazy, but I want to learn more about you. I want to spend time with you. I want more. And even if it's not a relationship. Even if it's just a friendship where we eventually joke about the great sex we had that one time, I just know that I'm not ready for you to be out of my life. I want an us, no matter what form that comes in."

I let out a breath when I'm done, and I'm kind of grateful she doesn't say anything right away. If it was going to be a no, she would have stopped me immediately. Izzy doesn't seem to be the kind of woman who beats around the bush. However, the longer the silence holds, the more worried I get.

"Yes."

I jump up from the couch in excitement. "Yes?"

"Don't make me say it again," she says. "But I do have a few questions I need answered before any of this happens."

Thank goodness this isn't FaceTime right now. She'd think I'm a loon based on how wide I'm smiling. "Ask me anything."

"Question one: are you a serial killer?"

I laugh. "Would a serial killer tell you they're a serial killer?"

"Well, no, but I think it's important to ask."

"Fair. I'm not a serial killer. I don't own a gun, and I'm not very good with an ax. But that's just based on my results from when I went ax throwing."

"Noted," she says. "Question two: who helped you this week with the deliveries? Because while I know most of it was you, there's no way you did it alone."

"Maybe I did?"

"I should have told you that if you lie, my answer turns to a no."

"Fine," I groan, hating that I'm going to have to throw my accomplices under the bus. "At first just Hazel. Then I got Jules in on it after the first day."

"Traitors," she grumbles. "I'll deal with them later."

"Don't be too hard on them," I plead. "They were just trying to help a guy out."

"Fair enough," she says. "Now, this last one isn't a question, but I need you to make me a promise."

At this point I'll promise her just about anything.

"You name it."

"Promise me that you know that just because I'm saying yes, it doesn't mean we're going to be boyfriend and girlfriend.

Promise me that you know this is just two people getting together. No expectations. And without a doubt, this is *not* a date."

Usually a smile doesn't come out when a woman tells a smitten man that their planned meetup is not a date.

But most smitten men aren't asking out Izzy McCall.

"I promise."

"Okay then," she says. "So what happens now? Do we meet somewhere? Are you one of those guys who has to pick the girl up?"

I laugh as I sit back down on the couch. "Absolutely not. I do have a question for you though."

"Shoot."

"Do you believe in magic?"

Chapter 10
Izzy

"DO YOU BELIEVE IN MAGIC?"

Those five words have been rolling around in my head all day since Oliver said them. Mostly because I don't know what they mean or what they have to do with what's in store for tonight. I might not know Oliver very well, but based on his gifts and notes this week, that could mean literally anything.

I don't like surprises. Or not being in the loop. Call it my Type A coming out to play. Call it my gut reaction from past traumas. I'm very uneasy when I don't know what's going on. Which is why I'm feeling all sorts of discombobulated as I stand on the sidewalk in downtown Nashville between a honkytonk and a cowboy boot shop.

"What do you have planned, Oliver? And why am I nervous?"

Shit, now I'm talking to myself. This man has me all out of whack. First I agreed to a date and now this. I think I'm officially losing it.

After I said yes to our date—which isn't a date but I don't know what else to call it—he informed me that he already had the whole night planned. Once I gave him shit for being cocky I'd say yes, he told me I'd be happy once he revealed his plans. But he wasn't going to tell me anything except where I was to meet him and that I should dress to impress.

So here I am, in a black cocktail dress and a pair of Louboutins in the middle of Nashville, looking like I'm lost. A bachelorette party stumbles my way, and the bride-to-be nearly trips right in front of me.

Maybe I should take a second to tell the bride that it's not too late, that she still has time to call it off. Better late than never, if you ask me.

Just as I'm about to approach the clearly drunk bride-to-be, I feel the gentlest touch to my elbow. I can't see him. Hell, his touch is so light I can barely feel him. But I immediately know it's Oliver. My body has never burned from the inside by anyone's touch. That is, not until my night with Oliver.

Fuck, this is bad.

I slowly turn around and I think my heel almost breaks off. That must be it. It's not because my knees are weak by the mere sight of this man.

I'm trying not to stare at him, but I can't look away. I think it's actually impossible.

His long blond hair is styled perfectly in an I-woke-up-like-this tousle. His scruff is that perfect length where it's not too long but you know you'd feel it if it was against your cheek. Or between your thighs. His light blue button-down shirt fits him perfectly. The top button is undone and his sleeves are rolled, showing off the forearms that have been haunting my dreams. He's wearing navy blue pants that I can tell are tailored perfectly for him.

Basically, he's fucking hot. And I'm fucking screwed.

"Hey, Red."

Fuck me sideways...

This. This is how he got me to say yes. Despite using that nickname, his voice puts me in some sort of hypnotic trance that makes me do shit I normally wouldn't. That must have been what he meant when he asked me if I believed in magic. Only explanation.

"Hey, yourself," I say.

"Have you been standing out here long?" he asks as he frantically checks his watch.

"Not long," I say. "But don't worry, you're not late at all. I'm the one who got here a half hour early."

He gives me a curious look. "Can I ask why?"

"I needed to get the lay of the land."

"Lay of the land?"

"Yes," I say firmly. "I don't like surprises. I like knowing what I'm getting into. And since you insisted on not telling me the details of tonight, I decided to do a little recon."

This makes him laugh. "And what did you figure out from this scouting mission?"

I shake my head. "Nothing. You've left me curious."

He smiles as he puts his hand on the small of my back. It takes all my mental fortitude to ignore how good it feels.

"Well, then, let's get you inside." He leads me toward the boot shop, which would have been my last guess as to where we were going. I honestly thought it was a decoy. "We have a magical night ahead of us."

It was right freaking in front of me, but I overthought it. I analyzed every detail and every syllable, thinking that there was meaning within his already cryptic question.

He took me to a freaking magic show.

It was in the basement of the boot shop. The only thing

that's making this not awful is the show is set in a hidden speakeasy. And they make a hell of a Manhattan.

"Ladies and gentlemen, the Amazing Marcello!" The crowd gives a round of applause as the magician/comedian/fraud takes a bow before exiting the stage. I clap, because I'm not an asshole, but his whole act was a bunch of crap.

Make an object disappear, my ass. And don't get me started on the "pick a card, any card" bullshit. They are marked. I don't know how, but they are.

"Wow," Oliver says when the applause dies down. "If he's the warm-up act, I can't imagine what the main attraction will be like."

I stare blankly at him. "Really? You're buying this?"

His face turns into shock in a nano-second. "You're not?"

"Come on," I say as I point to the stage where the wish.com Houdini just exited. "You know this isn't real."

"What if it is?" he says, turning to face me better. We're seated at a small round table, and it doesn't leave much room between us, which is a good and bad thing. Good because I can whisper my smartass comments to him during the show. Bad because I can smell his cologne and it's just as mouthwatering as I remember it to be. "Isn't it just fun to wonder about the possibility of magic?"

"No," I say pointedly. "All I wonder is how he actually got those cards to magically float in the air."

"Ah-ha!" Oliver points at me. "You said magically. You do believe!"

I shake my head. "Bad choice of words. Because I don't believe. Sorry."

Oliver leans his head on his hand. "What do you believe in?"

"Lots of things," I say as I take a sip of my drink. I happen to take a look at Oliver, who is looking at me right now like I'm telling the most fascinating story he's ever heard. "I believe in hard work. I believe only you can make your dreams come true. I believe in good whiskey, good sex, and the healing powers of a piping hot shower."

I take another sip of my Manhattan, running through that list one more time to see if I forgot anything. Nope. That about sums it up.

"Wow," he says, almost as if he's in disbelief. "That's quite a list."

"What about you? What's the belief system of Oliver Price?"

He shakes his head and looks away to take a sip of his drink, some sort of specialty cocktail that had one too many uses of the word "infused" for me. "I'd rather not."

"Oh no," I say, taking his chin in my fingers and turning his head toward me. "I told you mine; it's only fair that you tell me yours. Rule of the night: neither of us are allowed to deflect, though we both do it so well."

This gets him to let out a small smile. "Promise you're not going to laugh?"

I take my fingers off his chin to give his hand a squeeze. "I would never."

"Okay," he begins. "I believe in love. I believe in soulmates. I believe that people are stronger together than separate. I believe in family, both blood and chosen. And I believe in hope. Because if you don't have hope, then what do you have?"

"Wow," I whisper. I knew he was going to say something that dove into love and marriage and all that jazz, but I didn't expect all that. For a second, my cold, dead heart actually felt something.

I want to say more, but I'm stopped by the lights dimming. Good. I don't know if I could have said anything after that.

I look over to Oliver, whose bright smile has returned as he watches the magician enter the stage. I remember when I was like that. Hopeful. Not jaded by the world. Sometimes—not often, but sometimes—I wish I still had some of that spark. Then I remember I'm better off. Because what Oliver just listed? It's nice in theory. But all of those things are enough to break someone.

And I prefer to be whole, thank you very much.

"Now I know there are some skeptics in the house tonight," the magician says as he starts making his way through the crowd. "And I can always spot them a mile away."

I swear to God, if this man comes over this way I'm going to punch him in the junk.

"I can always tell who the nonbelievers are," he says as he continues to walk through the audience. "They always have the same look on their faces. Bored. Disbelieving. Wondering when the waitress is going to come over to get them another drink."

This makes the audience laugh, and I laugh as well. Not because it's funny. But because I have a feeling if I don't that this asshole is going to call me out. And I'm not going to be singled out in front of strangers as a nonbeliever. He'd probably do something like bring me on stage and make me part of the show. No, thank you.

"Well, this is interesting," the magician says as he approaches me and Oliver. "It seems here we have a bit of an opposite attraction."

He positions himself behind us, and just as he does, I'm blinded by the spotlight shining in my eyes.

"Ladies and gentlemen! Here we have a prime example of a nonbeliever!" I shoot this David Blaine wannabe a look that I hope can kill. He doesn't seem to notice. But you know who does? My date, who is currently snickering next to me. "And it seems she is here with a believer! What a match!"

I do my best not to roll my eyes, though it's a struggle.

"Sir, may I ask you your name?"

"Oliver," he says into the microphone.

"Well hello, Oliver. And may I ask who this beautiful woman is that you're here with tonight?"

If my look earlier could kill, this one could detonate the city of Nashville. Except it doesn't faze Oliver one bit. No, this motherfucker just wags his eyebrows at me, clearly loving this.

"This is the beautiful Izzy, who's with me on our first official date."

Of course, this gets a round of applause from the audience. I love that Oliver is eating this up right now. And when I say love, I mean loathe. I'm hiding behind my hands while he's waving to the audience in thanks for their enthusiasm.

Also, this isn't a date.

"So, Izzy," the magician says as he shifts over next to me. "Am I right to say that you're a nonbeliever?"

Talk about a pick-your-poison situation. I can either lie, which I hate doing, or tell the audience that just gave me a round of applause that, yes, I think all of this is a crock of shit.

"You're right. I am a bit of a skeptic."

There. Told the truth. And I didn't come off as a total bitch. I'm going to chalk that up as a win.

"What can we do to make you a believer?"

My brain immediately starts workshopping all the many things I wish I could say right now. I don't want to be basic and ask him for some lame card trick. I could ask him to make me disappear so I didn't have to be in this situation anymore. Or maybe I could shoot for the moon and ask him for a genie in a bottle to grant me three wishes—two of them being me getting out of here and him disappearing. But I doubt he has those kinds of powers, and that's conceding that he has any at all.

"I'm not sure," I say. "But it would have to be something pretty amazing."

"Then it's your lucky day!" he says, playing to the audience. "Amazing is my middle name!"

Funny. I would have gone for something like Vernon. Or Fraud.

"Ladies and gentlemen, how about we bring Izzy up on stage and show her that magic does indeed exist!"

The crowd starts wildly clapping as I feel every cell in my body turn cold. Fuck me. This is exactly what I didn't want—me, up on stage in front of a bunch of random people who have nowhere else to look except at me or junior varsity David Blaine, under unflattering lights. This is my own personal hell.

"Audience, I think Izzy here needs a little bit of encouragement. What do you say?"

On cue the room starts applauding, including Oliver. I could give him a pleading look, begging him to help me. But I don't. I can't let anyone see that this is the worst. I'll suck it up. Because that's what I do.

"You're going to pay for this later." I say as I stand up.

He takes my hand and gives it a reassuring squeeze. "I'll be happy to pay the price."

"All right, audience, one more time! Give it up for Izzy!"

You got this. This is supposed to be fun and harmless. No one is judging you. No one is whispering about you.

I let out a breath and suck up my courage as I follow the magician to the stage.

"What's about to happen?" I whisper, hoping the microphone isn't on. For my own sanity—and to not hyperventilate in front of an audience—I need to know.

"Don't worry," he whispers back. "Just go with it."

Sure...just go with it. He says it like it's so easy.

"Ladies and gentlemen, I did not intend on performing this trick tonight, so my apologies, but I only have this deck of invisible cards."

He holds up nothing and the audience laughs appropriately. I don't feel bad giving him a "what the fuck look" since I am the skeptic.

"Here," he says as he pretends to take a deck of cards out of the box. "Can you shuffle these for me?"

Really? This is what we're doing?

"You want me to shuffle air?"

"No. I want you to use your imagination and shuffle this deck of cards."

I look back to the audience and somehow through the lights, I see Oliver. He has his phone up, I'm guessing to record this, giving me a thumbs-up like a proud papa at his daughter's dance recital.

"Fine," I groan and go along with this charade. I take the "deck" out of the "box of cards" and shuffle it. Twice.

"Here," I say, handing it to him.

He shakes his head. "I think we need a few more times. Audience? What do you think?"

As if they were all given a script that I didn't get, they all start changing "Go! Go! Go!" Some are clapping, some are like Oliver and pumping their fists. So I do—unwillingly.

"Great. Now, what I need you to do Izzy is take a card out of that deck. Just one card. And I'm going to need you to show it to the audience."

Oh for fuck's sake...

I do as he says, because I've now learned that if I don't he's just going to tell the audience to "help" me do it. So I pretend to slide a card out of the deck and "show" the audience. This gets me a few chuckles, which I'm sure are pity ones.

"Now, slide the card back into the deck, but make sure it's facing the opposite direction of the rest of the cards. After that, put the deck back in the box and give it back to me."

I do as instructed while wondering how much longer I'm going to be up here.

"Now, Izzy, you pulled out one card," he says as he suddenly makes a real box of cards appear out of seemingly nowhere, though I think it was in his pocket and he just moved super quick. "What card was that?"

"There was no card. I pulled out air."

"But did you?" he says, giving me an elbow nudge. "Come on now. Don't be shy. What was your card?"

The quicker you answer the quicker you're done...

"Seven of spades."

"Seven of spades, ladies and gentlemen!" The magician makes a show of taking the cards out of the box. "Now, I told Izzy to put her card back into the deck facing the opposite direction of the rest of the cards." He fans out the deck, showing me and the audience all the cards face down...except for one card.

"Izzy, will you do me the honors of picking up the card that is currently face up?"

I can't believe my eyes as I take the card. Because it's the seven of fucking spades.

"Care to tell us what card it is?"

I don't think I've blinked. How the hell did he do that? "Seven of spades."

The crowd goes wild. He takes the card for me, tells me to take a bow—which I don't—before I head back to my seat. And when I say head back to my seat, I mean make a beeline. When I arrive back at my table, there's a fresh drink waiting for me, thankfully. I know Manhattans are meant to be sipped, but I chug it in one gulp.

What the hell was that? I mean, I thought of the seven of spades in an instant. He didn't tell me a card to say when we were walking up, and he had plenty of opportunities to do so.

Was it magic? No. It couldn't be.

But maybe...

"So?" Oliver begins with a sparkle in his eye. It reminds me of the look he had that morning in the hotel room when he was asking me out for the first time. "Are you a believer now?"

"No," I begin. "But, I can see where it might be a possibility."

I didn't know his smile could get so big. "That's all I needed to hear."

"Really? That's it? I could have avoided all of that if I would have just said maybe?"

He laughs. "No, because I appreciate that you don't bull-shit. You're a straight shooter, so I know what you're saying now is the honest truth. And I wasn't expecting you to believe something after one experience. I was just hoping that you would open yourself up to the possibility."

"The possibility?"

"Yes, the possibility," he says as he takes my hand and scoots in a little closer. "Because when you have a possibility, anything can happen. Possibility leads to hope. And hope can take you anywhere."

I don't know what has been happening on stage since I exited, but apparently something exciting as the crowd breaks out in applause. Honestly, I kind of forgot anyone else was in the room besides us.

"Hey," I say. "Can we get out of here?"

"Absolutely," he says. "We'll just start the second part of our date a little early."

Chapter 11
Oliver

"And that's how I wound up working at Left for Love."

I don't know if it's how Izzy tells a story, or if I'm honestly fascinated with every word that comes out of her mouth, but I don't think I blinked for the past five minutes as she recounts how she started working for Hazel and what brought them to Nashville.

"And you've been there ever since?"

She nods as we slowly walk through Riverfront Park. "Only job I've ever had."

"That's awesome. So it was your first job out of college?"

"Yup. Thirteen years later, and I've never regretted a minute of randomly jumping into a stranger's conversation."

"That's fascinating," I say. "Because you randomly went to a bar one night, your life changed."

I see her slightly tense for a second, but just like that, she's back to normal. Weird.

What isn't weird is how we've been walking for almost an hour now and not once has our conversation stopped or gotten awkward. I've been on some dates where I've been the only one talking, and some when I couldn't get a word in. This has been the perfect amount of back and forth. And I'm learning some very interesting things about this woman. I now know that she's not a chocolate fan, which I think is criminal. Then again, she thinks I'm insane because I will die on the hill that a hot dog is, in fact, a sandwich. The conversation only came up because she insisted on stopping by a hot dog cart as we were leaving the comedy show. I also now know that she hates surprises and that I should never do what I did tonight ever again.

All I heard in that last statement was that there was going to be an again.

"So, what does Oliver do? Let me guess. Sales. You scream salesman."

I laugh. "Strike one."

"Okay..." she says as she looks me up and down in deep thought. "Human resources."

"I guess part of my job is human resources. I do have to solve the conflict of why it's best to share the Play-Doh instead of stealing it."

"Huh?"

I laugh. "I'm a teacher. First grade. And a high school football coach. The Play-Doh negotiations are with the tiny humans. Most of the time. And like you, it's my first job out of college."

"Wow," she says, like she's truly in shock. "That one didn't even cross my mind."

"Why not? You don't strike me as the kind of woman who would genderize employment."

She shakes her head. "Not anything of the sort. I was just wondering how you, or really anyone, does that? I can't handle my niece and nephew, and I only see them through FaceTime at Christmas. And you deal with other people's children for an extended part of the year on purpose? It just baffles me."

This isn't the first time I've heard that, yet it always makes me laugh. "I do, and I wouldn't trade it for anything in the world."

She turns to look at me, almost as if she's assessing me. "You're quite the riddle."

"Meaning?"

"Just when I think I have you figured out, you throw a curveball."

"Apologies. I didn't realize I was that hard to get a handle on."

"In your defense, neither did I," she says. "But let's replay this. I meet you at the wedding. You're drunk as shit, and you ask me to dance. You don't take the hint. You proceed to get more drunk with me and at one point propose marriage. Even after I say no, you keep going on about love and marriage, and blah, blah, blah... At that point I had you pegged for a guy who had just gone through a breakup and didn't have enough time to get another date, so he was a little sad at a wedding alone."

"Actually, that's right," I say. "She actually broke up with me a few hours before the wedding."

"I'm sorry," she says. "Though I'm not sorry I at least got that one right."

"Glad to be of service," I tease. "But please, continue, this is fascinating."

Izzy hesitates for a second before continuing. "Can I be frank with you?"

"Well," I say in the most serious voice I can muster. "I prefer you just be Izzy, but if you want me to call you Frank, I'll do it."

She playfully slaps me on the arm as I laugh at my horrible joke.

"I'm sorry. Go on."

"What I was going to say...when we went back to your room, what transpired that night was not what I was expecting. At all."

I hurry and take a few steps so I'm now in front of her, walking backward. "Not expecting in a good way? Or a this-is-a-pity-date-because-of-how-bad-it-was way?"

This makes her smile. "Surprising in a very, *very* good way."

I'm so glad I moved in front of her, because now I can see the slight blush hitting her cheeks as she remembers back to that night.

"Well, I'm glad, then, that I could surprise you."

She stops walking, which I do as well. "Mission accomplished."

I've never had a poker face. So the fact I'm not jumping around, doing a happy dance, and immediately activating the group text is a big deal.

It's also taking every muscle in my body to not reach out and touch her. Nothing big. Just holding her hand. Or slipping my arms around her waist. Anything. But I know she was insistent this wasn't a date, so I'm respecting her wishes. She was also very clear that this wasn't going to lead to anything romantic. Therefore I know it would be in my best interest to keep this as platonic as possible. Which is so unlike me—my love language is physical touch. And acts of service. And gift giving. And of course I can't leave out words of affirmation. Yes, I know that is four out of five, but I have a lot of love to give.

"So back to the start of the conversation," I say, needing to get back on track so I don't keep thinking about how soft her skin looks. "Are you saying that you can't figure me out because one second I was a sad single at a wedding, then turned into a sex god—I know you didn't use those words but I'm assuming that's what you meant—and now you find out that I teach children for a living. Am I right?"

She nods. "Something like that."

I have a feeling there's a little more on her mind. "And?"

"And what?"

"And you weren't done with whatever you wanted to say."

"And how do you know that?"

"Because," I say, taking a step closer to her. We're now almost touching, and while I know exactly what I'm doing, this is *not* a good decision on the part of me who is trying to keep this night casual. "I can tell that there's something else on your mind. And I never want you to hold back."

This earns me a smile. "Okay. What I was going to also say is that yes, all of the parts of you seem random and no way can they be connected. But the more I get to know you, the more I'm realizing they actually fit perfectly together."

We share a smile as we turn around and start walking back toward downtown. I put my hands in my pockets, because otherwise I'm going to touch her. The small of her back is *right there.*

How am I not supposed to fall in love with this woman? She's beautiful. Funny. Seemingly gets me. And to top it off, she laughs at my stupid jokes. I really wish I would have told the guys about her, because I need all of them right now to tell me not to ask her to marry me.

Again.

But I don't. I take a few deep breaths, count to ten, and think about football stats and blue cheese dressing while continuing to walk with her. I keep my hands in my pockets for safety measures. Because I know me, and I know at some point I'll reach for her hand. And I'm not about to ruin this night because my hand doesn't know when to be cool.

"So have you always wanted to be a teacher?" she asks.

"Only thing I ever wanted to be," I say. "My mom was a teacher at Rolling Hills, as well. She taught older grades, but I remember sitting in her room and being in awe of how she connected with every student that came into her classroom. There were kids she didn't even have in class that came to her for advice. I remember the outpouring of love she got when she announced her retirement. That's why I work with young kids and older kids. The younger ones astound me with how their minds work. Knowing I get to have a part in helping them learn about the world, and themselves...there's just nothing else like it. And with coaching football, I can teach those kids life lessons and how to be good teammates and, in turn, good people. Because there are a lot of assholes in the world, and if I can do my part to make sure the future isn't filled with them, then that's what I'm going to do."

Izzy doesn't say anything for a second, which of course causes my mind to mentally beat myself up about talking too much. I have a habit of doing that. Or so I've been told by a few ex-girlfriends.

I'm so in my head about oversharing that it nearly makes me jump when I feel Izzy's fingers on my arm. I look down to see her wrapping her arms around my arm, her head tilting in toward me, as we continue our walk.

"You really are something, aren't you?"

I can't hold back my smile. Or keep my hands in my pockets as I bring her in closer.

"Thank you," I say.

"You're welcome."

"Not just for the compliment. But for tonight. I know that I pushed you out of your comfort zone with the magic show. I'm sorry, but also, I'm so proud that you did that."

"We exited the comfort zone when I agreed to go out with you," she says with a laugh.

"Very true. And I want you to know that I'm honored you took a chance on me."

"In my defense, you broke down my defenses with candy and flowers. And coffee."

"Just part of my arsenal," I tease as we come to a stop where the pathway intersects with Broadway. "And I meant what I said. I enjoy spending time with you. I know what you said, that you don't date, and I respect that. I'm just glad I got to see you again. And I hope it's not the last time. Because while you might say that I'm something, I think you're everything."

Fuck...why did I say all that? Why did I have to make this some sort of romantic hero monologue? Hell, I might as well just drop a "pick me, choose me, love me" line.

I said too much. I see her eyes growing wide. Similar to how she looked when I dropped the whole "will you marry me" question at the wedding.

"Everything, huh?"

No sense in covering my tracks now. "Yeah. I do."

"Wow," she says, taking a second before she continues. "I don't think anyone has ever said that about me."

"That sounds like a them problem."

She laughs quietly, letting go of my arm. "Every part of me is saying that I should say no, because that's what I normally do. But somehow I can't. Is that weird? Do you always get women to say yes to you after a speech like that?"

I let out a laugh. "Not even a little bit. In fact, I've never got a yes after that kind of speech."

She takes a step closer and leans up, giving me a kiss on the cheek. "Well, consider this your first yes."

I once again hold back from doing a little dance in front of Izzy and the crowds of people in downtown Nashville.

"Next weekend?" I ask.

She nods. "Yes, but this time I get to make the plans. And I have a few more stipulations."

"I expected nothing less."

"Again, this won't be a date."

I shake my head. "Of course not."

"And there will be no sex."

"I wouldn't dream of it."

"This is just two friends, who enjoy spending time together, hanging out."

And there it is. The word that I knew was probably going to be my fate. Funny, though, it doesn't sting the way I thought it would. Or how it's stung in the past when women have given me the "just friends" talk.

"I think that sounds like a great night."

She gives me the double blink, almost as if she's shocked that those words just came out of my mouth. "Really? You're good with that?"

I nod. "Yes. I told you, and I wouldn't lie—however I can have you in my life, I'm good with. I like spending time with you."

She gives a small smile. "I like spending time with you, too."

"Then I think this is the start of a beautiful friendship," I say as I casually wrap my arm around her shoulders and pull her into a side hug. "Now, I'm going to need another sandwich. Let's go back to the hot dog stand."

She shakes her head. "You're ridiculous."

"I know. It's part of my charm."

Chapter 12
Oliver

When I was a kid, I used to love the game at the county fair where someone would try to guess your age or weight. I'm not sure why, but everyone always underestimated me in the weight department. I never lost, which meant whatever girl I brought with me always took home the prize of her choice. If you wanted a giant teddy bear, then all you needed to do was date middle school Oliver.

I don't go to the fair anymore, but I continue to stump people. Izzy said I baffled her with all the things she's learned about me. I might be a romantic at heart, but many would be shocked to know that I'm a lover of horror films.

And then there's my gym playlist. There's a stereotype that every guy needs to be listening to either heavy metal or some sort of rap music to get them through their workout. Not me. My gym playlist is heavy on 2000s pop, boy bands, and of course, those classic hits from the 1980s that just make you smile.

Hall and Oates makes every workout better.

Take today, for example. My playlist is shuffling to the right songs, I had a good breakfast, and the reps are coming quick and painless. Then again, it could also have something to do with the fact I'm still on Cloud Nine after my date last night with Izzy.

I had no idea what to expect. There were parts of me that wondered if she'd cancel. When I found out she wasn't a fan of surprises, or magic, I figured she'd leave at the first possible opportunity.

But she didn't. She stayed. And not only did she stay, we probably had one of the best nights I've had with a woman in a long time. We didn't kiss. I didn't even hug her goodbye when I walked her back to her downtown Nashville condo. But knowing that we are going to see each other again is giving me a pep in my step I haven't had in a very long time.

I'm powering through this seated row, going faster than I normally go, when I feel a smack on the back of my head that nearly makes me lose grip of the handles.

I look over my shoulder to see Simon standing over me. "What the fuck!"

"What the fuck is up with you?"

I stop my set because clearly this is going to be a conversation. "Me? I'm not the one scaring the piss out of people mid workout."

"Well, I'm sorry. But every time I look over at you, you're wearing a smile that screams 'I got laid last night' and I can't do one more set until I hear every detail."

I'm known as the gossip of the group. Probably because I'm the talkative, most outgoing, of the four of us. Even when you throw Amelia in the mix, I'm still number one. But in reality, Simon is the worst of all. The man goes crazy if he doesn't know all the dirty laundry.

"What makes you think this is a sex smile?"

"Listen, you're the perkiest son of a bitch I've ever met,

and I love that about you. But no one, and I mean no one, should be this happy during a Sunday workout. That is, unless you spent it with a woman. That's the only reason for a smile like that. Add in the fact that you've been suspiciously quiet in the group chat, and Shane had to go get proof of life on you last week, I can only assume that you're dating someone new, having incredible sex, and that you haven't proposed because you didn't come crying to us yet that the tally has gone up."

"Close," I say. "No, I didn't have sex last night. I'm not dating anyone. And for your information, I haven't proposed to anyone since the wedding."

There. All truths. Not complete truths, but truths nonetheless.

"You realize you want me to be excited that you've gone two full weeks since proposing marriage? The fact that you need to be applauded for that means we really should have had that intervention a few years back."

I shrug. "You guys had your chance."

"It's not my fault that Wes couldn't get into town and Shane had to work. I knew I wasn't strong enough to face you on my own."

"All I hear are excuses."

I start making my way to the elliptical, because I know that's the quickest way to end this conversation. Simon hates cardio.

Which is why it shocks the hell out of me when not only does he follow me, but gets on one himself.

"Damn, you must really think something is up."

He pushes the buttons angrily, like they did him harm. "Something *is* up. Are you honestly going to stand there and tell me that you're in a good mood just because the sun is out today? Did the birds start singing at your window? Don't play this shit with me. I'm your best friend; I know you better than anyone on this planet."

"Really? You're my best friend?"

"Yes. Don't get me off topic here. Who are you seeing? Because I'm sorry, you're having regular sex. You have that glow. And I know you're not just hooking up with someone, so what's her name?"

"Maybe I am," I say, trying to divert. "Maybe I have a fuck buddy."

This makes him laugh. "Just hearing those words out of your mouth is ridiculous. I have fuck buddies. You do not."

That's very true. Our group has been, and is, so different when it comes to talking about the women in our life. I, until now, tell the guys everything. Wes doesn't normally hold back, but then again, he's only seriously dated his ex-wife and now Betsy. As for Shane...for all we know the man hasn't been with a woman in his adult life. I highly doubt that, but no one actually knows.

Then there's Simon. The man who will never get married, will never call anyone a girlfriend, and dare I say, is a man whore. I love him, but I'm going to have to call it like I see it.

"Okay, so maybe I don't have a fuck buddy," I say. "But I'm not seeing anyone. I promise you."

"Then what is it?" His voice is now serious and filled with concern. Oh shit, now he's serious. "Frankly, the longer you keep quiet about whatever has been going on with you, the more we're going to ask. Between the good moods, and you disappearing for days at a time, it's starting to worry us."

"Y'all have talked about it?"

He gives me a look like that was the dumbest question I could have asked. "Yes. We had to start a new group chat without you. I don't like using it, so I'm going to need you to fess up so we can go back to a world where we only have two chats, the one with Amelia, and the one without. That's the world I'm comfortable in."

I let out a breath, and it has nothing to do with the pace I'm taking right now on this elliptical. He's right. I've pulled a complete one-eighty with my friends since I met Izzy. I can see where that can be worrisome.

Should I tell them about her? I mean, there's no reason to keep her a secret. She's just a woman I've become friends with. That boundary was drawn last night. We're not dating, and I won't be proposing to her any time soon. I've never repeated proposals and that's not a bridge I'm ready to cross. Then the intervention would definitely need to happen.

So why not come clean? It would be easy enough to say that I met someone who I'm seeing as a friend. Is that why I can't bring myself to talk about her even now? Because she's put me in the friend zone?

"Okay, there is someone," I say. "But we're just friends. That's all. I promise."

Simon stops his elliptical so he can stare me square in the eyes. "That's it?"

I nod. "Yes. I did ask her out, but she was up front with me about not wanting anything romantic. We're just friends."

Yes I could have told him more. I could have told him about the wedding. And the night of the wedding. But this is all he needs to know. And in turn, what the rest of the group will know as soon as he sends off the text message I know he's dying to send.

"Who is she?"

I shake my head. "I promise you, I'll introduce her to everyone soon. Just not yet. I kind of want to keep this between her and me for a little while."

Simon nods. "I can respect that. You know I'm all about keeping women's identities secret for as long as possible."

This makes me laugh. I have a feeling he and Izzy are going to hit it off.

When the time's right. And the time isn't right. Not yet.

"Thanks, man," I say, stopping my machine. "I appreciate you."

"No worries," he says as we start walking back to the locker room. "What are best friends for?"

"I don't know," I say. "Maybe I should ask Shane?"

"Low blow, man. Low fucking blow."

Chapter 13
Oliver

"Hello?"

"Hey there."

Izzy doesn't say anything back for at least five seconds. I know because I had enough time to grab all of the ingredients I needed from my refrigerator and take them back to my kitchen counter.

"Hello?" I ask, wondering if the call dropped.

"Oliver?"

"Of course Oliver." I put my phone on speaker so I can start making my dinner. "How was your day?"

"How was my day?"

"Do we have a bad connection?" I check the bars on my phone to make sure nothing weird happened. "Can you not hear me?"

"I can hear you just fine. I'm just...why are you calling me?"

"Because we're friends."

"And?"

"And friends call each other."

"They do?"

How does she not know this? "Yes. They do. They call or text each other to see how their day went, to see if any new life events happened, or if there is something a friend needs to vent about, this gives them that open window for ventilation."

"You can ventilate words?"

"Of course you can, silly," I say. "So, let's try this again, how was your day?"

"Fine?"

I laugh under my breath. "Is it fine if you have to say it in the form of a question?"

"Probably not."

I smile, taking a seat on one of my kitchen bar stools as I cut the zucchini. "I didn't think so. Go on, tell me all about it..."

Izzy: Is ventilation allowed in the middle of the day?

I LAUGH as I read the text message. It looks like she's getting the hang of this.

Oliver: Yes, but only because it's after three and the students have left the building.

Izzy: Good. If one of them saw what I'm about to text they'd be asking you a lot of questions.

Oliver: Oooh! Not safe for work. I love these kinds of texts.

Izzy: This isn't the fun kind of NSFW. This is just a lot of cussing.

Oliver: I have the swear jar ready.

Izzy: It started when I burned my finger on my curling iron this morning, which is just a shitty way to start the day.

Oliver: I'm sorry. Want me to kiss and make it better?

Izzy: Friends don't kiss, Oliver. Not even burned fingers.

Oliver: Good to know the rules.

Izzy: Anyway, then I get to work and have to deal with an influencer who we are paying MAJOR fucking money to who thought it was a good fucking idea to fucking go on fucking ForU and make a fucking video about how many girls sucked his fucking dick during some fucking douche bag music festival. Maybe that's not the fucking image you want to portray when you're the spokesman for a fucking dating app that is anti-fucking hookup?

Oliver: That was a lot of fucks.

Izzy: It was.

Oliver: Feel better?

Izzy: Much.

Oliver: Did you let him go?

Izzy: Fuck yes. Fired his ass on the spot.

Oliver: That's my girl.

~

Oliver: How was your day?

Izzy: Are you really going to text me that every day?

Oliver: How else am I supposed to check on my friend?

Izzy: You could stop.

Oliver: That's not going to happen.

Izzy: Why did I agree to be your friend?

Oliver: Because I'm irresistible.

Izzy: Sure…we'll go with that.

Oliver: Oh! Speaking of being my friend, what are you doing tomorrow?

Izzy: On a Saturday? What every thirty-four-year-old woman does. I'm bringing home work, doing laundry, and grocery shopping only for me to use none of my groceries next week.

Oliver: Nope. Wrong answer.

Izzy: Fine, I'll bite. What's the right answer?

Oliver: Be ready at noon. Wear comfortable shoes.

"You HAVE GOT to be kidding me."

I look over to my passenger seat and can't hold back my laughter. "Not what you were expecting?"

"Hardly," Izzy says. "When you said to wear comfortable

shoes I figured we were going for a walk. Not the farmers' market."

"Nope," I say as I pull out my phone. "But first, selfie time."

"Really? Why?"

"Because. We take photos to remember the fun times. And I have a feeling this is going to be a very fun day."

"If I take this picture, will you get me a coffee?"

"It will be our first stop."

I hold my camera up and smile, while Izzy gives me an 'I hate you' look.

I've never seen a picture that represents two people more.

I get out of the car and hurry to her side, opening her door for her.

"You didn't have to do that."

"I know." I hold out my hand for her, which she eyeballs before she accepts. "But I need to ask, how many coffees is that today?"

"Just my third," she says defensively.

"Have you ever been told that you have a problem?"

She shakes her head as we start walking to the market. I put my hand on the small of her back but quickly realize what I've done. I slowly lower it, not wanting to make her uncomfortable. But I can't deny how good it felt to touch her, even if it was just that light, little touch.

"It's only a problem if you can't stop."

"And can you stop?"

"Of course," she says as she starts making a beeline toward the coffee cart. "Just not today."

~

"Favorite movie?"

Izzy looks up at me from dipping her tortilla chip into the salsa. "Really? How could I possibly answer that?"

"Easy," I say. "You name a movie you like a lot."

Izzy shoots me a look that I've learned today is her "no shit, Sherlock" face. She gave it to me no less than ten times during our farmer's market expedition.

"The last time I told you a movie I enjoyed, it ended up being used against me. Before I knew it we were drunk and naked."

I point my chip at her before drenching it in the queso. "I didn't use it against you. I used it to *woo* you. Totally different."

"Woo me?"

"Yes, woo you." I say. "Now, quit stalling."

She laughs in a huff. "Takes one to know one."

"What's that supposed to mean?"

"You're a deflector. So am I. It's something we have in common."

"Excuse me?"

"You heard me. It takes one to know one. I am a master deflector. No one does it better than me. Though I must admit, you're very close."

"Fine then," I say, though I'm not conceding to her accusation. "Right here, right now, we answer one question we honestly want to know about the other. No deflections. No excuses. Only truths."

This wipes the smile off her face. "Dammit. I walked right into that one."

I sit back and think for a second. I want to make this good. I'm not about to pass up my free pass to really finding out about Izzy.

"Okay," I begin. "Why don't you date?"

She narrows her eyes at me. "You went there, didn't you?"

"I had to take my chance while I had it."

She grabs her margarita and takes a sip. I'm guessing for courage, because it's a very large sip. "Because I don't believe that love exists for me."

Wow. Now I'm the one taken aback. "Why?"

Izzy shakes her head. "Nope. Just one question."

Shit. It might not be much, but at least it's something. "Fair enough."

"All right," she says, "Were you kidding at the wedding when you asked me to marry you?"

Out of any of the questions she could have asked, she had to go for that one. "No. I wasn't kidding."

Her eyes double in size before she nearly explodes in laughter. "You mean, if I would have said yes, we would be engaged right now?"

I shake my head and grab another chip. "Sorry. Can't answer that. We decided on just one question."

~

Izzy: I'm calling bullshit.

Oliver: Are you calling me a liar?

Izzy: I don't want to, but you're the one claiming that you own ninety pairs of socks. No man owns ninety pairs of socks.

Oliver: Cross my heart.

Izzy: How do I know you're crossing your heart?

Oliver: *Video crossing my heart*

Izzy: It was a figure of speech. I didn't need video evidence, dork.

Oliver: Better safe than sorry.

Izzy: I still think it's a load of crap.

Oliver: *Picture of two full sock drawers.*

Izzy: Well I'll be damned...

I LAUGH as Izzy rapid fires texts to me about my sock proof. Normally, a woman doesn't see the socks until at least date three—one ex-girlfriend, who I believe was proposal twenty-three, said it was weird so I never took a chance again—but I figured since Izzy and I aren't dating, I could break my rule for her.

I'm officially in the friend zone, and to be honest, it's not a bad place to be.

In all my years of dating, courting, and botched proposals, I've never been just friends with a woman. I like it. It's nice. No pressure. No worrying if I said or did the right or wrong thing. No worrying every day I'm accidentally going to propose.

It's freeing. I can just be myself. There's no hiding certain things because it might turn a woman off. There's also no getting into a certain hobby just because your partner is into it. Failed proposal nineteen was big into horseback riding. I bought boots and a twelve-gallon hat.

But with Izzy, it's just me. And I love it.

Oliver: You're trying to tell me you don't have an obscene amount of something?

Izzy: I mean, I have a lot of shoes?

Oliver: Come on, something better than that.

Izzy: I don't. I'm a minimalist.

Oliver: I don't believe that for a second.

Izzy: Are you calling me a liar?

Oliver: I don't want to...

Izzy: Want me to cross my heart?

Oliver: Only if you're telling me the honest truth.

Izzy: Fine. I have three cupboards of coffee mugs.

Oliver: Why am I not shocked it has to do with coffee?

Izzy: Am I that predictable?

Oliver: That's one thing I'd never call you.

Oliver: How was your day?

Izzy: Ugh...Not over.

Oliver: Are you still at the office?

Izzy: No, brought work home with me. I couldn't be in my office for another second.

Oliver: Why are you working so late?

Izzy: Hazel and I are going to a conference next week in Las Vegas, and there we have a big meeting about our London expansion. I need to make sure everything is set before we go.

Oliver: That will be fun!

Izzy: What part? The endless meetings or the boring conference?

Oliver: That's my girl. Always the optimist.

Izzy: Apologies. I'm getting hangry.

Oliver: You haven't eaten?

Izzy: Does a bagel this morning count?

Oliver: No.

Izzy: Then no.

Oliver: I'm grading papers. Want to do a double work night with a pizza?

Izzy: Get breadsticks.

Oliver: See you in an hour.

"Can I ask you a question?"

I lay back into bed, putting my arm behind my head as I put the phone on speaker. "Shoot."

"What made you a relationship guy?"

"Wow. I didn't see that question coming." In the last two weeks of us talking, she has never asked me one of these questions first. The get-to-know-you kind. She's been open when I've asked something. But I've kept them pretty tame. Nothing big like the day we said no deflections. Though I can tell by the tone of her voice, we might be leaning into that line of questioning.

"I don't know if anything made me, per se," I begin. "My mom never really dated and never got married. And while I don't think she was lonely, and I had an amazing childhood with zero bad memories, I always wondered what a nuclear family would look like. So I guess I became a relationship guy because in my mind, I couldn't have that without the relationship first."

"That makes sense, but I have one big question from that."

I chuckle, because I know what she's going to ask before it's even out of her mouth. "I'm adopted."

The silence says it all. Normally I don't drop it into conversation like that. Then again, that's not exactly the most natural thing to insert into any conversation.

"Wow," she says. "How old were you?"

"A baby. My mom had been trying for years to adopt. She wanted a child but didn't want to wait on a marriage that might never happen. But because she was going to be a single parent, a lot of people passed on her. Then one of her former students got pregnant with me. She was young, her parents told her they were going to disown her, and the sperm donor left the second she told him. So she asked my mom to adopt me. I've never met her, but given the circumstances, she probably protected me from a very difficult life."

"Well, fuck!" Izzy yells. "Why didn't you tell me that you were going to make me cry?"

"Sorry?"

"You should be. If I knew I was going to cry, I would have got tissues ready."

"I'll warn you next time."

"Appreciate it," she says. "In all seriousness, that's a beautiful story."

"Thank you." I take a second before I ask her the question I've wanted to ask for a while now, but didn't know how she'd react. Or if she'd just give me her famous short answers before moving on. "Speaking of family, you mentioned once that you had a niece and nephew, but you only saw them on FaceTime. Can I ask why?"

The line is silent between us, but I'm not worried. Somehow, I've come to know the silence moments between us just as much as the talking ones.

"My sister still lives in Nebraska, where we grew up. She married her high school sweetheart, had a few kids, and works in the office at my family's furniture store. She's living the life she always wanted."

"You don't go visit? Or they don't come here?"

"No."

Well, damn. Okay then. Clearly I went too far.

"I'm sorry I asked. Was just curious."

She lets out a sigh. "I'm sorry that was so short. It's just that I don't like talking about going back home. Or anything to do that part of my life. I left the second I could, and if I have my way, I'll never go back."

"Duly noted."

Shit...Now I feel bad. I knew Izzy had relationship hang-ups and for some godforsaken reason thinks that love isn't in the cards for her. I think if she opened up for the possibility of it, she'd love harder than anyone could ever love a person.

But I didn't realize there was family drama too.

"We are quite the pair, aren't we?"

I almost choke on my laugh. Shit, I wasn't expecting that from her. "You mean the guy who would start a family tomorrow being friends with the girl who doesn't talk to hers?"

This makes her laugh. "I was thinking more like the guy who loves love more than anything in the world and the woman who thinks it's horse shit. But yeah, yours works too."

In between our laughter, I hear Izzy let out a yawn.

"Go to sleep, Izzy."

This only makes her yawn again. "I'm okay."

"Go to sleep. I'm guessing you have an early day, and I have a first-grade art show to prepare for. We both need our rest."

"Fine," she says, though I think she's already half asleep. "Night, Oliver."

"Good night, Izzy."

Chapter 14
Izzy

Oliver: How was your day?

I READ THE TEXT MESSAGE, AND SHOCKINGLY, IT DOESN'T make me want to roll my eyes. If this were a few weeks ago, and it were any other guy, my immediate response would have been an eye roll. Granted, there have only been a few occasions where I would have given a man my number for these cheesy texts to even happen. But when they did, I would usually see it, let out a groan, delete the text, and then block the sender. Yes, I know I should have at least told the texter goodbye. But who has the time?

For some reason, though, when Oliver sends them to me, like he has every day since I told him that this was only ever going to be friendship, I'm not as annoyed. Maybe because our boundaries are clearly set. Maybe because I now know he's a truly nice guy. Maybe because as the days go by, this man is starting to really get to know me.

Izzy: Still going...

Oliver: Didn't you get to the office at like six today?

Izzy: Yes, stupid London meetings. I dread those days. I think Hazel does them to me on purpose.

Oliver: I'm sure she has a good reason.

Izzy: Yes. To torture me.

Oliver: Well, put the computer away. Go home. There's going to be a food delivery for you in approximately thirty minutes, and I'd hate for it to get cold.

This man...either he's the most stubborn and persistent man on the planet, or he's the best friend anyone could ever ask for.

Izzy: You know you don't have to send me food.

Oliver: Would you have remembered to eat if I didn't?

Izzy: Maybe. I might have eaten some popcorn?

Oliver: Is there anything else you have to get done tonight?

I think about what I was going to do if I stayed here for another hour. I mean, I'm trying to get ahead for the Vegas trip. At first, I thought the whole department was going to crumble because Jules was coming with me. But things came up and she can't get away. That helps slightly, but I really do need to get things prepared.

Then again, Oliver's right, there's nothing that is so pressing that it will make me push on to a thirteen-hour day.

Izzy: Fine, boss. I'll go home.

Oliver: I got you that manicotti from the Italian place we went to last week. Hope that's okay?

I smile, because pasta and sauce and a good glass of wine sounds absolutely perfect.

Izzy: It's more than okay.

Oliver: Good. Text or call me later. I'll be up.

I smile as I power down my phone, computer, and gather my things to leave the office. I'm the last one here, so it's eerily quiet as I take the elevator down to the ground floor and head to my car. I planned on driving home in silence, but my Bluetooth had a different idea.

For fuck's sake Oliver...

The first song that plays is some cheesy pop hit from the late nineties. I tried to tell him that I thought the song was stupid. So of course, when we went to the farmers' market again last week, he had it queued to play in his car. He called my bluff when I knew all the words. Though I didn't realize apparently he put it on one of my playlists without me knowing.

I laugh as I start up the car and make the short drive home. Everything about this man should annoy me. He's perky. He's a jokester. He's almost too sweet.

But the more we hang out, the more he's embedding himself into my life.

And the shocking thing about that is I don't hate it.

When I told him this was only ever going to be friends nearly a month ago, I assumed he would maybe try to hang around for a bit, see if I was actually serious, then slowly, but surely, go about his way. But no. This man has not only burrowed his way into my daily life, he's become my best friend. Well, my guy best friend. Whom I've seen naked. And whom I know can eat pussy like a champ.

I think about that more than I should.

Though if I'm being honest, it's kind of nice having someone check on me. The only people who check on me regularly are Hazel and Jules. And usually that's to make sure I stayed hydrated and fed. Granted, that's what Oliver does a lot as well, but add in some mundane texting and random conversations, and you have yourself a new go-to person.

As the song finishes, I call him, because I need to know when he managed to do this.

"So either one of two things have happened," he says instead of a hello. "Either your order is wrong or your playlist finally played my additions."

"Additions? As in plural?"

This makes him laugh. "Which one did you get?"

"The one about Michael J. Fox having a bunch of hits."

"Ah...a classic," he says. "Just wait. There are more from where that came from."

I fall back into my seat, letting the soothing tone of Oliver's voice relax me as I wait at a stoplight. Do I still find his voice sexy? Yes. Even though we're just friends I all of a sudden didn't quit having a pulse. But now I've come to associate it with comfort.

I won't tell anyone, but it's nice.

Since I moved from my small town in Nebraska, the only person I ever remotely had this kind of friendship with is Hazel. Hell, even back then I never had a ton of friends. I did have my sister, who used to check on me regularly. But the longer I've stayed away from the town I have very few fond memories of, the less frequent our communication has been. Occasionally, she'll send me a picture of my niece and nephew. Sometimes she wants to make sure everything's okay. But it's been months since either of those happened. Which is fine. I get it. We're living two different lives. Just like we should be.

"You know," I say. "You didn't have to order me food. I am capable of feeding myself."

"I don't know about that," he says. "Last night you said you ate a carrot for dinner. Did you even use ranch dressing?"

"Of course not," I say. "And it was *three* carrots."

"Well, then, that's a whole new ballgame."

"Whatever," I say as the light turns green. "How was your day?"

"Fine," he says. "I think I'm counting down the days until the end of the school year more than the kids are."

"What's it down to?"

"Three school days. One half-day for teachers. And then freedom."

"Nice. What are the summer plans?" I pull into my parking garage and slide into my parking space, which is right next to the elevators.

"For the first week, sleep. Relaxation. After a while, football practices will begin, so that will keep me busy. In between that I'll probably start the expansion to the back deck I've been wanting to tackle."

"You can build a deck?"

"Does that surprise you?"

"You don't strike me as the handy kind of guy."

"Don't let my boyishly good looks fool you. I'm a wiz with a hammer," he says. "Plus, I look hot as hell in a tool belt."

I laugh as I walk out of the elevator onto my floor. "I'm sure you do."

It only takes me a few steps down my hall before the aroma of the Italian dish hits my nostrils. Damn, that smells good.

"So that's it?" I ask as I let myself into my condo. "Football, sleep, and construction? No traveling? No fun outings?"

"Probably not," he says.

"Why?"

"Because I don't have anyone to go with."

"So?"

I drop the bag of food down on my kitchen island before pouring myself a glass of wine before I dig in. "So what? Go solo. Solo traveling is great."

"Maybe for you," he says. "But as you could probably guess, I'm not that kind of guy."

"I get that," I say, taking a sip of the crisp pinot grigio. "But have you tried it? Or is this you just having a feeling?"

"I actually tried it," he says. "I tried going to Savannah a few years ago. It's a place I always wanted to visit, so I figured there was enough to do that I could keep myself occupied for a few days. After day two, I got lonely and depressed and stayed in my Airbnb for the rest of the trip."

Well, shit...now I'm mad at myself that I suggested it. Oliver's such a sweet guy. I might not believe in love or marriage or any of that crap, but if there is one person who deserves the fairy tale story, it's Oliver. He should be able to have that partner to see the world with and go on cute vacations.

Well, I might not be able to give him the love stuff, but the vacation I can handle.

"Come with me to Vegas."

It takes him a few moments to realize what I said. "Did you just say come with you to Vegas?"

"I did."

"Are you sure?"

Am I sure? The fact I'm not freaking out that those words just came out of my mouth actually scares me more than the words themselves.

"Yes. I'm sure." I say confidently. "I have a fully paid for room with two double beds, and one is now open because Jules can't come. I'm sure I could even transfer her ticket to you. And it works perfectly because we leave the day after you're done with school. Plus, Hazel's bringing Knox, so you two can pal around together during the day while we're off doing boring conference stuff. Lay by the pool. Drink a mai tai. Find a buffet. Do whatever you want. Then after we're done, we can hang with them, or the two of us can paint the town while they're off doing romantic couple shit."

"I mean, I guess I could..." I can actually hear the wheels turn in Oliver's head as he thinks this out.

"Yes, you can. Your plans were to sleep this weekend. You can do that on a lazy river while sipping a pina colada."

"I thought I was drinking a mai tai?"

I smile, because it looks like I have a travel buddy for Vegas. "You can drink whatever you heart desires. It's Vegas, baby."

Chapter 15
Oliver

I LOOK AT MY BED, WHICH IS CURRENTLY COVERED BY everything I could think to pack for this three-day trip to Vegas. Outfits for the day and for the night. Swim trunks. Boxer briefs. And of course, twenty pairs of socks. I like to have options. What I make sure *not* to pack are condoms. It's not like I'm going to sleep with Izzy. And I wouldn't dare hook up with someone while I'm on a trip with her. Especially since we're staying in the same room. So no bother in packing those.

When Izzy asked me yesterday if I wanted to go to Vegas, I was hesitant for a few seconds. Then she sold me on lazy rivers, drinks with umbrellas, and a weekend away with no school, no kids, and no responsibilities. Now I'm a half day of work, cleaning my classroom, and turning in equipment away from slot machines, a sports book, and hopefully a show or two. Maybe I can convince Izzy to see Criss Angel?

I laugh to myself as I head to the bathroom to grab my toiletries. I hear my front door slam open, and just as quickly, slam shut.

"Oliver!"

Why is Shane here? It's seven in the morning. "In the bathroom!"

If there was anyone described in our friend group as the "mean" one, it would be Shane. But that's just to people who don't know him. Is he the brooding, silent type? Yes. Does he constantly wear a scowl? Also yes, but only when we're in public. In private it's only half of the time. I've even seen him smile more than twenty times; it's rare enough I keep count. I've known him since we were six years old, and there's nothing he can do to scare me.

Or so I thought. The look on his face right now is making me wish I didn't pack *all* my clean boxers.

"You're going to Vegas with a stranger, and you didn't bother to tell us?"

That's why he's here? "How did you find out about my trip?"

"Wes," he says as I head back into my bedroom, toiletry bag in hand. "He said when he talked to you yesterday that you were going to Vegas with someone we don't know, and you wouldn't say who it was."

"Oh. Well, then, you're all caught up."

I go back to putting all of the clothes I laid out into my suitcase. When I look back up at Shane, he's staring at me like I've grown a second head.

"What the fuck, man?" he says. "Why won't you tell us who you're seeing?"

"I'm not seeing anyone."

"Why are you lying?"

I look Shane square in the eye. "I'm not seeing anyone. At least in that way."

"Then tell me. Why the secrecy?"

He's right. I hid Izzy at first because something just told me I needed to. I think my subconscious was trying to protect me in case she kicked me to the curb. But now that I know she's going to be part of my life, and that I know there's nothing that's going to happen between us, I might as well come clean.

But not yet. When I get home I will. I'll show them all the pictures, tell them everything about how we met, my elaborate plan to try to get her to date me, and how she ultimately friend-zoned me. I'll even tell them that they can up their proposal count to thirty-four.

I just want one more adventure with her before we leave our bubble that I've come to love so much.

"I promise I'll tell you when I get home," I say. "But I want you to know, don't worry about me. I'll be fine."

Shane nods. "I know you will be. You just haven't been acting like yourself, and you're the one thing in my life that I can count on."

"Aw, you're getting sentimental."

His face goes back to the scowl. "Fuck you."

"When you say that, I know you really mean you love me. I love you too, brother."

Shane is unfazed by my words, a byproduct of nearly thirty years of friendship. "Promise me one thing?"

"Yes, I will bring you back a tacky T-shirt as a souvenir. Elvis or Blue Man Group?"

Shane doesn't laugh. Instead he puts on his mean "dad" look. "I need you to promise me you won't come back married."

I laugh, but I also understand his concern. "I promise."

I LOVE BEING A TEACHER. I don't know what I'd do if I wasn't. But there is nothing quite like the feeling of driving away, the windows of your car rolled down, the wind blowing through your hair, as you pull away after the last day of school.

It's a freedom that can't be replicated.

Instead of turning right to head to The Joint, where the rest of the teachers are going for a celebratory drink, I turn left to head toward the highway. It worked out that I was going to get done with my day in time to pick up Izzy and then head straight to the airport. As long as there are no delays, we'll be in Vegas just in time to get in a few rounds at the poker table.

Just as I turn onto Route 65, a call comes through the Bluetooth with the iconic song, "Fancy." Which means my mom is calling. Suzanne Price loves her some Reba.

"Hey, Mom," I say.

"Another year down! You did it!"

I laugh as she makes some sort of congratulatory sounds through the phone. This is a yearly tradition. It started in person as we were both teaching, though she was in middle school and I was down in elementary. Since she retired, she's kept it up through phone calls. It's my official start to summer.

"I did," I say. "I'm going to miss this group. They might have driven me crazy by the end of the year, but they were good kids."

"Of course you will. A good teacher never forgets her kids, no matter how many classes go through."

She would know. The woman taught for thirty-five years and can't go anywhere in Rolling Hills without a former student stopping her to say hello. I think she's been invited to every Rolling Hills class reunion, and she's attended most of them. She was invited to my class reunion, which she declined because she said I didn't need my mother there. So instead we all moved the party to her house and camped in her front yard.

It was worth it. She made us pancakes the next morning.

"I must admit, I'm kind of surprised you called," I say. "Aren't you in Missouri or something right now?"

"We are," she says. "We pit-stopped for the day. Carol

needed a day out of the car. But then we're heading for Oklahoma. Reba Museum, here we come!"

I can't help but laugh as I weave in and out of traffic. My Aunt Carol has been my mom's best friend since childhood. She helped raise me. I'm pretty sure she taught me my first swear word. I can't imagine my life without her. Or my mom's.

Neither of them ever got married, and for years called themselves Thelma and Louise. So for the past year, they've been planning a summer road trip on Route 66, with a few detours along the way. They were going to go see the sights, some shows, an exhibit of Reba McIntyre in her hometown—not a whole museum like she keeps saying it is—and maybe pick up a young version of Brad Pitt along the way.

"Well, I'm glad you two are having a good time. And actually, I'm about to go on a trip myself."

"Really? Are you and Simon going somewhere?"

"No, actually. Her name is Izzy, and we're going to Vegas."

The line is silent for more than a few seconds. I don't even hear her breathing. I also realize that, for the first time, I'm telling someone in my circle about Izzy. But it's my mom, and she should know. You know, in case I'm kidnapped and she needs to be briefed about my whereabouts and who I was with.

"Mom? Are you there?"

I hear a breath, which is good. I was scared for a second.

"Oliver, you always promised me that when you got married, I'd be there. I don't care if you elope, but I want to be there when my only child gets married."

"Mom, I'm not getting married." Why does everyone think that?

"Sure you aren't, sweetie."

Well if that wasn't Southern mama ridicule, I don't know what is.

"I'm not. We've been hanging out for a few months. She's

going for a work conference, and I'm tagging along. That's it."

"Is it?" she asks. "Oliver, I love you. But you've never been *just friends* with a woman."

"That's a lie. I have Amelia."

"I love Amelia, but she doesn't count."

"Why?"

"Because you've never wanted to sleep with Amelia."

"And how do you know I want to sleep with Izzy?"

I can't see my mother right now, but I can picture her face. Eyebrows up, gaze serious, head tilted. "Do you not want to?"

I start to answer, but quickly stop.

Do I? Obviously I did. Now I don't. But do I? If Izzy said this weekend, "Hey, I was wrong. Let's try this?" Would I?

Oh, who am I kidding? Of course I would.

"Fine," I admit. "But she has been clear that things are going to stay just friends between us. And I'm okay with that."

"You're sure?"

"Yes," I say as I pull off the highway toward Izzy's condo. Luckily, traffic is light so I'll be in front of her building before I know it. "You don't need to worry about me."

"You know I do," she says. "I'll always worry. That's what moms do."

I smile, because she has said that to me many times over the years. Every time she does, I always think of what would have happened if my biological mom hadn't given me to her. What if she would have been chosen by the adoption agency before that? What if I wouldn't have been put up for adoption? It's a rabbit hole I could get lost in.

But then I remind myself that everything happens for a reason. And I'll always let my mom worry, because I'm glad that I'm here for her to worry about.

"Okay, Mom. I'm picking up Izzy," I say. "I'm going to go."

"Oh no you don't," she says as I pull up to Izzy, who is

waiting for me in front of her building. "I want to say hi."

I put the car in park and turn on the hazards. "Are you serious?"

"As a heart attack."

I quickly get out of the car and meet Izzy at my trunk to help her load her bags.

"Warning," I quickly say before she starts talking. "My mom's on the phone in the car. She wants to say hi to you. I don't know what else she's going to say, but I wanted to warn you."

Izzy just laughs. "Of course you'd be the one to talk to your mom before going on a trip."

I shut the trunk and both of us get into the car. "I'm back, Mom."

"Hi. Izzy, is it?"

I look over to Izzy, who all of a sudden doesn't have much color to her face. "Yes. Hi."

"I'm Suzanne Price."

"Nice to meet you, Ms. Price."

"Call me Suzanne, dear. Now, I need a favor from you."

Izzy shoots me a confused look. I shrug my shoulders, because I'm just as clueless as she is.

"Sure."

"I need you to make sure my boy doesn't get married in Vegas," she says. "I'm sure you've heard about his propensity to propose. Please don't marry him in Vegas, or allow him to marry anyone else. However, if he's insisting on it, I'd like to be there, so please call me and let me know."

This makes Izzy laugh. It makes me want to slam my head against the steering wheel. "That will be no problem, Suzanne. I'll take good care of him."

"Good," she says. "Because sometimes what happens in Vegas doesn't stay there."

Chapter 16
Izzy

"First we need to play a slot machine, because I'm still mad you didn't let me play at least one at the airport. Then we're going to get settled into our room. Then I thought we'd meet up with Hazel and Knox to say hello and then maybe take a walk on the strip. It's your only day to do it, so I figured if there was anything you wanted to see, we should do it today. Oh! And there's a show—"

"Oliver!" I don't mean to yell—or scare our Uber driver, a very nice lady named Juanita—but my head is spinning and we're not even to our hotel yet.

"What?"

"Take a breath."

"Oh," he says as he realizes that he hasn't stopped talking since the second we landed in Vegas. "Sorry. I'm just excited. I've never been to Vegas."

"Neither have I," I say. "But we don't have to do everything today. We have two more days. Plus, Hazel and I have to meet with some people this afternoon."

He looks out the window, then turns to smile at me—a

mischievous smile that usually means he has an idea I'm not going to like. "Well, then, I know the first thing we're going to do. Juanita! Can you stop up here for a second?"

"Sure thing, Mr. Oliver!"

Juanita, also known as Oliver's new best friend after he made small talk with her at the airport, pulls to a stop, and I look to see where we are. I should have guessed.

"The Fabulous Las Vegas sign?"

"Yup. We're taking a picture."

I shake my head. "No, we're not."

Oliver shoots me a look I'd guess he gives his first graders on a regular basis. "And why not?"

"Because," I say, though I don't really know why. "Because I don't want to. And there are a bunch of tourists and it will take forever."

There. Those are pretty good reasons.

"Nope," he says, grabbing my hand and pulling me across the backseat of the SUV. "We're doing it."

I moan and groan, but eventually exit the car. One thing I've learned about Oliver is he loves taking pictures. Selfies, posed, random things, his food. The man captures everything. Then there's me. The only pictures I have on my phone are of my niece and nephew, one of Hazel and I from I don't even remember when, and now a few photos of Oliver and I that he sent me. The first from our day at the farmers' market, a random one he took some night when he came over because we were both bored, and then one this morning when we made it to the airport.

"Why do you like taking pictures so much?"

He looks at the sign, then down to me. "It's all about the moments. I want to have my life documented so one day I can sit around with my grandkids and tell them about all the things I got to do. Tell them about all the people I loved and who helped make me the man I am. I don't want to miss a thing. And I damn sure don't want to forget one."

Oliver has this way about him that makes me feel inspired, and yet also makes me feel like I really am a soulless bitch, all at the same time.

I think about his words. Do I have any experiences I wish I would have documented? The sad thing is, I can't think of any. Sure, there are fun moments with Hazel that I would have liked to relive in picture form, but all in all, I can't think of a single one. Have I really become that closed off? I mean, I know I'm a workaholic with no social life. But I think at some point that went from a defense mechanism to simply becoming who I am.

That is, until fucking Oliver Price asked me to dance with him. Now here I am, taking pictures and going to fucking farmers' markets. I bet he's going to make me see a show this weekend.

"Our turn!" he says, grabbing my hand and pulling me toward the sign.

"A little over to the left," Juanita says, who somehow got Oliver's phone when I was in my own thoughts. "Oh, come on, Miss Izzy. Show me that smile. You're in Vegas, baby!"

Oliver wraps his arm around my waist, pulling me so close that I don't have a choice but to also put my hand around his. "Come on. Smile. I have a feeling we're going to want to remember this trip for the rest of our lives."

~

"Holy shit..."

I look over to Oliver, whose eyes are wide and unblinking as we walk into Caesars Palace.

"All right, I'm going to go check in," I say to Oliver, who is still taking in every inch of beauty that is the Caesars' lobby. "You...well, just don't run away."

He nods and waves me off as I make my way to the line. I have a few seconds, so I shoot off a message to Hazel. She and Knox flew in last night so they could have an entire day just for themselves.

Izzy: In the lobby. What room are you?

Hazel: 1811. How was the flight?

Izzy: Fine.

Hazel: How's Oliver?

I look over my shoulder, where I see Oliver taking a picture of every angle of the fountain.

Izzy: He made me take a picture at the Vegas sign.

Hazel: LOLOLOLOL. And you did it?

I tap away from the text into my photos, where Oliver already airdropped the photo to me. It really is a nice picture...

Izzy: Begrudgingly.

Hazel: Well, if you're in a picture-taking mood, then we're taking all of them this weekend. Remind me to buy Oliver a drink for opening that door for me.

Izzy: Oh I will...

"I can help who's next!"

I put my phone away and wheel my luggage over to the check-in desk. "Hi. Reservation under McCall."

I slide my driver's license and credit card to her, knowing the drill. "Ah, yes. Elizabeth McCall."

"Your real name is Elizabeth?"

I whip my head around. "Shit, I thought you were still playing at the fountain."

"I wasn't playing," Oliver says, holding up and waving his phone. "I was documenting."

I shake my head. The man is so damn glass-half-full sometimes I wonder how he doesn't spill over.

"Okay, Miss McCall. I have you in the Palace tower. One king bedroom."

Did I just hear her right? "Did you say king room? And one bed?"

"Yes, ma'am," she says. "That's what I have the reservation under."

How did this happen? I didn't make the reservation; Jules handles all that for me.

"There has to be some sort of mistake," I plead. "I need a room with two beds. Whatever size doesn't matter to me. I just need there to be two of them."

"What's the matter?" Oliver leans down to whisper in my ear. "Can you not resist me if we're in the same bed?"

I snap my head so hard to Oliver I think my hair smacks him in the face.

"You shush."

I turn back to the attendant and do my best to keep calm, because it's not her fault. I think. "Ma'am. Is there any way we can change rooms? I don't care what tower or floor we're on."

"Let me check, but I honestly doubt it. Besides the convention your room is blocked under, we also have MagicCon happening," she says. While she's searching, I see Oliver out of the corner of my eye, who's doing a shit job of holding in his delight.

"You're loving this, aren't you?"

Oliver tries to wipe the smile from his face, but he can't. "I don't know what's better, you freaking out over the beds or knowing that we could be next door to a magician."

I turn back to the attendant while wondering how much cash I have on hand to bribe her. "Is there anything?"

She shakes her head. "I'm sorry, ma'am. We're all booked."

"It will be fine," Oliver says. "Is there a pullout couch?"

She shakes her head. "There is a couch, but it doesn't extend. But if you need extra blankets or pillows, we'll be happy to send them up."

I let out a sigh of defeat, which also serves as a breath to calm myself down. I feel Oliver's hands on my shoulders, which does relax me. Slightly.

"We'll figure it out," he says. "Look at it this way, now we can build a pillow fort so you don't have the urge to seduce me in the middle of the night."

"Sure," I say, though I can't hold in my laughter. Probably because he's doing this ridiculous eyebrow wag. "I guess it will be fine."

"It will be," he says as he grabs the keys and we make our way to the elevator. "Now. Let's go put our stuff down. I need to find a slot machine, and you, my dear, need a drink."

Chapter 17
Oliver

I KNOW IZZY IS STILL IN A HUFF ABOUT THE BED situation, but I must say, this room is really nice.

The view is amazing. The bathroom, with its white and gold tile and walls, is probably the nicest one I've ever used. It even has a bathtub that might make me change my views on baths. And these pillows? I wonder how much we'd get charged if I took one home?

Today has been a chill day, which I didn't mind. After our room check-in debacle, Izzy only had time to drop off her things and get quickly changed. She and Hazel had to meet with some potential clients and collaborators, so Knox and I took the opportunity to walk around and get the lay of the land. We checked out the pool and the pool bar, played a few hands of blackjack, and sat in the sports book for a bit. I even won fifty bucks on a horse race.

I look over at the clock to see that it's nearly nine-thirty. Shit, I didn't realize it was that late. Though now that I know that, it makes sense that my stomach has suddenly started growling.

Oliver: You still going strong?

Izzy: Almost done.

Oliver: Have you eaten?

Izzy: What do you think?

Oliver: Figured. I'll order room service.

Izzy: Some sort of wrap. And maybe a salad.
Or pizza. Or fries. Cheesecake?

Oliver: Haha. I'll get a little bit of everything.

Izzy: I freaking love you.

I set down my phone and grab the menu from the bedside table. I order more food than either of us will probably eat before lying back in the bed and turning on a random baseball game. What I don't do is overanalyze the phrase, "I freaking love you."

That's what old Oliver would do. He'd analyze it six ways from Sunday to see if there was any hidden meaning. New Oliver knows it's a figure of speech and to not read into it.

"Look at me. Growing," I say to myself as I get up off the bed and head to my suitcase. Just as I'm pulling out a T-shirt and pajama pants, I hear the sound of the door opening and Izzy slowly walking through.

"That was quick." I put down the clothes and watch as Izzy slowly walks into the room.

"Nothing about this day was quick," she says, falling back onto the bed in perfect snow angel form.

I walk over to the bed and sit down at her feet. "I thought you only had one meeting today?"

She looks up at me, and I don't know how to describe her look right now, but the word annoyed is definitely somewhere in there. "We were. Then Hazel saw a friend from college, so we sat with them for a while. I didn't mind that so much, because at least it was in one of the lounges and I could get a drink. But then as we were walking back, we passed a conference room and saw one of the keynote speakers that Hazel is friends with. What started as a quick chat turned into two hours of computer shit that I don't understand. I'm tired. Hungry. My feet hurt. And I've been in Vegas for a day, and I haven't bet one dollar on anything."

"I'm sorry," I say, reaching over to grab one of her feet. I slowly take off her high heel and start working her arches with my thumbs.

"Oh, fuck me," she moans.

Football stats and blue cheese. Football stats and blue cheese.

"I don't know where you learned to do this, or who taught you, but I'm grateful."

"Thanks," I say, using a little more pressure, which apparently Izzy likes. Believe me, I remember her cues for the "I really like that" body movements. "I don't know if anyone actually taught me, but never has an ex complained about it, so I just figured it was one of my hidden talents."

"Can I ask you a serious question? And you can't deflect." Izzy leans up on her elbows, and I take the opportunity to switch feet.

"Must be serious if you're putting in the deflection clause early."

"Why are you single?"

"Wow," I say, a little shocked she went there. "Going right for the big one."

"Yes, but it's been something I've wondered more and more since we've started hanging out. I know I didn't want to date you, but that was a direct reflection on me. But are these other women crazy?"

I can't help but laugh. "If you ask my friends, they'd probably say yes."

Izzy sits up, taking her foot back with her so she's now sitting. "I'm serious. I mean, you're the nicest guy I've ever met."

"One broke up with me because I was too nice."

"Okay, so at least one was crazy. But I'm not done. You're nice. You have a good job. You seem to love your family, which I might not be able to fathom, but I do get that not everyone had my fucked-up childhood. And then there's the fact that if I would have let you keep rubbing my feet, I'm pretty sure I would have had an orgasm. And I also know that you can fuck like a champ. So what's wrong with them?"

When hearing it like that, I truly don't know what to say. While on one hand, I'm glad Izzy thinks all of these things about me. Especially that last part. Then again, I can't help but feel a touch of depression, knowing that I do bring things to the table, yet for some reason, I'm still not enough.

"I wish I knew," I say. Luckily for me, I don't have to think of anything else as there's a banging on the door.

"Room service. You go clean up, put on your pajamas, and get comfy. I'll get dinner set up."

I give Izzy a hand to help her off the bed as I head to the door. I bring the food back and put it all out on the coffee table that's in front of the couch, also known as my bed for the night.

"I don't know what you ordered, but it smells amazing."

I look over to the bathroom where Izzy was changing, and I'm pretty sure that if I were holding something I would have dropped it.

I've seen Izzy in a lot of forms over the past few months. But my favorite was that morning after the wedding. Her hair was mussed, her body was relaxed, and there was a glow about her that I'll never forget.

This right here? I don't know if it takes over the number one spot, but it's definitely trying to. Her red hair is piled up on the top of her head. Her face is freshly cleansed, exposing her freckles that get covered when she's wearing makeup. She's changed out her business clothes for an oversized T-shirt, and if she's wearing anything underneath, I can't tell. Which might be hotter than lingerie. Actually, it is. Yes, lace and silk are great. But an oversized T-shirt, especially if it's one of yours, is without a doubt the hottest thing a woman can wear.

Stop it, Oliver. Don't let your mind go down that path.

"Dinner's ready," I say, quickly, turning back to the food. If she realizes I'm now thrown, she doesn't say anything. Instead she just shimmies up next to me and starts making herself a plate before sitting down on the couch.

"So, are we going to talk about it?"

I look over to her in confusion. "Talk about what?"

She looks over to the bed and back to me. "The sleeping arrangement."

"Oh," I say, grabbing a slice of pizza and a helping of salad. "I can sleep on the couch."

She shakes her head. "You absolutely will not."

"I won't?"

"No. For one, this thing is not suitable for sleeping in terms of comfort. Number two, half of your legs will hang off. Three, I don't feel bad often, but I'm pretty sure you sleeping over here while I have a gigantic king bed for myself will make me feel slightly guilty."

"Okay," I say. "And you're positive you're okay with us sharing a bed?"

Izzy nods in between bites. "I am. Why do you keep asking me?"

"Maybe because a few hours ago I didn't know if you were going to show up on a viral video about customers gone crazy."

She hangs her head. "I know. I acted like a lunatic. I think I was just taken by surprise. And I was tired from the travel. And you made me take a picture."

"Oh no. Don't you go blaming this on me. A photo did not almost make you a Karen."

She slaps me on the shoulder. "How dare you!"

"Ow," I say. Though it didn't really hurt.

"Oh, stop. I barely touched you," she says. "Back to the subject. The bed is plenty big. I think that we are adult enough to be able to share a bed without needing to build your pillow fort."

"Speak for yourself. I always take the opportunity to build a pillow fort."

"You're ridiculous," she says, yawning between bites.

"You're going to fall asleep in your salad."

"No, I'm not," she says while yawning.

"Okay, then," I say, setting down my now empty plate. "I'm going to go get ready for bed. Twenty bucks you're asleep when I get back."

She gives me a thumbs-up while yawning. "You're on."

I grab the T-shirt and pajama pants I pulled from my suitcase earlier and head to the bathroom. I could make this whole process five minutes—all I need to do is change, brush my teeth, and take out my contacts. But I know she's going to fall asleep, and while I'd never collect on the bet, I know she's tired. And the quicker I go back out there, the more she'll fight it.

She's a stubborn one. But that's what makes Izzy Izzy. She's like no one I've ever met.

On one hand, she's fierce in a way that is damn impressive. Sometimes a little bit scary, though I know it's just a front.

She's smart and witty. Funny with a dry, sarcastic humor. That's the part of her that she lets be seen to the world.

Then there are the parts I'm now getting to see when it's just the two of us. Softer. More relaxed. Like she can let her guard down and not have to keep putting up this impenetrable front that she insists on maintaining.

The one who is currently asleep on the couch, plate still in hand.

I smile as I walk over to the bed, bringing the covers down. I have to hold in a chuckle when I hear a slight snore from her. I gently take the plate from her hand, which makes her blink her eyes open slowly.

"Shhh," I say, scooping her under her legs and behind her back. "Let's go to bed."

In the most un-Izzy move I think I've encountered, she doesn't argue with me. Instead, she brings her arms around my neck, placing her head against my chest as I carry her the few steps it takes to get to the bed. I slowly lower her onto the mattress and bring the covers up to her chest before leaning down to place a gentle kiss on her forehead.

"You owe me twenty dollars."

She doesn't hear my whisper, which is fine. I'd never make her pay. Nope, seeing her like this is the best payment there is.

Chapter 18
Izzy

Jesus tap dancing Christ...

Oliver Price in dress pants and a button down is fucking sex on a stick. And I can't stop staring at him.

This isn't the first time this weekend I've had to remind myself that Oliver is not on my Vegas to-do list. One was last night when I could feel his chest under me as he carried me to bed. Another was this morning when I woke up, and even though I know he didn't mean anything by it, his arm still ended up lazily draped over my waist.

I selfishly didn't move it for a few minutes.

I thought the most tempting time was this afternoon when Hazel and I found him and Knox lounging on the pool deck. Yes, I've seen Oliver shirtless. I've touched it, licked it, and held onto it for dear life. But there was something about him, laying in the sun in his swim trunks and skin glistening, that made me immediately need a cold drink to cool down.

But none of those instances compare to right now. Watching Oliver button his crisp white shirt and rolling his sleeves is better than porn. I don't know what it is about watching a man getting dressed, especially if they throw on some cologne, but it is one of the sexiest things he can do.

"Are you staring at me?"

"No. Of course not."

"Liar," he says with a wink. "It's okay, though. I know I'm irresistible."

If he only knew...

No. No, no, no. I internally scold myself as I get up to finish getting ready. I have to keep repeating that Oliver isn't the guy you have a fun vacation fling with. Or *any* kind of fling.

And I don't want him to be. Despite my carefully constructed walls, Oliver is breaking them down daily. He's become the friend I didn't know I needed. I just have to remind myself that I can't sleep with him. Or stare at him. Or get lost in the sound of his voice.

If I do all of that I'm fine.

"What time are we meeting Hazel and Knox?" I ask.

"Twenty minutes. Are you going to be ready?"

"Yes," I say, though I'm not sure if I'm lying. "All I have to do is finish my makeup and get dressed."

"The timer starts now."

I laugh and shake my head as I carefully start applying my eyeliner. Somewhere today while Hazel and I were doing our things at the conference, Knox and Oliver were busy planning our night. First, dinner at a Michelin-rated steakhouse, followed by a night of gambling and dancing and, of course, checking out the fountains at the Bellagio.

Not wanting Oliver to be right—I need to knock him down a peg after that whole irresistible comment—I quickly put on the dress I picked for the night. Is it a little revealing? Maybe. Did I do it on purpose? No. Maybe. I still haven't decided.

I slip on the little black number before finishing off my lipstick. After giving my hair one more shake I exit the bathroom, only to find Oliver lying on the bed, head propped up on his hand, looking like he's better than anything that's about to be on the menu tonight.

I don't know what is happening right now. Our eyes are locked on each other, and I know I for sure can't tear mine away. He starts to get up, but that doesn't break our gaze. I feel my mouth getting dry with every step he takes toward me. And the closer he gets, and the more powerful his cologne becomes, I wonder if my knees are going to give out. And it has nothing to do with my four-inch heels.

"I need to say one thing." His voice reverberates through me as I look up at Oliver. We're mere inches apart. My mind immediately goes back to the hotel room after the wedding.

Fuck...I need to quit being in hotels with this man...

"Okay..."

"I know I need to be a gentleman right now. I know we're friends, and the line has been drawn in the sand. And I respect that. But I need you to know...there is nothing gentlemanly about the thought I'm having right now. Because I would love nothing more than to fuck you in that dress before ripping it off just so I can fuck you again."

Oliver's eyes are on fire right now—I should know. Because there isn't a cell in my body that isn't burning.

"Good to know," I say, not backing down. "Makes me feel better about staring at you earlier. Because believe me, those thoughts were not very lady-like."

Neither of us move. I don't know if—or when—we would have, if a knock didn't startle us at the door.

"You two ready?" Hazel yells. "I'm starving!"

"We should go," I say.

"I guess we should."

I don't move. Neither does Oliver.

"Do we have to go?" he says.

I laugh, loving that no matter what the situation, I can always count on Oliver to lighten the situation. Even if he's minutes removed from talking like the dirty man I know he is.

"Come on," I say, finally taking the first step so I can grab my purse. "If you're lucky, maybe you can help me take the dress off later. That zipper is tricky."

He groans, which only makes me laugh harder. "You're killing me, woman," he says, grabbing my hand and opening the door. "You're fucking killing me."

"I'd like to make a toast," Oliver says as he holds up his glass of bourbon. "To Left for Love. Even though I was on the app for many years without any luck, I can't help but be thankful for it. Not only did it bring Hazel and Izzy to Tennessee and into our lives, but it brought us all here this weekend."

Knox raises his glass. "I'll toast to that."

The four of us clink glasses before Knox and Hazel break away for a tender kiss. I take a sip of my Manhattan, but happen to catch Oliver looking at me out of the corner of my eye.

"What?"

He smiles behind his glass. "Just thinking."

"About?"

He looks down, then back up to my eyes. "Stuff."

I shake my head, but a smile escapes. "You're ridiculous."

He leans in closer. "If you didn't want me to think bad thoughts, you wouldn't have worn that dress."

I can't help but shiver as his words run through me. "Should I apologize?"

He shakes his head as he backs away. "Never."

"Ladies. Gentleman. I think it's time we hit the tables," Knox says. "Who's with me?"

"Let's go!" Hazel says. Oliver doesn't answer. Instead he gives me a wink as he helps me off my barstool.

The four of us start walking toward the casino, but Hazel suddenly grabs my hand, pulling me back behind the guys.

"What was that!" she whisper-yells.

"What was what?"

"You two eye fucking each other during dinner. And at the bar. I thought you two were just friends?"

"We are," I say. "Things have just got a little..."

"Have you slept with him again?"

I shake my head. "No. But the room only has one bed."

"What!" she yells. Knox and Oliver both turn around and look at us. I wave them back around before answering. "How are you just telling me this?"

"I didn't want you making a big deal out of it. Because I know you're Team Oliver."

"I would not do anything of the sort. And how do you know that?"

I shoot her a look. "You would and you did. I know you helped him with all those gifts and deliveries."

"Fine. I helped. Guilty as charged," she says with a huff. "So there's one bed. And you're both...just sleeping in it?"

"Yes," I say firmly. "Though there was a...*moment* tonight."

"A moment! What kind of moment?"

"I don't know. A moment," I say.

"Like a 'you wanted him to kiss you' moment? Or a 'we're not making it to dinner because we never made it out of the room' moment?"

"The second one," I admit. "Definitely the second one."

"Damn," Hazel says.

"Exactly."

The guys head toward one of the craps tables, but the two of us hang behind.

"Can I ask you a question you're going to hate?"

I let out a humorless laugh. "Even if I say no it won't stop you."

"You're right. But I have to know, why *not* Oliver? Because, as someone who has made her career on love and relationships, I don't think you'd do better than him."

"You know why."

"Seriously?" she says. "Why, after all this time? Why are you still holding on to this notion that love isn't for you?"

"Because it's not," I say firmly.

"Bullshit."

I turn my head to her. "Excuse me?"

"You heard me. It's bullshit. It's a line you've said for so long that you believe it."

"Because it's true."

"It's not." She stops and grabs my hands, turning me toward her. "I've known you for more than a decade, and I've always respected your privacy. I've never pushed on why you hate this notion about love or who hurt you to get you to this place. But I know it was a long time ago. You, Izzy McCall, are an amazing person. You deserve to be loved. And you might not know it, but you have love to give."

Hazel stops for a second and motions over to Oliver. "That man over there? You might not see it, but he looks at you like you're the only one in the room. Every time you spoke at dinner tonight, he couldn't take his eyes off you. He memorized every word you said. And the way you look at him? You don't realize it, and maybe I'm the only one who does see it, but you look at him in a way I've never seen before. That has to mean something."

"Yes, it means he's my friend."

She shakes her head. "No. He's more than a friend. And one day you're going to realize that. I just hope that day isn't when he's found someone who wants what you were too scared to give him."

Hazel walks away, leaving me standing in the middle of the casino floor staring at Oliver. Sweet, handsome, sexy, too-good-to-be-true Oliver.

She's right. He would be the one. He'd be the one to help me finally forget the past. He'd be the one that could help me erase the pain I've been carrying for sixteen years. He'd be the best boyfriend. He's going to be the best husband and father. If I had to pick anyone, it would be Oliver a hundred times over and again on Sunday.

But he deserves more than a broken woman who has forgotten how to love. He deserves more than a woman who can't give back even a fraction of what he gives. So I'll take his friendship. I'll take moments that will never amount to anything. Like he said before, friendship is better than nothing.

"Hey," he says, wrapping me in his arms. "You okay?"

I hug him back, needing this contact more than he could ever know. "Yeah. Just tired. I think I'm going to go back to the room."

He backs away but doesn't take his hands off my arms. "Okay, let's go."

I shake my head. "No. You stay. Have fun. Gamble. Plus, you wanted to see the fountains. Don't let me ruin your night."

"I can see the fountains tomorrow," he says, taking my hand. "If you're going to the room. I'm going to the room."

"But—"

He puts his fingers to my lips. "But nothing. I do have one request, though. I'm going to need ice cream."

I smile as he lowers his fingers. "Ice cream sounds good."

"Then let's go get some ice cream."

He puts his arm around my shoulders nonchalantly, but I take a little more, leaning my head on his shoulder.

This. I'm getting used to this. I'm starting to need this in my life more than anything. Yes, I might have to fight back the urge and temptation from time to time. But I can do that. Because I'm not about to let this friendship be ruined by bringing love into the picture.

Because love ruins everything.

Chapter 19
Oliver

"Go! Go! Let's go!"

I stand up and pump my fist as the horse I bet on crosses the finish line.

"You know that's not a real race?" Knox jokes.

"Yes, but the money is real. And that horse right there won me a crisp hundred bucks."

Knox gets up as I head over to cash out my bet. "I never pictured you as a gambling man."

"Why's that?"

"I guess it's the whole teacher thing," Knox says. "I guess I could never imagine the teachers we had in school gambling or cutting loose."

"Well, you have to remember, our first-grade teachers were Mrs. Eshelman, who had a pet skunk, and Mrs. Eaton, who had three dead husbands."

Knox tips his beer to me as we make our way out of the sports book. "Very true."

I've enjoyed hanging out with Knox these past few days. I've known him for years through Jake, and he's fixed my car more than once, but we've never really hung out. He's cool. His knowledge about cars is insane. I've learned more this weekend than I knew in my entire life. I also didn't realize how big of a Nashville Fury fan he was, which provided us hours of conversation at the pool yesterday.

In a perfect world, Knox would be the best bro-friend ever. As in, the husband or boyfriend of the girl your dating's best friend. I can see it now. Board game nights. Double dates. Concerts. Birthdays and Super Bowl parties. We'd be the best couple of couples that ever coupled.

And yes, we might still hang out as the four of us. I can see that happening. But I also know now that at the end of the night when Hazel and Knox head back home together, Izzy and I will be going our separate ways.

This weekend has proven how hard it is to be friends with a woman you're attracted to. And while I love this friendship, and I want to keep it more than anything, I can't deny that I still have feelings for Izzy. But I'm going to do what I promised I would. I'm going to put them aside.

Even if it might be the hardest thing I've ever done.

I let those feelings slip last night when we were getting ready in the room. I couldn't help myself. Izzy is sexy in jeans and a T-shirt. But in a skin-tight black dress and her silky, long red hair calling to me like a siren? She's the most irresistible woman I've ever met. It doesn't help my peace of mind that I think something might have happened if Hazel hadn't knocked when she did. Actually, I *know* something would have. I wouldn't have stopped it, and I don't think Izzy would have either. It also doesn't help that I know for a damn fact I wouldn't have had one regret. Not a damn one.

Though considering how the night ended, I'm glad it didn't. I don't know what Izzy and Hazel were talking about, but I know Izzy barely said two words the rest of the night. We got our ice cream before lying in bed and watching television the rest of the night. She fell asleep with her head on my chest, in that T-shirt I'm going to have dreams about for years to come.

I watched her sleep for hours, her holding on to my shirt for dear life, like she needed to hold onto me or I might go somewhere. I've figured out Izzy doesn't have a lot of friends besides Hazel and I, at least people that she truly is herself around. I'm honored I'm in that small circle. Because I think that's where she needs me. She needs me as a friend. As a confidant. As a pillow when she's chasing away the bad dreams.

And if that's where she needs me, then that's where I'm going to be. For as long as she wants.

"I'm going to run," Knox says, giving me a pat on the back. "Hazel and I are headed out for a helicopter ride, so I should probably be ready when she gets back from her last lecture."

"Sounds good."

Knox heads off to the elevators, and I find myself in front of one of the many bars around the hotel.

Hmm...

Izzy said she's going to be done around two today, which by the look at my watch, is in fifteen minutes. She's not let loose once since we've been here. And if anyone needs to let loose for a night, it's that girl.

"Two margaritas please. And an extra shot of tequila in each."

The bartender whips me up the drinks, I charge them to the room, and head off to her conference rooms. Just as I'm approaching a door, Izzy comes walking out, looking like the bad ass business woman she is.

"What are you doing here?" she asks, eyeing the two drinks in my hand. "Isn't it a little early to be double fisting?"

I hold out one of the drinks for her. "This, my dear, is for you."

"Well, thank you," she says, taking a sip of the blended beverage. "Shit that's strong."

"I got them with an extra shot. I thought you might need it."

"I do," she says, taking another sip, only this one lasting a little longer. "What's the occasion?"

I loop my arm around her shoulders as casually as I can. "The occasion is that as of two minutes ago, you are officially done with business. For the next however many hours we are in Vegas, we are going to have nothing but fun."

"I like the sound of that," she says. "Except we can't start it quite yet."

"And why not?"

She looks down at herself then back up to me. "Because I'm still in my work clothes. And because I have a laptop and folders in this bag. Let me go to the room, drop this stuff off, and change. "

"Fine," I say with a groan. "You have ten minutes to go upstairs, put on your best Vegas outfit, drop your laptop, and promptly meet me in the lobby."

"Yes, sir," she says with a mock salute.

"Smart ass. Go change."

I walk her to the elevator, each of us finishing our drinks before we get there.

"Shit, that went down smooth," she says.

"Is that a bad thing?"

She shrugs. "Depends on what you have planned for the night."

The door opens, and I take the empty glass from her hand. "No plans. We're just going to see where the night takes us."

Chapter 20
Izzy
~~ Ten hours later ~~

"CAESARS! AND STEP ON IT!"

I think our Uber driver mumbles something, but I don't hear what it is. I really don't care, either. Tonight is the best night of my life, and I have Oliver to thank for it.

I've never felt this free. Or light. I don't think in my entire adult life I've truly ever let go like this.

We danced. We drank. We gambled. We drank. Oliver finally got to see the fountains. And then we drank some more.

Did I mention we drank?

I think we did some other stuff, including seeing an actual Elvis impersonator. And a good one. Not just a fat old guy with black hair in a gold jumpsuit. But now all I want to do is go back to the room and fuck this man.

Cause I can.

"What are you doing?" Oliver mumbles as I begin to kiss his neck.

"Kissing you."

"I thought friends didn't kiss?"

"Who said that?"

"You."

I swing my leg over so I'm now straddling him. "You should really quit listening to me."

Oliver doesn't respond, unless you count a slur of moans and grunts a response. I feel him hardening against me as I continue to kiss his ear and neck. Did I know he was that sensitive here? I don't remember. All I remember is that Oliver is the only man who has ever made me speak in tongues, and I'd like that to happen again tonight, thank you very much.

"Hey, you two," the driver said. "I know it's a big night for you and all, but you have to be in your seats or my ass gets a ticket."

"You're no fun," I groan as I go back to my seat.

"It's okay," Oliver whispers to me as he takes my hand in his. "You can have your way with me as soon as we get back to the hotel."

"Really?"

He nods. "Really really."

And like we've done it a thousand times, Oliver leans over and takes my lips with his.

I'm a fucking idiot. Why have I been denying myself this? Oliver makes me feel good, and I like feeling good. Who doesn't like feeling good? Feeling good is grrrrreat.

Like right now. His lips feel good. His hand that's currently cupping my pussy feels good. I know his dick is going to feel good.

Yup. I've been an idiot.

Who knew all you needed was ten shots of tequila, two bottles of champagne, and a few margaritas to not be an idiot? Someone should tell people that.

"We're here," the driver says. "And please give me five stars since I was an unwilling audience to your porno."

"You got it man!" Oliver says as he helps me out of the car.

As soon as we're in the lobby, we make a beeline for the elevators. We're not even two steps into the elevator when he starts kissing me again. We nearly fall out of the elevator when it stops on our floor, which luckily isn't too far away from our room.

"Oliver," I whisper as we stumble to the door. "I'm having déjà vu."

Oliver stops for a second before looking at me. He's in deep thought. At least he looks like that to me. All three of him.

"We did! At the wedding! When I fell in love with you!"

"Yes! That night!" I yell, nearly falling over in my excitement. "So why can't you ever get into rooms?"

"Becaussse," he slurs. "I'm not very good with my hands."

I try to step toward him, but I'm pretty sure I trip into him. Either way, I got the card, which is all that matters.

"You are very good with your hands. And your tongue. And when we get in that room, you're going to use both of them."

Oliver nods his head, but it keeps bobbing up and down like a doll. "Yes, ma'am."

I turn around and tap the key to the lock and luckily the green lights appear.

"We're in!"

I try to take a step in, but Oliver surprises me by picking me up, one arm under my legs and the other around my back.

"What are you doing? You're going to drop me."

"I would never drop you," he says. "Never ever."

He carries me into the room, and I throw down the key and my purse in the process. One of my shoes falls off, which is fine. My feet were hurting so bad. Heels are stupid.

"My lady," he says, lowering me down on the bed, and I don't know if he planned on coming into it with me, but he did. I'm fine with that. Makes it easier for me to take his pants off.

That is, if I could get his shoes off. It's not easy. He has them double knotted. And I'm really drunk.

"Oh!" Oliver yells suddenly, nearly making me fall off the bed. I look up at him, and his eyes are doubled in size. "I just realized something."

"What?"

"We like to have sex in hotels!"

It takes me a second to process, but he's exactly right. "Oh my God, we do! We're hotel fuckers!"

He lies back, and I get back to work on the extremely complicated shoes. "It's our thing. We're the people that have sex in hotels."

"Fuck yeah we are," I say as I'm finally able to start working on his pants.

"Izzy?"

"Yeah?"

"What are you doing?"

I look up at him and even though we're both drunk, I thought it was pretty clear what I was doing. "I'm trying to give you a blow job."

"Why?"

Wow, he's drunker than I thought. Which means he's really, really, really, really drunk. Instead of just really, really, really drunk. "Because you didn't let me last time. And I wanted to. But now I get to do it."

"Well, then, by all means. What's mine is yours."

I smile as I start handling his cock, which is already hard and ready.

"You have a nice dick," I say, my head on his thigh as I stroke him up and down.

"Thank you."

"I mean it," I say, because I don't know if he realizes what I'm saying. "Dicks aren't pretty. But yours is. You have a pretty penis."

"Thank you, dear," he says.

I think he was about to say something else, but he didn't. Instead all I hear is a weird combination of a groan, moan, and swearing as I wrap my lips around his cock.

That. That's why I have always enjoyed giving blow jobs. Hearing them speak gibberish as you hold them in your mouth. There's no greater turn on. Well, maybe a few other things that I can't think of right now because I'm concentrating too hard on what I'm doing, but this is right up there.

"Izzy," he says as I feel him collect my hair into his hands. "Take it. Take it all."

Holy fucking fuck. Even drunk his voice makes me want to come in my pants.

But I do as he says. I double down on him, making sure I'm stroking in tandem with my mouth, taking as much of his girth as I possibly can. I should be choking, but my gag reflex likely went out the window sometime after the eighth tequila shot.

"Fuck, Izzy!"

Oliver startles me by pulling me up by my hair. At some point he sat up, making us now eye to eye.

"I'm going to fuck you now. And just like last time, I want you to wake the neighbors."

I nod. "Yes, please."

"Good girl."

The room starts spinning as Oliver somehow grabs me and scoops me underneath him. Before I even have a second to get my bearings, I feel him enter me. Every last...delish...inch.

"Ahhhh!"

I don't know if he really wanted me to wake the neighbors, but I think I just did. And I don't care. Because I'm having sex with a man who is fucking me like his life depends on it.

"Give it to me, Izzy."

He lifts my legs up, putting them both on his shoulders as he continues to drive into me. I reach up and claw at his chest, wishing I had something—anything—to hold on to as Oliver fucks me into the next time zone.

"Fuck me, Oliver," I say as I feel my orgasm start to build already. "Make me yours."

Because I'm drunk, I don't think about those words. And honestly, I mean them. If this man fucks me like this, maybe we should be together. No way I'm going to get fucked this good ever again in my life.

Oliver suddenly lets go of my legs so they open as he falls on top of me. Nearly all of his weight is on me, but it doesn't stop his momentum.

"You're mine," he growls into my ear. "Now come for me."

I can't even answer. Oliver has lifted my hips up slightly, finding that perfect spot that sends me over the edge.

Oliver lets out a grunt as he spills into me. He doesn't move for a second, but I can see him breathing. Which is good. I really don't want to have the conversation with Hazel where I explain I literally fucked Oliver to death.

"I think I'm going to pass out right here," Oliver says, slightly moving off me.

I'm barely keeping my eyes open as I wrap my arms around him. "Sounds good."

Oliver turns his head slightly, kissing my cheek sweetly. Such a contrast to the way he just literally fucked my brains out.

"Goodnight, wife."

I lean down and kiss the top of his head. "Goodnight, husband."

Chapter 21
Oliver

I now pronounce you husband and wife. You may kiss your bride...

I jolt awake right at the good part. Though for some reason I feel like I can taste her lips. Weird.

Damn, that was one hell of a dream. In all my years of proposing, not once have I ever dreamed of a wedding. But there it was: Izzy standing in front of me. She was wearing the outfit she had on last night, and we were getting married by Elvis. Clearly, my likely-still-drunk mind is playing some fucked-up tricks on me.

I try to open my eyes, but I immediately shut them the second the morning light hits me. However, that little dose of sunshine has seemed to wake up every part of me. It's then I realize I'm completely naked under these covers. And there's an arm draped over me. And a naked woman is spooning me. I want to freak out—for good and bad reasons—but that requires movement. And I don't think I can do that right now.

I try to push through the haze of last night, and the headache of this morning, to piece together what the hell happened. There were shots. So many shots. There was gambling and the fountains. I do seem to remember the car ride back to the hotel when Izzy started kissing me, but the rest is pretty foggy.

Where were we coming from?

"Uggghhh."

I want to laugh at Izzy's groan, but just the thought of laughing makes my head hurt even worse.

"Too loud," I whisper. "Suffer silently."

"Am I naked?"

"Yup."

"Are you naked?"

"Yup."

"We had sex, didn't we?"

"Yup."

"Fuck..."

I open my eyes and roll over to look at Izzy. Her hand is still on my chest, and her blue eyes are tired but still beautiful. I take her hand and lace our fingers together. I have a feeling I know what she's about to say, but I think since we're currently naked, I can hold her hand.

"I'm pretty sure we need to stop going to hotels together."

This makes her laugh. "Apparently. But Oliver—"

"I know," I cut her off. "I know this doesn't change anything. I know we were drunk and in a vacation bubble. You don't have to give me the spiel."

"I'm sorry." Her words are sincere and her eyes are sad. "I wish I could be more for you."

I bring her hand up to my lips, placing a kiss on her palm. "I've told you once, and I've told you again. I don't want you to change a thing. Because you're amazing just the way you are."

She nods but doesn't say anything. She does pull her hand from mine and slowly begins to get out of bed.

"I don't remember the last time I was this hungover," she says as she bends down and picks up a random piece of clothing. "Or that I blacked out."

"Same," I say as I slowly sit up in bed. "Actually, that's a lie. My twenty-first birthday."

I watch Izzy put on a T-shirt and am immediately confused. "Whose shirt is that?"

She looks down, then back up to me. "I have no idea."

The shirt she put on is one of those black tuxedo T-shirts. Where in the world did that come from?

"You're going to wear a shirt that somehow ended up in our hotel room, but we don't know how it got here?"

"Oliver, I couldn't give a flying fuck right now if it came here from the Tooth Fairy. I need to go to the bathroom and find some aspirin."

I look around to the floor and see my pants thrown to the side. I'm guessing my phone is still in the pocket. I hope it is. I also hope there's a bottle of water in the mini-fridge, because I need it more than anything in this world right now.

I gingerly get out of bed and slowly bend over to pick up my pants from the floor. I can feel my cell phone in the pocket, which I take out before throwing my pants toward my suitcase. I grab a clean pair of boxer briefs and slip them on before finding and chugging the cold bottle of water. I know we probably need to start getting ready to leave, but I need a few more minutes for my head to stop spinning.

I drop back on the bed and power up my phone. Huh... that's a different background. Yesterday it was the picture of Izzy and me at the Vegas sign.

Today it's still a picture of me and Izzy, only now I'm kissing her while she's wearing a veil and I'm wearing a black T-shirt.

And I might not be able to see the front of it, but I guarantee there's a tuxedo on it.

Holy shit...

My fingers start pushing every wrong button as I frantically open my phone and go to the photos. If sober me takes a million pictures, I can only imagine how many photos drunk me takes.

"Oliver?"

I look up to see a very pale and wide-eyed Izzy standing in front of the bed. "Yeah?"

She holds up her hand. The one that now has a ring on it. "Care to tell me what this is?"

I look down at my hand, and fuck—how did I not realize that I have a ring on myself?

Holy fuck...

"Well, I think I know where that T-shirt came from."

I hold up my phone as she takes a few steps closer to the bed. She looks at the phone, then back to me in a panic.

"Did we...get married?"

"THE FOUNTAINS ARE SOOO PRETTY. And romantic."

I look up to the famous Bellagio fountains and am getting lost in the lights and the water. It doesn't help that I quit feeling my face about an hour ago and am pretty sure that most of the liquid in my body is tequila.

"Oh look!" Izzy says as she tugs on my button down and points toward our right. "They are getting engaged!"

"No fair," I pout. "I want to get engaged at the fountains. But no one loves me. Or wants to marry me. So I don't get to get engaged at the fountains."

I stumble as I look away, but notice Izzy isn't next to me. I mean, she's not that much shorter than me. Where'd she go?

"Izzy?"

"Down here."

I look down to see Izzy on one knee.

"What are you doing?"

"Proposing at the fountains."

How drunk am I? Is this happening?

"You're what?"

I think I see her almost fall, but she rights herself. Then again, that could have been me. "Oliver Price. Will you marry me?"

Oh my gosh, this is happening!

"Yes!" I yell as I take her hands and she stands back up. I hear a round of applause from the crowd as I bring Izzy in for a kiss. Because that's what you do when you get engaged. You kiss your fiancée.

Our kiss is broken up by a crowd of people coming to congratulate us. Luckily, strangers took pictures and videos. Thank goodness. I never would have forgiven myself if this moment wasn't captured to remember forever.

"You've made me the happiest man alive, Izzy McCall."

"Just you wait," she says with a grin, pulling me toward the street. "Because in a few hours we're going to be husband and wife!"

~

"I DIDN'T EVEN GET to propose? I'm married, and I wasn't the one to propose!"

Izzy shoots me a look, and I swear daggers are coming out of her eyes. "That's what you're mad about? Everything that happened last night and that's your biggest problem?"

I shrug. "I'm just saying, it would have been nice if I finally would have got a yes."

"For fuck's sake, Oliver..." Izzy trails off and begins pacing the room. I want to smile that she's still wearing my tuxedo T-shirt, but I keep that to myself. "Okay, so I apparently proposed? Which for sure means I was drunker than I've ever been in my entire life. But you can't get married drunk. I mean, someone has to realize that you're drunk and tell you that you can't do it."

I continue to scroll through the pictures and stop on the one of Izzy posing with our marriage license. The next one is both of us holding it. And the next is the same, only this time Izzy is kissing me on the cheek.

"No one stopped us," I say as I turn the camera so she can see the phone. "Not one single person."

"Fabulous."

I continue scrolling when I realize there's more than photos on here. "Oh, shit."

"What?"

I look up at Izzy. "There's a video."

~

"THAT WAS SO EASY! We're getting married!"

I laugh and Izzy waves our marriage license in the air as we walk toward the taxi. I didn't know taxis still existed. I also didn't know you could actually get married by Elvis, which is what we're about to do.

"To the King and Bling Chapel," Izzy says as she falls into the backseat. "And step on it!"

I bring her in for a selfie, which she doesn't fight. Drunk Izzy likes taking pictures a lot more than sober Izzy.

"I'm really proud of you," she says.

"For what?"

"For taking charge in there," she says. "No one questioned us."

"Right?" I say. "I think I did a really good job acting sober."

Izzy leans over and kisses my cheek. "You did. Good job, future husband."

"Thanks, future wife."

Izzy lays her head on my shoulder as we make our way to the twenty-four-hour chapel.

Holy crap, I'm going to get married. Which on one hand makes me sad that Shane and Simon and Wes aren't here. On the other hand, I'm marrying Izzy, and she's just the best.

"We're here," the driver says. "Happy wedding day."

We get out of the car and all but race inside.

"We have a reservation. Price!"

The older lady squints as she looks at the computer. "Yes. Price. I have here you want the deluxe package, which comes with rings, pictures, a video, and your very own Elvis officiant?"

"You're damn skippy we do."

She nods her head to the left. "Come on back. Last couple bailed. Bride got cold feet. We'll get you in and out in a jiffy."

Izzy and I start walking behind the very nice lady when I stop.

"What?" Izzy asks. "Everything okay?"

I look down at my shirt then back up to Izzy. "I can't get married in this. I need a tuxedo."

Izzy looks around before running over to the gift shop portion of the lobby. "Here! This will do."

I hold up the T-shirt she just threw me. If you can't get married in a tuxedo, then a tuxedo T-shirt is the next best thing.

"Perfect," I say. "You ready?"

Izzy nods her head. "Yup. Let's fucking do this!"

I start walking down the aisle, only to see Elvis in front of me—in his famous white jumpsuit. I hurry and grab my phone, needing to take a picture of this. The guys are never going to believe this when I show them.

"Congratulations," he says. "Your bride is beautiful."

I turn to see Izzy walking to me, a borrowed veil on her head and a bouquet of flowers in her hands. She's all smiles as she walks toward me to the sound of one of Elvis's iconic love songs. I hold out my hand for her, and for a second, I feel as sober as I have all night.

Holy shit, I'm marrying Izzy McCall.

And holy shit, Elvis is actually singing!

"Today Oliver and Izzy come together to become husband and wife. These fools might be rushing in, but their love will always be burning."

Izzy smiles at me, and I hope the photographer is getting all of this. I need to see it sober tomorrow.

"Oliver," Elvis says as he hands me the ring. "Do you take Izzy to be your wife?"

I nod and slip the ring on her finger. "I do."

He turns to Izzy, handing her the gold ring. "And Izzy, do you take Oliver to be your husband?"

"Fuck yeah I do!"

"Then by the power vested in me by the state of Nevada, I now pronounce you husband and wife. You may kiss your bride."

And I do. I take Izzy, dip her nearly to the ground, and kiss the living hell out of her.

"I now pronounce you Mr. and Mrs. Oliver Price."

Chapter 22
Izzy

"Where the hell have you two been? Our flight is boarding in ten minutes."

Oliver and I share a guilty look before looking back to a confused Knox and a slightly angry Hazel.

"We overslept."

"Overslept?" Hazel says. "Our flight is about to board, and you two decided to not answer your phones or return any messages. And all you have is that you overslept? I thought something was wrong."

Knox raises his hand. "For the record, I didn't and told her everything would be fine."

Hazel snaps her head toward her husband. "You stay out of this."

"I'm sorry," I say as I put down my carryon bag. "We were... in a rush, and I honestly didn't check my phone."

Hazel narrows her eyes, trying to see if I'm spewing a line of bullshit. Which is half true. I would have texted her if I had checked my phone all morning. Which I didn't. I was scared to touch it. Yes, I know that most of the evidence of what happened last night is on Oliver's phone, but I know there's a chance more is on mine. I convinced myself that if I looked and it's there, then somehow the situation is even more real than it already is.

"I'm going to go get a bottle of water," Oliver whispers to me. It's also at that point I realize he's kept his left hand in his pocket. Is he still wearing the ring? "Want anything else?"

"Crackers and a Gatorade, please."

He nods his head and gives my hand a squeeze before heading to the snack station at the airport.

Knox pops up out of his seat. "I'll come with you!"

I look to Hazel, who clearly told Knox to go with Oliver. Great. Here we go...

"Seriously, what the fuck?" Hazel begins. "And don't give me this bullshit that you overslept. Because Oliver looks like he's about to be called to the principal's office, and you look like you got caught with your hand in the cookie jar."

"I..."

I trail off, because I honestly don't know what to say. Oliver and I have barely had time to process. Once we finished looking at the photos and putting together the pieces of last night, we had to scramble to make the plane.

Then again, this is Hazel. She knows most everything about me. And she clearly knows something's up. I could continue to try to bullshit my way out of this situation with lame excuses like oversleeping, but the woman knows me too well.

I motion for her to sit down next to me and to come closer. If I'm going to say this, it's going to be a whisper.

"Oliver and I got married last night."

Hazel slowly backs away and doesn't say a thing. It's a little bit scary.

"Hazel, blink twice if you're alive."

She does. She actually blinks about ten times. "I'm sorry. I think I misunderstood you. And I did have a few too many martinis last night, so I might be a little more hungover than I thought, but I could have sworn that you just said that you and Oliver got married last night?"

As if on cue, Oliver and Knox come walking back toward us. I couldn't tell you what Knox has in his hand, because I can't stop staring at Oliver's haul of waters, snacks, and other drinks being held by his left hand, which is still sporting the wedding ring.

"Holy shit, you two got married!"

Oliver sits down next to me as Knox takes a seat on the other side of Hazel, who I think is trying not to faint.

"Yes, we did," Oliver says. "We are an official Vegas cliché."

"Wow," Knox says. "How did it happen?"

"Tequila," I answer. "That's how it happened."

"How many did you have?" Hazel asks. "Because for as long as I've known you, you've been completely anti-marriage. You haven't even dated anybody seriously. So by my calculations, that means you have had to have drunk at least a bottle of tequila for this to even be plausible."

"Judging by my headache, that sounds about right."

"How do you know you're married?" Knox asks. "Maybe it was just some sort of show you were part of and it wasn't real?"

Oliver shakes his head and tosses his phone to Knox. "The videos, photos, and marriage license seem to prove that point otherwise."

Knox and Hazel start looking and scrolling through the phone. If it wasn't me, I'd be laughing at their reactions.

"Dude, is that the rugby player Renn Brewer?"

"Yup," Oliver says. "Apparently they were the ceremony after us."

"I can't believe this," Knox continues. "I didn't realize this could happen in real life. I thought it only happened in the movies."

"Oh, it can," I say. "And you can even get yourself an Elvis if you want."

"No fucking way." Knox starts scrolling faster, which leads to him getting slapped in the arm by his wife. "What? You gotta admit this shit is funny."

Knox is right. This shit is funny. Part of me wants to laugh because of just how outrageous all of this is. Here I am, the woman completely against all things love and marriage, who goes to Vegas and ends up getting super drunk and being in her own worst nightmare.

"So what are you going to do?" Hazel asks as Knox gives Oliver his phone back. "Can you get it annulled?"

"We haven't talked about it," I say quickly. "We'll figure something out."

I look over to Oliver, who is returning my look with a sad smile. I hate that what I call my worst nightmare is his dream come true. Because if this were any other person, I'd have rebooked my flight, stayed in Vegas for another day, and figured out how the hell to end this sham of a marriage. I mean, there has to be a thirty-day return policy on drunken marriages, right?

But I saw the look in his eye this morning when he realized we were married. The man who has searched for love his whole life finally has a taste of it, even if it's not real. When he first told me the story of him being adopted and always wanting to know what a traditional, nuclear family was like, my heart broke. Which is crazy because I didn't think I had one. But apparently I do when it comes to Oliver. And in just a few months, this man has become one of the most important people in my life. I know I can't be cynical or rude about this. I have to consider his feelings.

Which means letting this cool down and figuring it all out when we get back to Nashville.

"Now calling flight number 1240, Las Vegas to Nashville, now boarding."

The four of us stand to start getting in line, Oliver and I a little more slowly than Knox and Hazel.

"You okay?" Oliver whispers, taking my hand in his as we walk to the boarding area. It's at that moment I feel the metal of the ring on his hand. I look up at him and somehow he knows exactly what I'm thinking.

"I know I should probably take it off," he says with a sadness in his voice that once again puts a dent into my cold, dead heart.

"No. Keep it on."

"Really? You're not wearing yours, and I shouldn't have even—"

"No." I interrupt. "That's me. Who knows how long we're going to be married. Have some fun with it."

He smiles the smile that gets me every time. The one that reminds me how good of a person he is, and how much better off he is with me just as a friend.

"Thank you, Mrs. Price."

"Oh no. No, no, no. I will not be changing my name, and that's even if we were staying married. Which we're not."

"That's fine. Izzy McCall-Price has a fine ring to it."

"I was thinking more like Oliver McCall."

He smiles and brings me in for a quick kiss on the temple. "If that's what needs to happen so you stay married to me, consider it done."

Chapter 23
Oliver

"Okay, so what are we going to do about this?"

I nearly get whiplash as Izzy storms into my house and sits down on the couch. "Nice to see you too, my wife."

"Stop with that wife shit," she says. "I'm not your wife."

"The state of Nevada begs to differ. Also, where's my nice wife from yesterday? The one who told me to wear the ring?"

She lets out a deep sigh like she's already had enough of my shit. "That person was tired, hungover, and confused. But Oliver...we need to figure this out. Right now."

It's been twenty-four hours since we returned from Las Vegas, and I still can't wrap my head around the fact I'm married. I knew Izzy needed some space to think after we got back, and honestly, so did I.

Though judging by the way she stormed in here this morning, I assume we were thinking about very different things. If I had to go back to Vegas to make a bet, I'd put money on the fact she had already drawn up divorce papers. Then there's me, who used the last day to try to figure out how I can convince her to stay married.

"Do we? Do we really need to figure it out? I feel like it can wait." I know I shouldn't be messing with her right now, but it's too much fun.

Izzy looks at me like I'm nuts. "Yes. We do."

"For the sake of argument, can I ask why?"

"Because, Oliver. We were drunk and didn't know what we were doing. Because I don't believe in marriage. Because you live in Rolling Hills, and I doubt you're about to move to Nashville. Because I love our friendship, and I don't want it to be thrown away because of our Elvis wedding. Did I mention because we were drunk and didn't know what we were doing?"

"Once or twice," I say with a smirk.

"How are you smiling right now? I know I said you could keep wearing the ring, but maybe you need to take it off, because this whole husband thing is going a little bit too much to your head."

"Nope. You said I could keep it on. So it will be on my finger for the next sixty days."

Izzy stops moving. Maybe stops breathing. I think she's more shocked at this moment than when she realized we were married.

"What do you mean *sixty days*?"

"Married. We have to be married for sixty days."

"Says who?"

"The state of Tennessee."

"Who the fuck does Tennessee think it is, telling me I have to be married for sixty days?"

I give my head a shake, because never did I think that Izzy would come to this conversation unprepared and unresearched. "Did you not look up divorce laws in Tennessee?"

She furiously shakes her head. "No. I was so confused and tired when I got home I developed a migraine. I walked into my house, popped a pill, and immediately passed out. I woke up and drove straight here."

"Wow." I wipe my hand over my face, because this was not what I was expecting when Izzy barged in. I expected a full presentation with citations and flow charts about when, how, and why we are getting a divorce. "Okay. Let's regroup."

Izzy's face is now buried in her phone, her fingers frantically typing away.

"Do you just want me to tell you what I found?"

She shakes her head. "No. Because I need to see with my own eyeballs that the patriarchy is telling me I need to stay married for sixty days. Because you know for a fucking fact a man wrote that law."

I sit back on the couch and wait for her to come to the same realization I did last night. Then I actually look at Izzy for the first time today. I'm not going to lie; she looks rough. Hair is a mess. No makeup. Dark circles under her eyes. Yet, she's still more beautiful than she was yesterday. And the day before. And the day before that.

That's how I know I love her. I tried fighting it. I tried telling myself these feelings were just a byproduct of our whirlwind and untraditional timeline. But they aren't. The more time I spend with her, the more I love her. And I know that's going to wreck me when this marriage ends.

I laugh to myself as I let myself think this for the first time. Only I would find a woman, fall in love with her, drunkenly get married to her, only for her to want nothing to do with me.

But hey, at least it wasn't another engagement on my wall of shame.

"Fucking shit fuck," she mumbles.

"I didn't know that was a phrase."

She looks up at me, worry and dread lining her face. "Oliver, I can't be married."

I move next to her on the couch, and in the most shocking move of the day, Izzy falls into my arms and starts crying. I didn't know she *could* cry.

"I'm sorry," she says, wiping away her tears. "I don't know where that came from."

"We don't apologize for letting out our feelings," I say. "It's been a lot to process. You do what you need to do."

"I'm fine," she says, though I know she's the opposite of fine.

"Let's take a breath," I say as I hold her hand. I'm ready for her to jerk away, but she doesn't. She didn't yesterday, either, when we were at the airport. Or when we were driving home and she hadn't said a word. That just further proves my point that the tough person facade is just that—a front.

"I'm trying," she says. "And what I'm about to say has nothing to do with you and everything to do with me. But I made a promise to myself sixteen years ago that I'd never let anyone in. That I wasn't built for love. And I would never, ever get married. It was the one thing I promised myself, Oliver, and I can't go back on that."

"Okay, let's start over," I say. "I know all of the reasons why you want to end this, and I get every single one of them."

She tilts her head like she doesn't believe me.

"I swear I do. I know I tease, and you're right, I'm a hopeless romantic, and you're a cynical love hater. I wear fun socks, and you don't own clothes with patterns. But what you just said, and that look of pure fear on your face, that's more than us being opposites and the state of Tennessee having a stupid rule. So the question is, do you want to talk about it?"

Izzy doesn't look at me, instead choosing to focus on our joined hands. "I want to. But I can't. I've never told anyone about my past, not even Hazel. I think about it every day, but I'm too ashamed to talk about it."

"Okay," I say. "I won't push you. But if you ever want to talk about it, you know I'm here, right?"

She nods. "I do. And that's another reason why we can't stay married. I like you too much."

"Izzy, I don't know what happened in your past, but usually liking a person is part of a reason to *stay* married."

This makes her laugh a little. "In theory, I know that. But in my messed-up head, letting you in any more than I already have means I run the risk of losing you. And I can't lose you, Oliver. Somehow, in a matter of a few months, you've become my best friend. I know you don't think you do, but I'm pretty sure you know more about me than Hazel does. I don't know what I'd do if I couldn't call you tomorrow or if you didn't text me to remind me to eat. But I made a promise to myself."

I hold open my arms, and Izzy comes right back into them. I can tell she's crying again, but not as hard as last time. I let my head fall back against the couch as I think about the words she just said. I had a suspicion that Izzy was hurt in her past, but I never wanted to push it. I still won't. But I'm now certain of the fact that this woman—this beautiful, intelligent, sexy, strong, woman—was hurt. Deeply.

I'm not a violent man. I don't believe anything can be solved with fists. But I swear if I ever figure out who hurt her, I will beat them within an inch of their life. And then I'll call Simon, and he'll call his guy to dispose of the body.

"I'm sorry," she whispers. "I want you to know that if I were ever to get married, it would be to you."

I laugh. "You forget, my wife, you're stuck with me for sixty days. So, you do get to be married to me."

She sits back up, tears still coming down her face despite her laughing. "Okay, so this week, we call a lawyer and file for divorce. In the meantime, we're the same Izzy and Oliver. Two friends who talk every day and laugh about the time they had sex."

"You mean times. It's now in the multiples."

This gets me another laugh. "I thought the wife was always supposed to be right?"

"So now you want to play the wife card?"

"If it means I get my way, then of course I'll play it."

"Anything you say. Happy wife, happy life, right?"

She takes one of my pillows and playfully smacks me with it. "You really are ridiculous, you know that?"

"So I've been told."

Chapter 24
Oliver

Oliver: Everyone come to my place for dinner tonight. Six. BYOB.

Wes: What's the occasion?

Oliver: Do I need to have an occasion to invite my best friends in the world over?

Amelia: You don't, but when you're inviting me and not just the guys that means something is up.

Simon: Once again, Amelia proves why she is the smartest in the group.

Oliver: Whatever, just everyone come, okay?

Simon: Is it thirty-four? It's thirty-four, isn't it? OLIVER PROPOSED AGAIN!

Oliver: It's not thirty-four.

Shane: I want garlic bread too.

Simon: Shane, focus.

Shane: I am, on food.

Oliver: Of course there will be garlic bread. Any other requests?

Simon: Yes. You owe me $20 because I was convinced you'd come back from Vegas with thirty-four under your belt. I'm kind of disappointed in you.

I don't even bother responding to the last text as I start making my signature dish of macaroni and cheese with blackened chicken. It's the thing I make for every dinner function, and it was the one thing I knew would get my friends over here.

Because I need to tell them. About everything.

Part of me is scared as to how they're going to react to the news that I came back from Vegas married. The other part of me can't wait to see their faces, especially Simon's, when I tell them that thirty-four happened weeks ago, and I never got to thirty-five.

If I had to predict how tonight's going to go, I'd say they're going to start as shocked. Then they're going to think that I'm fucking with them. Then people are going to start screaming—likely Shane and possibly Wes. Then Amelia's going to calm them down while Simon says something borderline inappropriate. When everyone's got that out of their system, they're going to ask me if I've lost my mind, especially when I tell them that actually I'm in love with my wife.

Speaking of...it appears she is sending me a text, and I have a feeling I know what it's about.

Izzy: You're really telling your friends tonight?

Two days into marriage, and I'm already reading her mind. I'm the best husband ever.

Oliver: Yes.

Izzy: Do you have to?

Oliver: Yes.

Izzy: What can I do to keep you quiet?

Oliver: Nope. Hazel and Knox know. I've wanted to tell my friends about you for a while. I just didn't realize it would be in this context.

Izzy: It still can be. You can tell them I'm just your friend. I'll even come to Rolling Hills and meet all of them and be the best female friend you've ever had.

Oliver: You'll have to fight Amelia for that title. Though she's never seen me naked *wink wink*

Izzy: Can you see my eyes rolling?

Oliver: Clear as day.

Izzy: What are you going to tell them? Do we need to coordinate stories? Is this going to be like when couples say they didn't meet from an online dating app when they really did? What do I need to prepare for?

I suddenly get an idea, though I don't know if she's going to go for it. I also need to take the temperature of my friend group before I put this idea into motion.

Oliver: I plan on telling them the truth. I'll let you know if I deviate from that when you meet them.

Izzy: WHEN I WHAT?

Oliver: Gotta go! Time to put the mac and cheese in the oven!

Izzy: OLIVER WHATEVER THE FUCK YOUR MIDDLE NAME IS PRICE YOU ANSWER ME!

Oliver: It's Michael. And relax. Everything's going to be fine.

Izzy: So you've said.

I laugh as I toss down the phone to start mixing together the noodles and cheese. Everything is going to be fine. I just know it.

~

"WHAT IN THE fuck is that? You had one thing to *not* do in Vegas and it was *that!*"

For a second, I'm completely confused as to what Shane could be talking about. The door hasn't even been open for ten seconds. Then I remembered that I didn't take off my ring, and Shane is staring right at it.

I planned on taking it off. I swear.

"How about you sit down and wait for the others to get here?"

"They're right behind me," he says as he walks to my couch. I'm a bit unnerved because he hasn't taken his eyes off me. Not when he walked in. Not when he sat down. Not even when he grabbed a bottle of beer from the six-pack he brought with him. He doesn't even flinch when the next knock comes to my door.

I quickly slide the ring off and put it in my pocket. "Welcome."

I open the door to find Simon, Amelia, Wes, and Betsy standing in my doorway. "Betsy! I'm glad you could make it."

She reaches out to give me a hug. "I'm here for the macaroni and cheese. And to see who wins the bet."

"What bet? Wait, Simon said something about how I owed him twenty bucks. Was that not him being, well, him?"

"Nope," Betsy says. "Once everyone found out you were going to Vegas with a mystery woman, and knowing that you've been holding back on us for months, we all put twenty bucks in with our guesses about what's really been going on with you."

"Wow," I say. "I don't know whether to ask for a cut on the winnings or wonder what y'all thought I was getting into?"

"My guess was that you got into a relationship with a dominatrix and she had you tied in a sex dungeon," Simon says.

"I thought you had my guess that I proposed?"

"That was my second guess. I couldn't decide so I bet twice."

"Well, both are wrong," I say. "Technically."

Simon's eyes go wide. "What do you mean technically?"

"I'll explain later," I say as I turn to Wes. "What was yours?"

"That you had long since been a closet gambler and had lost your money in an underground poker game. You were going to Vegas with a hit woman to settle your debt."

"Really? My practical, logical, friend is going to go with that?"

"I didn't want to be boring," Wes says. "I had fun with it. I even let the kids help."

"But their ideas were more PG-rated," Betsy adds on. "We took it up a notch."

"Clearly." I look over to Amelia. "What about you?"

"I played it safe with you having a girlfriend and being cautious. This was you changing ways of the past and making sure she was here to stay before introducing her to us."

"As always, Amelia proving that she's the most level-headed of all of us."

Her eyes get big with excitement. "Did I get it right?"

"No. But close."

She lets out a sigh as I look over to Shane, who because of his earlier arrival is the only one who actually knows the secret. "What was yours?"

"Pay up."

Everyone starts talking over each other as Shane and I stare each other down. This man would be the one to get it right.

"Whoa! Everyone calm down," Wes says, standing up and looking between the two of us. "Shane, what do you know that we don't?"

"Take it out of your pocket," Shane says. "And then everyone pay up. And none of that Venmo shit. I want cash. Because our little Oliver went and got himself married."

Shane sits back on the couch, signaling for me to pull the ring out of my jeans pocket. "One of these days I'm going to be able to keep a secret from you."

I take the ring out and show it off before slipping it back on my finger. The room is quiet for at least ten seconds before pure chaos ensues.

"What the hell?"

"Holy shit!"

"Are you fucking kidding me?"

"I knew it was the right decision to come and leave the kids at your moms."

"You told me it wasn't thirty-four!"

"Is everyone done?" I ask, sitting back down.

"Depends," Wes asks. "Are you finally going to tell us everything that's been going on?"

"I am," I say. "But warning, it's a lot."

I start at the beginning. I tell them how I met Izzy at Jake and Whitley's wedding. I tell them I spent the night with her, and that's why they couldn't find me that morning. I tell them every part of my elaborate plan to get her to go out with me, and how I was immediately friend zoned.

"Okay, before you go any farther," Amelia interrupts. "Why didn't you tell us about her before Vegas? It seems like a harmless relationship that doesn't require secrecy."

"I honestly don't know," I say. "I think part of me didn't know if she'd be around, and I didn't want to get shit from anyone about another failed attempt at a relationship. And part of me liked having a person outside of you guys that was just for me."

"I take offense," Simon says. "But I get it. I wouldn't introduce anyone to me either."

"Continuing on," I say. "We started spending a lot of time together, so when she had an extra ticket for Vegas, she suggested I go. I figured why not? What could be the harm?"

Wes signals to my hand. "I think the harm is around your finger."

"I don't know how it happened," I say. "It was our last day, and Izzy had been working nonstop since we got there. So I surprised her with a margarita that might have had an extra shot in it."

"Tequila once again proving that it's the devil," Betsy says.

Amelia nods in agreement. "That's true. It's how I ended up pregnant at eighteen."

"Anyway," I say, wanting to get this back on track. "I'll admit, the weekend had been a little...tense."

"Tense how?" Betsy asks. "Tense as in you two were about to fight or tense as you were about to fuck?"

Simon raises his hand like he's in my classroom. "I'm going to guess the fuck one."

I let out a frustrated breath. "Yes. But that's not the point. Or maybe it is. I'm not sure. Either way, the weekend had been a lot, and I thought Izzy could use a night to unwind and have a little fun. One margarita turned into two, two turned into five, and well, things got out of hand."

I stop to pull out my phone, which makes everyone start asking me at the same time what the hell I'm doing.

"It's going to be easier to show." I click a few buttons on my phone to put my screen on my television.

"Oh my God! There are photos?"

I nod to Betsy, who looks so excited she might burst. "There are."

Everyone simultaneously moves to the front of their seats, like getting three inches closer is going to somehow make them see better.

"This is the first picture of the night." I bring up a selfie of Izzy and me at a slot machine. I can't help but grin just looking at her smile. She doesn't do it often, especially that big.

"Holy shit, dude. She's fucking hot."

I shoot a glare at Simon. "You fucking watch it."

He holds his hands in the air in surrender. "Just making an observation."

I continue scrolling, which is mostly pictures of us at the casino, us taking many shots, and us in front of the fountains at the Bellagio.

"Everyone ready?" I ask, knowing what's coming next.

After a chorus of agreement I scroll to the video and hit

play. I don't watch it. I've seen it plenty of times to know what's coming. I decide to watch all of my friends' faces when they realize that I'm not the one who proposed.

And by the way their jaws drop a little more each second, it was the right call.

"Wait...wait, wait, wait," Shane says. "You mean to tell me that Oliver Price, the man who has proposed more times and places than anyone on this whole green planet Earth, *did not* propose to his now wife?"

"Nope," I say, letting the 'p' pop for emphasis. "Turns out the thirty-fifth proposal was me."

Simon glares at him. "Bullshit. I think that still counts in the bet. Wait, did you say thirty-fifth?"

"I did." I can't help but flash a smug look. I love fucking with Simon. "I actually proposed to Izzy at the wedding, the first night we met. That was thirty-four."

"Fuck you," he says. "That should still count."

"Focus," I say, getting his attention back to the screen. "There's more."

We bypass the photos of us celebrating and the random ones we took while getting our marriage license.

Me and Izzy standing at the altar. Me and Izzy sharing a smile as Elvis says whatever he said. Me kissing Izzy so hard I think we might have fallen over. Me and Izzy holding our hands up in celebration after being pronounced man and wife. Other random pictures celebrating our nuptials with everyone we could find.

"Holy fuck," Wes says.

"I can't believe it," Amelia adds.

"I can't believe y'all got married the same night as Renn Brewer and Blakely Evans," Betsy says. "That news was *everywhere.*"

"I can't believe I wasn't there to be your best man," Simon chimes in.

"You wouldn't have been his best man," Shane says before turning to me. "But the question begs to be asked, what's next?"

And there's the million dollar question. I knew it was either going to be Shane or Wes to ask. Doesn't mean I was any more ready to answer.

"Well, according to law in Tennessee, sixty days is the minimum length before a divorce can be final."

"This is true," Wes adds. "Longest sixty days of my life."

"So, as much as I enjoy wearing this," I say as I hold up my hand, "it will only be on my hand for two months. Izzy wants a divorce, which I'm going to give to her."

Amelia stands up, only to come to sit next to me. "What do you want?"

"What?"

"I said, what do you want? Because the Oliver I know wouldn't get divorced so quickly. Even the version of Oliver who got drunk and married in Vegas."

"It doesn't matter what I want," I say.

"Yes, it does," Betsy adds. "Because you love her, and your feelings are valid."

"Who said I love her?" I mean, I know I do, but I didn't realize they already know I do.

"Do you think we're blind?" Shane says. "I've been there for nearly every woman you've dated. And I've been there for every failed proposal. In all of those years, you've never *not* told us about a woman. You've never kept a relationship to yourself. You sure as hell didn't kiss any of them like you did in that picture. You also need to remember, I saw you the morning after the wedding. Did I think you were being dramatic when you said she was the one who was getting away? Of course, because it's you. But I'll admit that I was wrong. You've never looked at a woman like that. Not in the thirty years I've known you. I'm sorry to say it, but you're in love with your wife, Oliver."

I look back to the screen, which is now showing a picture of us kissing before we got back into our car. "What am I supposed to do? She doesn't believe in love. She's against marriage. Every time it gets brought up a look of terror runs over her. And I told her when this was starting, being in her life as a friend was better than not being in it at all. And I mean that. So if she wants a divorce and to go back to how things were, then so be it."

"Nope. Bullshit," Simon says as he stands up and blocks the television. "That's not how this is going down."

"Then please tell me, so-called best friend, how is it going to go down?"

"First we need to know the answer to a couple of questions. One, do you love her?"

No sense in lying. "Yes."

Wes stands up and walks next to Simon. "You said before she was different. Do you still feel that way?"

"I do."

"Do you want to be married to her?" This comes from Shane, who joins the others.

"Yes."

"Then you need to fight," Amelia says, taking my hands in hers instead of joining the three musketeers. "You need to show her that love with you is different. You have to show her that it might have started as an accident, but sometimes that's how the best things begin."

"You have sixty days," Betsy chimes in, sneaking a glance at Wes. "A lot can happen in that amount of time."

She's right. They're all right. I love Izzy. And I know, in my heart of hearts, she loves me in some way that I don't think she's realized yet. And I can fight. I can wait. I can do whatever I need to do.

Sixty days. Two months. In that time, I have to slay a few dragons and make my wife fall in love with me.

Easy enough.

"Last question."

I look back to Shane, who's still standing with Wes and Simon. "What's that?"

"When are we meeting Mrs. Price?"

Chapter 25
Izzy

"You ready?"

I shoot a look over to Oliver, who has the most shit-eating grin on his face that I've ever seen. "Have I told you today that I hate you?"

"Nope," he says, bouncing out of his car that's currently sitting outside The Joint. By the time he gets around to my side, his smile has gotten wider. "But in fairness, it usually takes a few hours of being around me to get to that point. I just figured it was a matter of time before it happened today."

I can't help but to shake my head as I get out of Oliver's car. Am I really doing this? Am I meeting his friends? His friends who now know the whole story. His friends who probably think I'm either a crazy woman for doing what we did or a bitch for wanting to get a divorce the second we can.

"Why am I meeting them again?" I ask. "We're going to be not married before we know it."

"Yes, but you're still my friend," he says. "And I want my friends to know each other. Plus, they have questions."

I snap my head to him. "Questions? What kind of questions?"

Oliver puts his hand on the small of my back as we start walking inside. "Now, what would be the fun in that?"

"I really, really hate you."

He leans in and gently kisses me on the temple. "I know. Now let's go. They can't wait to meet you."

I focus on Oliver's hand on my back as he leads me into the bar. I know that all eyes are going to be on me when we enter. I just have to keep reminding myself they aren't looking at me in pity, or because I'm the butt of a joke I didn't know about.

Oliver's here, he's with you. Lean into him.

"Hello!" Oliver yells as we walk into cute dive bar. Actually, I wouldn't even call it a dive bar. It's the perfect small-town spot. Enough tables for small or big groups. Local signs and jerseys along the walls. Pool tables and dart boards, and a bar that lines the wall. On a good note, there aren't a lot of people here. On the other hand, everyone who is here is looking at me like I'm an exhibit at the zoo.

No one says anything as Oliver and I approach the table that currently has three men and two women sitting at it. The silence would be deafening if it wasn't for the sound of the vintage video games from the corner of the bar. I see a small girl standing on a chair playing pinball, a preteen girl making sure she doesn't fall, and a little boy at the other video game getting very into whatever he's playing.

"Everyone, this is Izzy," Oliver begins before he starts pointing to the people at the table. "Izzy, this is Wes, his girlfriend Betsy, Amelia, Shane, and Simon."

I raise my hand slightly to give a wave. "Hello."

Awkward greetings are exchanged, which is to be expected. I start to sit down, but before I can pull out my chair, the man who I believe was introduced as Simon does it for me. "Here you go."

"Thank you," I say, though I'm not sure why he did that. But before I know I can ask him or Oliver, the little girl from the pinball machine is standing very, very close to me.

"Are you Uncle Ollie's wife?"

Wow. Okay. I didn't expect direct interrogation from the kid...

"Technically, yes, I am."

"I'm Magnolia. I'm almost seven years old, and Wes is my dad. Betsy's my bonus mom and my best friend."

"Nice to meet you Magnolia, I'm Izzy."

She holds out her hand for a handshake, and I don't know whether to be impressed or terrified of this child.

"Can I ask you another question?"

"Sure."

"My whoooooooolllle life I've dreamed of being a flower girl. I don't know when my dad and Betsy are getting married, and I don't want to age out. When you and Uncle Ollie redo your wedding because none of us were invited to the last one, can I pleeeeeeease be a flower girl? I promise I'll be the best flower girl there ever was."

"I..." I blink rapidly and do my best on how to answer this. Because I've known this child for two minutes, and I feel like if I disappoint her I will hate myself forever. Then at the same time I don't want to lie to her.

It's then I happen to catch a glimpse of Simon, who is watching this interaction a little more intensely than a spectator should be. Don't get me wrong, the others are as well. But their looks are more of shock and awe. But Simon...it's like he's watching a script he wrote play out in real time.

All right, that's how we're going to play this? Game on.

I turn to whisper to Oliver. "Hey, can I fuck with Simon?"

I feel his smile against my cheek. "Abso-fucking-lutely."

"Magnolia, it would be my honor for you to be our flower girl."

Her eyes grow wide with excitement. "Really?"

"Of course. And you get to pick the color of your dress."

"Pink. Obviously."

"Obviously." I can't help but laugh. This kid is fucking great. "Now, I know you can handle it, but can you go ask your Uncle Simon if he can handle being the flower man? I'm picturing him in all pink, to match you, of course, throwing petals from a rhinestone fanny pack."

Magnolia turns back to Simon, who is doing a simultaneous glare and glass tip to me. In the business world, that is the ultimate sign of respect. "Uncle Simon. She wants you to be a flower man. So I'm going to need you to do this, because I really want to be a flower girl. Deal?"

"Deal," he groans.

"Oh, Magnolia?"

"Yeah, Izzy?"

"Tell your Uncle Simon that if he wants to use you to freak me out, he better pay you more money. Because next time I want to screw with him, I'm going to pay you double and make sure it's at the time he doesn't want it to happen."

Magnolia gives me a firm head nod with a handshake to go with it. "Got it, Izzy."

The table erupts in laughter as Magnolia holds out her hand for Simon, who gives her two twenty-dollar bills.

"Well played," Simon says to me. "Well played, indeed."

"I must admit, you had me for a second. Next time, try not to look so smug."

"Sorry to burst your bubble, but that will never happen," Amelia says. "Simon has looked smug since the day he was born."

"Not true. I was an adorable baby. The smug came when I moved here."

Amelia rolls her eyes as the table continues to laugh.

"That was the most amazing thing I've ever witnessed," Oliver says.

"Which part? Me or Magnolia?"

"Both. But especially you and Simon. Not many can handle him at the first meeting."

"Oh please...I've dealt with plenty of Simons in my day. They think they're so tough, but they are the easiest to knock down a few pegs."

"I'm going to keep you around just for that."

We share a smile, which I'm finding that we do a lot. I notice it because I generally don't smile. At least I used to not smile. But freaking Oliver and his freaking nice guy persona and his freaking voice and his freaking dimples get me every damn time.

"So you two crazy love birds," Wes says. "Tell us the story. And leave nothing out."

I give the table a confused look. "Don't you guys already know everything?"

Simon nods. "We do. But we're going to need to hear it from you to confirm. Especially the proposal. We're going to need every second of that."

"You know I was drunk and I remember only pieces?"

Magically, a pitcher of beer appears on the table and more appetizers than I've ever seen a small group eat.

"Even better," Shane says. Shit, he was so quiet I almost forgot he was there. "Now tell us everything."

~

"OKAY, now it's my turn to ask the questions," I say. I've been playfully grilled for the past hour about our Vegas nuptials. I had prepared myself for the worst, but Oliver's friends are pretty amazing. Even Simon. I feel a strange kinship to him—probably because he's an asshole, and I've been called way worse than that in my life.

"Yes," Simon says, rubbing his hands together. "We'll tell you everything you could want to know about our boy over here."

"The proposals," I say. "He's hinted that there have been many. I need to know how many."

I think all of the guys start actually bouncing in their seats. That's until Oliver stands up.

"Nope," he signals all of the guys to follow him to the bar. "All of you. With me."

"But it was just about to get good!" Wes says with a whine. "I was going to tell her about the scoreboard proposal!"

Oliver grabs them all and pulls them toward the pool tables. "Not today you're not."

Amelia, Betsy and I laugh as the guys head to the other side of the bar.

"Is this the part of the night where the two of you grill me without the guys around?"

Betsy shakes her head. "Absolutely not. It's the time when you answer a question we've been dying to know."

"*She's* been dying to know," Amelia says. "I've known Oliver since we were six, and he's basically a brother to me. Hearing what I'm about to hear is going to potentially scar me for life."

"Are you about to ask...?"

"Yes," Betsy says. "The whole nice guy thing. I don't think it's a front. I genuinely believe that Oliver is the nicest guy in the world. But, I believe that in bed he's a freak. Like pull your hair, tell you your praise kink, and leave you wondering what the hell just happened."

"And I think that he's a gentle soul and that translates into every facet of his life."

I turn to look at Oliver, who's now playing pool with the guys, and I can't help but bite my lip as I remember the time he did call me a good girl. The time his hand was perfectly gripping onto my throat. I don't know if he can feel me looking at him, but at that moment he turns and we lock eyes. Does he know what I'm thinking about? The way he's looking at me makes me think so. It makes me wish I wasn't keeping him at arm's length, because the way he's looking at me right now makes me want to take him into the bathroom, lock the door, and have him fuck me senseless.

"Yes!" Betsy's yell brings me back to the conversation.

"Yes what?"

"Yes, I was right."

"How do you know?" Amelia asks. "She hasn't said a thing."

Betsy picks up her drink and takes a sip, looking very pleased with herself. "Because I know the look you give to a man who's made you forget words. And that look she just gave can only mean that our Izzy has called out to gods she doesn't believe in because of our sweet and beloved Oliver."

I smile and tip my drink to her. "Let's put it this way, if the mothers at Rolling Hills Elementary knew what that man was like in the bedroom he'd need a security detail outside his door."

"I don't want to hear this," Amelia says, covering her ears. Which of course makes Betsy and I laugh.

"Welcome to the club, Izzy," Betsy says. "I think you're going to fit in with us just fine."

Chapter 26
Izzy

"Why was I scared to meet your friends again?"

"I'm not sure," Oliver says as he pulls his car out of the parking lot. "Probably because you like to psych yourself out about situations that you didn't have forty-eight hours to prepare for, and you always think the glass is half empty."

I start to answer back, but I don't, because he's right. On everything.

"When did you get to know me so well?"

"Probably sometime between when I found out what your lunch order was and when I realized that you don't own any clothing with color."

"Hey!" I say, looking down at my all-black outfit. "I own colorful stuff."

"The gold dress you wore to the wedding doesn't count."

"I have more," I say. Though now as I mentally think about the options in my closet, I can't seem to think of any.

"Exactly. Face it. I know just about everything there is to know about you."

"No, you don't," I say. "There are plenty of things about me that you don't know."

"Really?" he asks as he turns onto his street. "Well, then I think since we're going to be married for the next sixty days, and plan on being friends long after everything is finalized, I feel like we should put all the cards on the table."

I know Oliver means this playfully—like he wants to know what my top milkshake flavors are—but my mind immediately goes to the things I don't tell anyone. I've come so close to telling Oliver, but I knew I needed to keep them to myself. But the more these conversations pop up, the more I worry that pretty soon I'm going to slip.

"Not tonight," I say as he pulls into his driveway where my car is parked. "It's late, and I have an early morning. I should get back to Nashville."

He turns off the car and gives me a look I'm guessing he uses on his students when he wants them to tell the truth. "I'll give you that it's late. But it's Friday. You don't have to work tomorrow, and I remember you telling me earlier that you couldn't wait for this weekend to, and I quote, do jack shit."

How dare this man use my own words against me?

"I don't have pajamas or a toothbrush."

"Izzy, I have a T-shirt, which due to our pre-wedding trip, I know is your preferred mode of sleep attire. Also, because I'm an adult, I have a spare toothbrush that can be yours. I'll even get out my label maker and put your name on it."

"You own a label maker?"

"Yup. See, one more thing you've learned about me. Let's go."

I let out a groan as I open the car door and walk into Oliver's house. Every time I come here, I find something else that just makes me smile, because this house is so Oliver. From the light blue paint, to the plants, to the bowl of Skittles that's always on his coffee table, this house is Oliver through and through.

Take the pictures on the wall. The first time I came over and saw them, I think I stared at them for hours. I mean, the pictures in and of themselves don't surprise me. It's Oliver, after all. But the fact that he took the time to print, frame, and hang them in a perfect display is what puts it over the top. There are pictures of him and the guys. Some from classes over the years he's taught. There's one of him and his mom next to a birthday cake that melts my cold, dead heart every time I see it. Maybe because they are so happy. Maybe because they are wearing those silly, pointy birthday hats. I don't know. But I can't help but smile every time I see it.

"That was from her sixtieth birthday party," he says, coming to stand next to me. "She had just retired from teaching and had decided that day she was going to take her first of what was going to be many road trips."

"She seems great," I say.

"She is," he says. "She'll be back in town in three months. I'd love for you to meet her."

"Does she know?" I ask.

"No," he says as he starts walking over to his couch. "I have a feeling if I told her, she'd turn her car around, and I'm not about to be the one that ruins her Mother Road voyage."

"That makes sense," I say. "By the time she's back, we'll be divorced. We can tell her then and all have a good laugh about it."

Except neither of us are laughing. But we should be. Tonight was a fun night. We drank, we laughed, we cracked jokes on ourselves that we can only do now in hindsight of our antics. For the first time since I realized I was married to Oliver Price, I felt okay about it. I felt good, even. I didn't feel like a weight was on my chest and the only thing that could alleviate it was the signed and finalized divorce papers.

"So what did you think of them?" Oliver asks. I don't know if he could tell that I needed a topic change, or if he did, but I'm glad for it.

"They are great. Even Simon."

This makes him laugh. "He's something, isn't he?"

"That's one way to put it," I say as I make myself comfortable. "I will say, your group is an interesting dynamic."

"Meaning?"

"You guys seem so different," I say. "First off, I want to go on record saying that Amelia must be a saint to have put up with all of you over the years."

"She is. We've nominated her many times."

"Good," I continue. "So you have Wes, who at first seems very even keeled. Then I saw him with Betsy and the kids and he was this big, goofy guy. Then there's Simon, who's just a different brand of cocky. Shane, I think, said three words all night. Then there's you."

He leans his head on his hand against the back of the couch as he shows off that smug smile. "What about me?"

"You really want me to go there?"

"More than anything."

I bring my feet up under my legs, getting a little more comfortable. "You're loud and bright and freaking cheerful."

"I don't know why you needed to use the word 'freaking' there, but go on."

"Because you are. You're freaking cheerful. You make friends with strangers standing in line. You somehow got me to go to a farmers' market and do other people-y things. I hate people."

"No, you don't," he says. "Just certain ones."

"Most," I say. "Anyway, it's so interesting to see you in your group of friends. You're so you, and so different from them, but somehow you all work. It's something you don't see every day."

"Do you have that? Or did you back before you moved?"

Fuck, I walked right into that one, didn't I? It's a perfectly normal question. And it's very normal for people to ask questions back to the other person when you're getting to know them. I don't want to answer. My mind and defensive reflexes are screaming at me to change the subject. That if I tell Oliver a little, he'll want to know everything. I'm definitely not ready for that. But part of me also thinks one day I might be, and I'll never know if I don't start somewhere. I must have had more to drink tonight than I thought...

"I didn't," I say. Oliver's eyes go wide as he realizes I'm actually answering a personal question, but he quickly corrects himself. "I had a few friends, but nothing like you guys. I had my priorities in high school, and safe to say, a group of friends was not that priority."

There. Easy. Told the truth, opened up a little, while not letting the whole damn can of worms explode.

"Thank you," he says.

"For what?"

"For that. I know talking about your past isn't something you like to do. I appreciate knowing that you trust me with that."

"I wish I could tell you more," I say, suddenly feeling vulnerable, but in a good way. Like I'm safe if I open up just a little bit more. "But just the thought of saying words out loud makes me want to vomit."

Oliver holds out his arms, which I go into without question. I know I shouldn't. I know in my head I'm taking advantage of his feelings. But here, in Oliver's arms, is the only place I feel safe. That I feel like the demons from my past aren't controlling my every move.

"You know when the day comes that you're ready, I'm going to be here. No matter whether or not I have a ring on my finger or if one of us is living in a different time zone, I'll always be here for you."

"I know," I say, snuggling in a bit closer. "You're too good to be true, you know that right?"

Oliver laughs a little. "I appreciate the compliment, but I know for a fact that's false."

"Why do you think that?"

Oliver doesn't answer for a few seconds. The silence seems familiar. It reminds me of me when I'm broached with a topic I'd rather not talk about.

"You know how the guys joke, and even I joke, about the amount of proposals I've made?"

"Yes."

"Have I ever told you the actual number?"

I go still in Oliver's arms. It's a question I've always wanted to ask, but dared not to. "You haven't..."

I feel him take in, then let out a deep breath. "When I proposed to you at the wedding, that was my thirty-fourth proposal."

I don't know if Oliver can see me right now as my back is against his front, but I've stopped breathing. I've stopped blinking. I've ceased all movement.

"Wow," I whisper. "That's...a lot."

"You could say that," he says. "I know it's a running joke, and I'm fine with that. I get why. Honestly, it is funny. But in the back of my head, I have to wonder, what's wrong with me? Why, out of thirty-three women, did none of them want to marry me?"

There was a moment in the *Wizard of Oz* when the Tin Man realized he had a heart. Right here is my Tin Man moment.

"You know it's them, right?"

Oliver starts gently brushing his fingers on my arms. I don't know if it's for my benefit or his, but I don't stop him. "So I've been told. Though I'm the common denominator in all of those relationships."

I sit up so I can turn to look at him, and my newly-found heart breaks a little more when I see the utter defeat written all over his face. "Oliver Michael Price."

He seems shocked by this response. "You remembered my middle name..."

"I did. Now focus. You are the best man I've ever met. I wish I could stay married to you. In another life, in another time, I'd marry you ten times over. Because you are the type of man who deserves all the love in the world. And there's some woman out there watching some romantic comedy, eating Skittles, wondering where her happily ever after is, and it's you."

He nods, though I don't know if he believes me. "Thanks. I appreciate that."

I tip his head up with my fingers, wanting him to look at me for this. "I'm not just saying that. I don't lie, Oliver. I told you that from day one. I might not be forthright with information, but honesty is a deal-breaker for me. There's never a word that has come out of my mouth that I didn't mean. You, my friend, are the biggest catch of all. Hell, I'd make you a part of a dating app campaign if you'd let me. Wait, will you let me? Nevermind, we can talk about that later. But in all of this rambling, please know this: There is not one single thing wrong with you. Not one, single, thing."

My finger is still under his chin, and for some reason I have this sudden urge to kiss him. It would be so easy to do it. The moment is here. And so are his lips. Lips that I know taste like the best thing in the world. Lips that have the power to make me feel treasured and sexy all at the same time. Lips that don't lie to me. Lips that have made me start to feel like there might be light in the darkness.

I quickly drop my finger, sense somehow smacking me upside the head. I can't kiss Oliver. I'm already blurring lines. I'm already playing with fire.

But man, that fire would feel so good...

"I should go to bed," I say, quickly moving off the couch.

"Yeah, sure." Oliver stands up and points me down the hall. "You can grab a T-shirt from my drawer. Toothbrushes are in the medicine cabinet."

"Thanks," I say, quickly turning to head down the hall. Why am I nearly running? That would be because I feel a fucking tear threatening to leak, and I do not cry. Except when I realize I'm married, apparently.

"Hey, wife?"

I stop at Oliver's words and quickly take a breath. Luckily, that's enough to push back that fucking tear that was threatening to escape. "Yeah?"

"Whoever he was who hurt you, you know I want to kill him, right?"

I laugh as the tears start falling from my face. There's no holding them back this time. "I don't know if you have enough swords to fight all these dragons."

"Try me."

Chapter 27
Oliver

I didn't think anything of it when Shane sent a message in the group text this morning seeing if we all wanted to go to breakfast at Mona's Diner. In fact, I kind of expected it. I mean, my friends did just meet my wife for the first time, so that calls for coffee and waffles.

I might have expected the text, but I didn't expect this.

Then again, I should have remembered who my friends are and their penchant for decorations and sign making. Because when I walk into Rolling Hills's favorite small-town greasy spoon, I'm greeted by balloons, streamers, and a big sign that says "He said yes!"

"What the fuck?"

"Everyone! The guest of honor has arrived!" Simon announces from the table he's currently standing on. "Ladies, you've had your chance. Gentlemen, you have one less man to contend with for the affections of the woman you're trying to court. Because it's my great pleasure to introduce the no longer single and looking to mingle...everyone's favorite elementary teacher...Oliver Price!"

I send a glare to Simon, who looks all too pleased with himself as he causes a commotion in the diner. And not just him. Shane and Wes are standing on either side of him, making sounds with some sort of noise maker you get at a party store.

"You guys are idiots," I say as I slide into the booth under the sign that was apparently made for me.

"Hey, this is all your fault," Simon says.

"How so?"

"Because," Shane says. "It was your idea to decorate Wes's car after his divorce. Which brought out the decorating bug in all of us. So really, you only have yourself to blame."

"Again, idiots," I mumble as I grab a menu to look at it.

"Give me that." Wes rips the menu out of my hand. "You can recite this menu front and back, so don't hide in there. What happened last night after you two left?"

I can't help but smile, even though nothing happened.

"We almost kissed."

I watch as every person's eyes grow wide in shock. Wes is the first to speak up, but only because he was the first to pick his jaw off the table.

"Can I ask why it was an almost?"

"Because it wasn't the time," I say. "Izzy's a hard nut to crack. The little tidbits I've got from her about her life, and what makes her tick, are few and far between. And last night I felt like we really made some strides. I wasn't going to ruin that by taking a chance on a kiss."

But damn if I didn't want to. She did, too. I could tell. The way she looked at me. The few times she accidentally licked her lips. Kissing her last night would have been the perfect ending to a perfect evening.

"Okay, that makes sense," Shane asks. "But was that the chance? Did you miss it?"

I think about the question for a second, even though I've

thought about this exact thing at least twenty times since last night. And every time I come up with the same answer.

"I didn't."

"Are you sure?" Shane leans in like he really wants me to hear this. "I'm not saying that you did or didn't, but you're the only one who knows."

I nod. "I didn't. We talked...a lot. She revealed some stuff about herself, and I opened up as well. If anything, not kissing was the best thing we could have done."

Wes pats me on the back. "Then I'm glad. Because I get why you've acted so different the past few months. She's it. You've finally met her."

Wow. I didn't expect that seal of approval. "You think so? Do you all?"

All three of my friends nod their heads in agreement.

"I know Betsy and I are very much Team Izzy," Wes says. "And Magnolia would like it on record that she will, in fact, be a flower girl when you two renew your vows. She might have said that stuff because Simon said to, but that didn't change the sentiment."

I laugh and look over to Simon. "I can't believe you tried to screw with her and use your goddaughter as the bait."

"I have no regrets, and I'd do it again," he says as he sips his coffee. "If a woman can handle Magnolia, she can handle any of us."

"That's true," I say. "So you approve?"

"Very much. In fact, if for some reason it doesn't work out, please let me know."

"Don't you fucking dare."

My snarl only makes Simon smile like the evil mastermind he is. "That's all I needed to hear."

I turn to Shane, who besides his noise making when I walked in, hasn't said a lot. Even for him.

"Shane? Care to weigh in?"

"She's great," Shane says.

"I feel like there's a but coming on..."

Wes tips his coffee mug toward him. "It wouldn't be a Shane conversation if our friend didn't play the devil's advocate."

"I like her. I do. Amelia likes her, too."

"You talked to Amelia about her?"

Shane seems thrown off track for a second before he quickly recovers. What the fuck was that about?"

"Amelia and I chatted a little last night after you guys left."

"No, you didn't," Simon says. "Amelia left before everyone else did."

"I mean this morning. It doesn't matter. What I wanted to say is yes, she's great. She gets along with everyone, and she even fucked with Simon, which you always know scores points in my book. But I only needed to see you with her once to know that you, my friend, are in love with this woman like you've never been before. I know you thought you were in love with those other women, but it only took one look at you last night to know that you are gone beyond belief. And I'm happy you've found that."

Here comes the but...

"But how sure are you that she's going to come around? Because if she doesn't, you're going to be wrecked. And I'll be there to help pick up the pieces; we all will. But I want you to really understand that if this doesn't work out, if the clock runs out and she wants you to finalize the divorce, you're not going to be okay. Are you prepared for that possibility?"

I can always count on Shane Cunningham for a dose of realness.

"I am."

"Really?" Wes asks. "Because that even freaked me out."

"Yes, really." I sit up a little straighter. "You guys have been with me during a lot of shitty relationships."

"The yoga teacher who you proposed to on the meditation retreat."

"The bartender you tried to propose to while reenacting a scene from *Coyote Ugly*."

"Wasn't one in a cult?"

"Yes," I say to all of them as they snicker about my stellar dating history. "But what I've come to realize is that from the beginning, Izzy was different. I never sleep with women on the first night, yet I did that. I always tell you guys about every detail, I didn't do that."

"I'd like to say thank you for that one," Wes says.

"Anytime," I continue. "I didn't tell you guys about her at all. I wondered for weeks why I was doing that. Why I didn't just come clean. But I figured it out. It's because she's different. *We're* different. We've done nothing in the right order or traditionally. Hell, I'm married, and I just said that it was a good thing that my wife didn't kiss me. So yes, I know that I'm taking a huge leap of faith by letting her figure this out. But there are times when it's just the two of us, and I can tell she loves me too. She just doesn't know it yet."

The table falls silent. No one even moves after an order of waffles that I didn't order magically appears from our waitress.

"No one? No one's going to say anything? Simon, you have to want to say something."

"I do," he says, but he turns his gaze to Shane. "Can we please go back to the part of the conversation when you lied about when you talked to Amelia and why you stuttered and sounded like you got caught doing something you shouldn't have done?"

I laugh as I sit back and enjoy not being in the spotlight for the first time in a few months.

"I misspoke, is that a fucking crime?"

"I don't know, Officer Cunningham, is it a crime?"

Wes and I try to keep our laughs to ourselves, but fail miserably.

"I hate every one of you assholes," Shane says as he stands up and storms out of Mona's.

Simon watches him leave before turning back to us. "Was it something I said?"

Chapter 28
Izzy

Oliver: What do you feel like for dinner tonight?

Izzy: Hmm…maybe Mexican? I could go for some queso.

Oliver: That will work. Maybe a few margaritas to go with it?

Izzy: No. Never again.

Oliver: Oh come on, what's the harm? We can't get more married.

Izzy: Let's just play it safe…

"Look at our girl, Jules. Who knew she could smile like that?"

"I know, Hazel. It's like every day is filled with rainbows and sunshine in this office."

I put down my phone and shoot a look at my two supposed friends. "Very funny."

"We're just making an observation," Hazel says as she and Jules take a seat in my office. "We like to call this The Oliver Effect."

"The Oliver Effect?"

"Yes," Jules says. "Since Oliver came into your life, you've become more...pleasant."

"Pleasant?" I wasn't expecting that word to be used. "Are you saying I wasn't before?"

"No, that's not what I'm saying...it's just..."

Hazel holds up her hand. "What Jules is trying to say is that there were times when everyone in this office was mildly terrified of you. But since Oliver came into your life, those times are...well...gone."

"Interesting. I didn't realize that."

"Which part?"

"All, I guess," I say. "I mean, I knew I could be a little standoffish at times. But I didn't realize it was that bad."

"We're exaggerating...slightly," Hazel says with a smile. "But in all seriousness, I hope that when you two get divorced he stays around. Because he's good for you."

The mention of divorce immediately puts a knot in my stomach. Which is the opposite response of what I want to happen. The thought of not being married should make me excited. Giddy, even. But instead, every time I think about actually signing those papers, a sense of gloom overtakes me and my stomach gets all weird.

I don't know how, but this is Oliver's fault.

"When are you two going to see the lawyer?"

"Tomorrow," I say. "Oliver's actually coming into town tonight and staying over so that way we can go to the office first thing in the morning."

"Oooh, a sleepover!" Hazel teases.

"Not like that," I say. "We've spent the night at each other's places before. The guest bedroom at his place has now become mine, and he insists he finds my couch more than adequate."

"I don't know how you do it," Jules says. "If a man that hot was in my house, I don't know if I could resist."

"Easy. I remind myself that if Oliver and I do find ourselves in the same bed, we usually sleep together or end up married. This is the only way to ensure that doesn't happen."

"But would it be so bad? I mean, the man is sex on a stick."

"Jules! What would your fiancé say about that?"

She shrugs. "Honestly, if he met Oliver, he'd probably get a crush on him. And I wouldn't blame him one bit."

I mean, Jules isn't wrong. Oliver is sexy in all the stereotypical ways a man can be. Good jawline. Perfect hair. Piercing eyes that make you feel like you're the only one in the room when he fixes them on you. A voice that never fails to send shivers down your spine.

And yes, all of those are a thing. It's what outsiders like Hazel and Jules see. But Oliver is sexy in so many other ways. He knows exactly when a small touch does wonders. His jokes and little quips turn your mood around in an instant. He's a great friend. He's the best listener. And there's no one, I mean no one, whose shoulder and chest I'd rather cry into when the day has become too much.

"Izzy? Earth to Izzy?" Hazel says, snapping her fingers to get my attention. "You there?"

"Yeah," I say. "Just thinking."

"Thinking about how you love your husband and that's fucking with your head?"

"What? No!" I say, though I know what she said was damn close to the truth. But hell if I'm going to admit that.

"It's cute you think that," she says. "Because I remember when you once called me out for having feelings for my fake boyfriend. But if I'm reading that far-out look on your face correctly, you're in love with Oliver, and that's scaring the shit out of you."

"You're ridiculous," I say. "It's nothing like that. We're just friends."

"Sure. Friends. Let me know when you're done lying to yourself."

"I'm not lying to myself," I protest. Though I don't say any more as something, or should I say someone, catches my eye at my door.

"Knock knock? Delivery for Mrs. Izzy McCall-Price."

Hazel and Jules giggle as Oliver waltzes into my office, a big brown bag in hand that smells delicious. I really try not to smile —I have a reputation to hold here, and I was doing a great job at denying things just a few seconds ago—but I can't help it. It also doesn't help that Oliver's wearing a T-shirt that says "World's Best Husband."

"Hello ladies," he says to Hazel and Jules as he sets the bag down on my desk. "I hope everyone is hungry. I brought enough for you as well."

"Well aren't you just the sweetest," Hazel says. "What a guy, right, Jules?"

"Right Hazel. There aren't many men out there who would not only surprise their wives with lunch, but also bring enough for her friends as well."

"Those are the guys you don't let go of."

Oh, for fuck's sake...

"You two, out!" I say, pointing to the door.

"Fine, but we're taking our sushi with us."

Hazel and Jules each grab their dishes and wave to Oliver as they exit my office.

"Thanks, ladies! I appreciate the kind words!"

"Don't encourage them," I say.

Oliver smiles as he hands me my California rolls. "Well I'm

not going to stop them from saying those very nice things about me. That would just be silly."

"Speaking of silly. What the hell is that shirt? And I'm really going to need to know when you purchased that."

"What? This old thing?" Oliver says, playing dumb as he looks at the shirt then back at me.

"Drop the innocent act. It doesn't go well with your complexion."

Oliver sends me one of his devilish smiles as we take a seat on my couch. "It's actually a gift from Simon. He wanted me to tell you that he found a matching shirt for you, but didn't know your size."

"How nice of him. Make sure you tell him my size is whatever works best for him to shove it up his ass."

"Will do." Oliver laughs as he lays out all the sushi options he picked up. "Lunch is served."

"I wasn't expecting this," I say as I take one of the rolls. "I thought you weren't coming down until after I got off work?"

"Can't a guy want to surprise his wife?"

I raise an eyebrow, wondering what he's up to. I've also realized that I don't even flinch anymore when he uses the word "wife."

"He can. But that doesn't mean I'm not going to be suspicious."

"Fine. I was bored."

"Bored?"

"Yes, bored," he says. "We had football practice this morning, but Wes and Betsy were leaving for their vacation right after, so he was gone. Shane was working. Simon's out of town. Amelia had something with her kids. So that means you get me early!"

"So I was your last choice?" I tease, though I do my best to keep my voice level.

Oliver leans in. We were already close, but right now I feel like he's overtaking every one of my senses.

"You're never my last choice. And don't you ever forget that."

Oliver doesn't pull away. In fact, he might inch a little closer. Our mouths are inches away from touching. I feel my breathing pick up the longer we stay like this. It's like I can't move. Without even touching him, I can feel his lips against mine. I can feel my fingers in his hair as his hands wrap around my waist, bringing me to his lap.

What would that be like? Taking a minute in the work day to share an intimate moment with your partner? To show how thankful you are to them when they surprise you with your favorite sushi? To close the blinds, blocking the outside work out, and have a little extra fun that no one could see?

I could do it. I'm the only one stopping this. Yet every time I think maybe I could do this, something in my brain pops up that says this is only good because it's not for real. If this was real, it wouldn't be this easy. It wouldn't be this good.

Because love doesn't feel good. Love hurts, love sucks, and most of all, it breaks you down to where you don't feel like you'll ever get back up.

"Are you going to get that?"

"Huh?" I say to Oliver, because I honestly have no idea what he's talking about.

He tilts his head back to my desk. "Your phone. It's been vibrating for the past two minutes."

"Oh." I sit up and give myself a shake as I walk to my desk. When I pick up my phone, I realize it's the last person in the world I expect to be calling me right now.

"Mom?"

I fall into my seat as I hear my mother's voice on the other end of the phone for the first time in sixteen years. I didn't even know she had my number. Before I can grasp what is happening, Oliver is on his knees, holding my free hand with the most concerned look I've ever seen in my life.

"Hello, Elizabeth."

I flinch at the use of my full name. Funny how something so simple can have such an impact on you.

"Is everything okay?"

"No," she says evenly. "Your father is dead."

"Dad's dead? What? How?"

Oliver must see the shock in my eyes because he immediately brings my hand to his lips, trying to comfort me anyway he can.

"He had a heart attack last night."

"And you're just calling now to tell me?

"Your sister wanted to, but we needed to make arrangements, and I figured we'd get to you when we did."

I can't even laugh at that, because it doesn't surprise me in the least. "Well then why didn't she call me today?"

"We needed Jessie at the store," my mother says in her even, heartless tone. "She's doing what a good daughter would do at this time."

Oh, here we fucking go. Even when a family tragedy is happening, my mother can't help but get in a few digs.

"I'm sure you could close the store for a little bit, Mom. I'm sure the four families in that town can buy a couch next week."

"This is why I didn't call you. I didn't need to hear your attitude."

"Well, then, why *did* you call, Mom?"

"Because you need to be at the funeral."

Now I can't hold in my laughter. "You want me to come home for the funeral? The daughter who can't do anything right? The disappointment of the family?"

I hear her let out a sigh. I should know what those sound

like. I heard them repeatedly in the first eighteen years of my life. "Despite our differences, you should be here to pay respects to your father. The funeral is in two days. And please, don't cause a scene. For once in your life, have a little decorum."

My mom hangs up on me before I can do it to her. "My dad's dead."

"I'm so sorry," Oliver says, helping me stand up as we go back to the couch. Oliver brings me into his arms, I think expecting me to cry. But I don't. There's not one ounce of emotion coming from me.

"I have to go back for the funeral."

"Of course. I'll check for our flights."

It takes me a few seconds, but I realize that Oliver said "our." I sit up so I can look and make sure I heard what I just heard.

"What do you mean?"

"I mean, I'm going with you."

"No, you aren't."

"Yes I am."

"Oliver," I say as he starts doing something on his phone, presumably looking up flights to nowheres-ville Nebraska. "Stop."

I put my hand on the phone and lower it for him. I need him to look me in the eye for this.

"Oliver, I love that you want to come with me and support me. But I haven't been back to Nebraska in sixteen years. This is going to be ugly, messy, and downright horrible. And that's just my family."

"I know. That's why I'm going with you."

"You're making zero sense."

"For a smart woman, sometimes you just don't get it." Oliver takes my hands back in his. "I'm going with you. I know that this is going to be hard. I know from the little bit you've told me that this actually might be hell on Earth. Do you think that I'm about to let you go do that without me? Without support? Because if you think that, then well...I don't know what to say."

Shit. I think I'm going to cry.

"I don't want to go back. But I have to."

Oliver brings my hands to his mouth, placing a gentle kiss on my knuckles. "I know. But you aren't going to have to do it alone."

I fall into Oliver's arms, letting tears escape for the first time since I got the call. "I swore I'd never go back. I don't know if I can face everything."

"I know you think that. But you're strong. Plus, you've got me. And mothers love me."

This makes me snort-laugh. "You've never met my mother."

"Unless she's auditioning for the title role in *Mommy Dearest* I think I'll be okay."

"I wouldn't put it past her."

Chapter 29
Oliver

For my entire life, I always thought Rolling Hills was the epitome of a small town. I mean, everyone knows everyone. When we got our fifth traffic light it was a very big deal. And don't get me started when the first fast food chain restaurant came to town. It happened when I was in sixth grade, and it was a big deal.

I didn't think towns got smaller than Rolling Hills. Then I arrived in Smallwood, Nebraska. Hell, it has the name small in it. If that didn't give it away, the tumbleweed I was racing as we drove into town was a dead giveaway.

I look over to Izzy, who fell asleep on the two-hour drive from Omaha to Smallwood. For the first time since we left her office yesterday afternoon, she seems at peace. Once she got the call, she quickly wrapped up anything she had to figure out before she left the office. It was my job to call the lawyer to tell him we wouldn't be able to come in today to start the divorce proceedings. I got my wish of delaying the inevitable, but I didn't want it to be like this.

She still hasn't told me what she's walking into here, but I know it's bad. After we left the office, she barely said two words as she packed for our morning flight. She fell asleep early, but tossed and turned all night. Normally when I stay at her place, the couch is my best friend, but last night I couldn't make myself go out there. I tried to hold her, but she wasn't having it. Her nightmares were getting the best of her.

I turn the car off, which jolts Izzy awake. "Are we here?"

"Yeah. Just pulled in."

There were no hotels in a thirty-mile radius, so we are staying at the Husker Bed and Breakfast. And considering we are the only car in the parking lot, I have a feeling we have the place to ourselves.

Izzy lets out a yawn and stretches as much as she can in our rented sedan. "Sorry I fell asleep."

"No worries. It was a stimulating drive through the cornfields."

She silently laughs as she takes off her seatbelt and turns to face me. She also grabs her purse from the floor and sets it on her lap. "Okay, so there's something I should have told you before I let you come here."

"Besides the years of trauma that stem from here?"

"Yes. I'll get to that, but this is first," she says. "This town is...well, how do I say this nicely...is...conservative."

"Okay..."

"There are going to be a lot of dirty looks toward me, and you because you're with me. If we ask for two rooms, we'll get weird looks that I'm traveling with a man who I'm not married to. If we stay in the same room, there will be talks that I'm a harlot and staying in the company of a man."

"But we're married."

Izzy nods. "For the next few days, yes, we are."

She reaches into her purse and pulls out the gold band I haven't seen since Vegas. I try not to smile. I really, really,

really, try. But I can't help it. My wife wants to be married to me, and well, I think that's just neat.

I hold up my ring and flash it to her. "I'm already there."

She lets out a small laugh, the first one she's had since yesterday. "If anyone asks, we didn't get married in Vegas. Small ceremony in Nashville will be just fine."

"Whatever you say, my dear."

She looks toward the bed and breakfast then back to me. "I don't know if I'm ready for all of this."

I take her hand, the one that now has a ring on it. I want to revel in the fact that I'm feeling the metal against my skin. I want to kiss her hand, knowing it's wearing the companion piece to mine. But I don't. Not now. Izzy needs me to be her rock. And dammit, that's what I'm going to be.

"We need a sign," I say.

"A sign?"

"Yeah. Or a code word. If for some reason I get pulled away from you and you need to be saved, or if the conversation is getting to be too much and you need an escape, a sign that I know to take over and remove you from the situation."

"That could work," she says. "Except what if I do it by accident?"

"Well, what's something you'd never do or say in front of the people you're about to be around?"

"Probably swear. I might want to, but it's easier if I don't."

"Then that's it. Give me a really loud fuck or shit or your classic for fuck's sake and you'll be as good as removed from the situation."

"Now I kind of want that to happen just to see their faces when I drop any of those words."

"Honestly? Me too."

~

"You ready?"

I look over to Izzy, who looks like she's psyching herself up to go twelve rounds in an MMA cage. "As I'll ever be."

I turn off the car and walk around to help her out. She gives me her hand, which I don't let go of as we start walking toward Izzy's childhood home.

"You know you don't have to hold my hand," she says.

"If we're going to be real husband and wife, I have to look the part. We're not going to get called out as fakes or frauds because I'm not playing my part."

"You're ridiculous," she says as she turns and smiles at me. "Thank you."

I lean in and kiss her temple. "Anytime."

She takes a deep breath and squeezes my hand for good measure before opening the door. Now, I had a feeling a lot of people were over paying their respects, as the driveway, and street, are full of cars. But I wasn't expecting this kind of crowd. The second we step through the door, the room goes quiet and all attention turns to us. Izzy flinches, immediately pulling into me, as it seems like every pair of eyes in the room is staring at her. Which by my rough estimate right now is no less than fifty people.

"I got you," I whisper. "I'm right here."

"Elizabeth, it's nice to see you."

The woman, who I'm going to assume is Izzy's mother—simply based on their same color red hair and taller stature—doesn't reach out for a hug. I don't even think she blinks.

"Hello, Mom. This is Oliver."

"Hello, Mrs. McCall. I'm Oliver Price."

I reach out to shake her hand, but I'm not met with a return gesture. I'm only met with her grabbing my hand, staring at the ring, before she turns her eyes back to Izzy.

"Married?"

Izzy nods. "Yes. Earlier this year."

"At least you could find a man to marry you. Come, everyone is in the living room."

My mother-in-law turns her back to us, walking the way she came without ever checking to see if we were following behind her.

"I can't believe a mom didn't like me. *Every* mom likes me."

"I told you, Constance McCall doesn't like anyone. Don't take offense."

We start walking toward what I'm assuming is the family room as every person we walk past either whispers about us or just flat out mumbles something under their breath about Izzy. I want to tell them to speak up, but I'm not ready to cause a scene this early.

"Should I ask what she meant about you and me getting married?"

Izzy shakes her head. "Just my mom being my mom."

I have a feeling there's more to the story, but this isn't the place. Not as we're about to walk into the lion's den.

I don't think I've ever seen a living room look so sterile. The walls are a boring beige. There is exactly one couch, one recliner, and one coffee table. No television. No pictures. There's not even a blanket on the back of the couch or flowers in the windows. Nothing.

"Where are we?" I ask.

"My childhood."

Like in the other room, every set of eyes is staring at us, which is unnerving. The only difference is there's a few people who aren't looking at Izzy and me with confusion and disgust.

"Aunt Izzy!"

A little boy, probably around Magnolia's age, runs up to Izzy and launches himself into her arms. She was startled at first, but catches him at the last second so he can give her the biggest hug I've ever seen a tiny human give. And I've been on the receiving end of some epic tiny human hugs.

"Hey, Benji."

"Mommy said you were coming but I didn't believe her because you never come here, but you came and I'm so happy."

"I'm so happy to see you buddy. So happy."

I see Izzy blink hard, meaning she's trying to hold back the tears. I put my hand on her back, hoping that I can give her some sort of support through this emotional moment. Hell, I feel the tears welling up.

"I was hoping he was running to you."

Izzy sets Benji down. "Hey, Jessie."

The two wrap each other in a hug that I can tell has been years in the making. Tears are flowing, and not just from them. I'm a mess.

"Are you crying?"

I look down to Benji, who is looking up at me like I'm the most fascinating thing he's ever seen.

"Happy tears," I say as I wipe the wetness from my eyes. "I'm Oliver. Nice to meet you"

Benji looks me up and down, clearly assessing whether or not I can be trusted. "Are you with my Aunt Izzy?"

"I am. I'm actually her husband."

"Husband!" Jessie yells pushing Izzy away and grabbing her ring finger. "Why didn't you tell me?"

"We don't have time for that today, I'm afraid," Izzy says. "Where's your husband and the other child?"

"Home," she says. "After I begged Mom to let me close the store for today and the funeral tomorrow, she then insisted we all come over here to greet the people coming to pay their respects. We were all set to come until Macy decided to get sick in the car. Jimmy took her home, and Benji and I came here."

"Poor girl," Izzy says. "And poor Jimmy."

"Believe me, he'd rather take care of a sick kid then deal with all of this."

The three of us look around the room and it seems as if for the time being, the focus isn't on me or Izzy.

"Where are my manners?" Jessie says, extending her hand to me. "I'm Jessica. Or Jessie. Izzy's older sister and interference runner."

"Nice to meet you. I'm Oliver. The husband and situation saver."

"See, I'm all covered," Izzy says. The three of us and Benji walk over to a set of doors that leads out to a patio where luckily, no one is currently sitting.

"Go play on the swings," Jessie says, shooing Benji away. "I need to talk to Aunt Izzy."

Benji turns to me before he goes. "Will you come push me?"

I look over to Izzy, who is already nodding in approval. "Go."

"Yes!" Benji says as he runs away.

"You sure?"

She nods. "I'm sure. I'll be fine. Plus, if I need to scream the signal, it will be great getting to yell it across the yard."

I give her a kiss on the head. "You sure?"

"I'm sure. Now go."

I head down the lawn and over to the swing set, where Benji is already locked and loaded into position.

"All right, Oliver. Let's see what you're made of."

Chapter 30
Izzy

"Where did you find that one?"

I laugh at my sister as we watch Oliver push Benji on our old swing set. "Got drunk with him at a wedding. Haven't been able to get rid of him since."

"And your wedding?"

"Drunk in Vegas."

My sister starts laughing so hard I think she's going to rock out of the chair she's sitting on. Which of course, only makes me laugh as well.

This is where we had to go to laugh in this house—outside, on the porch, away from our parents. I don't think I'm putting words into my sister's mouth when I say we grew up in a bleak home. There wasn't an outpouring of love. There wasn't color or fun. The mantra was that families only existed to do work and eventually produce more family members. I don't think in the eighteen years I spent in this house I ever saw my dad kiss my mom. I don't know if my mother knows how to smile.

The only thing that kept me sane growing up was Jessie. Yes, we followed the rules because it was easier than not, but once a day we'd come out here, when Mom was on the other side of the house cooking dinner, and have an hour of smiles and laughter. It's where she told me she first kissed her now husband. It's where I told her about my first crush. It's also where she held me and let me cry when my world fell apart.

But I choose not to remember the sad days out here. Because the good far outweighs the bad.

"Why didn't you call me about Dad?" I ask. "I know I'm the black sheep, but it's still pretty fucked up that it takes twenty-four hours to get a call that he was dead."

"I'm sorry, I wanted to," she begins. "I was at the store when Mom called to tell me. At first I was so frantic to get over here I barely remembered to call and tell Jimmy. Then once I got here Mom had me doing so many things—all of course while she was showing no signs of grief or loss—that it honestly slipped my mind. I'm so sorry, Izzy. You know I didn't do it on purpose."

I reach over to hold her hand. "I know. I don't blame you. Though I much rather would have heard the news from you than Mom."

"Try being the one who had to see her as the paramedics wheeled him away. Believe me, I'd have taken the awkward phone call anyday."

"Has she cried at all?"

Jessie tilts her head down and raises her eyebrows. "What do you think? Constance McCall does not cry. Or emote."

"I figured, I just had to ask. Oh, and why the quick funeral? Not like I expected a long mourning period, but this seems fast, even for her."

"Something about inventory coming into the store next week and she didn't want to change the schedule."

All I can do is laugh. "Of course. Why does that not surprise me?"

My parents have run the town furniture shop for forty years. My grandparents opened it fifty years before that. When Jessie and I were fifteen and thirteen, they sat us down and told us that it was our legacy and birthright to continue to operate the store. When I told them I didn't want to—I believe at that age I wanted to be an actress—I was told that I was a disobedient and terrible child. I was then forced to work at the store every day until the day I left Smallwood.

"Did you ever think of moving?" I ask Jessie. I might be talking to my sister, but I can't stop watching Oliver with Benji. He's currently throwing a football with him. It's adorable.

"Once."

I turn my head in surprise. "Really? It was more of a rhetorical question. I didn't think there was an actual answer."

"I'm not the only sister who fantasized about getting out of this two-horse town."

"Yes, but in my defense, when I did leave, it wasn't because of the grand plan I came up with when I was going to run away at fourteen."

"True. But yes, I did. Jimmy and I talked about what it would be like to start fresh. We've always had dreams of opening a restaurant. Nothing big. A family-style restaurant with games for kids and free pie night on Wednesdays."

"Jessie, you guys would be amazing at that." I say. "I know I haven't had your cooking in years, but I doubt that's something you get bad at."

"It's just a dream. We know we can't leave. Mom and Dad would have lost their minds if I wasn't there to help with the store and 'keep it in the family' for the next generation. And Jimmy has a good, steady job at his uncle's construction business. We're happy. The kids are happy. This is where we belong."

We sit and rock for a few seconds, neither of us saying

anything. Yes, when I was a tween, I had dreams of moving far, far away to a town that had tall buildings and wide skylines. But at one point, I was planning on living the life Jessie is living. If life would have worked different, I'd have been here when my dad died. I would have been next to her at that furniture store. I would have gotten married, built a house, had kids, and lived the life my parents always wanted me to.

That's what you do when you're young and in love and you think it's forever. Throw in wanting to please your family and you have a recipe for a life you didn't choose to live, but were forced to.

But I'm not that girl anymore. That girl is long gone.

"There you are, girls, I've been looking all over for you. Why are you out here and not talking to the guests?"

"Sorry," I say, taking the heat for Jessie. I am the one who gets to leave in two days. "I just wanted to talk to her for a few minutes."

"Well, that's over. Go inside. Talk to the people who came here to pay their respects."

Jessie gets up and starts walking to the door, but I don't move.

"Elizabeth. Go with her."

"Do you really want me talking to people, Mom? You know what they're going to say and ask me about, and then you're going to get mad about that. So how about I just stay out here and mind my business?"

"You're so selfish," Mom says, her voice getting louder. Though I don't look, I'm pretty sure I see Oliver out of the corner of my eye, closely watching this interaction. Jessie is standing by the door, knowing it's best not to open it for the next few minutes.

"I'm selfish? Me? Please tell me how that's even an option on the table."

"Because you left."

Here we go. The fight sixteen years in the making. "Did you expect me to stay here? I couldn't step foot outside without people laughing and pointing at me. With no support or help from you or Dad, by the way. And they didn't even know the whole story. So what did you want me to do?"

"You should have taken Matthew back. He made a mistake. It wasn't worth ending your relationship over."

Oh my God, she took his side then, and she's doing it now. Un-fucking-believable.

"He fucked my best friend for months! Months, Mom! She was pregnant with his child at my wedding, and you expected me to take him back like nothing happened? Did you want us to be some sort of fucked-up Brady Bunch? Maybe play the role of the fun bonus mom? I know you aren't a person who has feelings, but that's low, even for you."

My breathing is heavy, but I feel good. Strong. Right there is just the tip of the iceberg that I've been wanting to get off my chest for so long.

"I swear, Elizabeth, you've always been so dramatic."

"Dramatic? That's what we're going with?"

"Yes, dramatic. It wasn't that bad. You've blown it out of proportion. Plus, you know we needed his family to save the business."

I throw my hands up in the air, completely exasperated by this conversation. "Of course. Always the business! Never mind that this man hurt me deeply. Never mind that two of the closest people in my life betrayed me. Never mind what he put me through mentally and emotionally. No, just worry about the business, Mom. The business that is so stressful it's probably why Dad died. The business that you think is the end all be all of your life. The business you pimped your own daughter out for. Yes, Mom, that should be your priority. Not your daughter. Never your daughter."

Mom doesn't say another word, instead turning on her heel and walking back into the house. Jessie follows her, but not without mouthing a "holy shit" to me before she walks in.

I try to slow down my breathing as I turn toward the yard where Oliver is standing, just staring at me with...is that a look of pride?

"That's my girl."

I feel the biggest smile I think I've ever had on my face, only for it to be taken away by two words that I never wanted to hear for the rest of my life.

"Hey, Red."

I slowly turn around as I come face to face with the man who ruined my life in more ways than I can count. And he's standing next to Riley, my former best friend and would-have-been maid of honor and their fifteen-year-old son.

None of us say anything for I don't know how long. Eventually, Riley awkwardly waves to me as she leads their son into my childhood home. I wonder if she remembers where everything is. She should. She spent enough time here growing up.

"How many years has it been?"

"Not enough."

Matt takes a step toward me, which immediately means I take a step away.

"Oh, come on, Red. After all these years, you can't be near me?"

I do my best to tamp down my anger. For the sake of not causing more of a distraction than I already have, I need to get away from him and get the fuck out of here.

"I'd rather not."

"Oh come on," he says, putting his hand on my arm. "That was a lifetime ago. We're different people now."

I try to rip my arm away from him, but he only holds on tighter. Panic starts to flood through me, but I do my best to push through. "It could be a hundred years and you'd never change."

"I'm not like this with Riley, it must be you who makes me this way."

Before I can reply, I feel Oliver pull me back from Matt as he inserts himself between us.

"I think it's time that you step away from my wife."

"Your wife?" Matt says with a snarky laugh. "You married her? You know she's damaged goods, right?"

Oliver starts to pull back his fist, but I grab it to make sure she doesn't swing. "For fuck's sake..."

This gets Oliver's attention. He slowly lowers his arm, quickly taking my hand in his as we walk away.

"That's right! Run!" Matt says as we exit the porch to head back to our car. "That's what you're good at."

I stop and turn to look at the man I once thought was going to be my whole life.

"Then you do what you're good at. Go fuck yourself."

Chapter 31
Oliver

I DON'T KNOW HOW I MADE IT BACK TO THE BED AND breakfast without ripping the steering wheel off the car. To say my knuckles were white the entire drive back is the understatement of the year. Now, even being back in the room, I am pushing down the urge to punch a wall.

Then there's Izzy, who's wrapped herself in a ball on the bed. She hasn't said a word since we got in the car.

Fuck, I need to be strong for her. Yes, I want to turn around, go back and punch that asshole in the fucking face. Maybe that can be on the list for tomorrow. Tonight, I need to be there for Izzy. In whatever way she needs me to be.

"Hey," I say, laying on the bed behind her, wrapping her in my arms. "It's just me. Just you and me here."

Izzy doesn't say a word, but she does take my hand to wrap it tighter around her body.

"I'm sorry I flew off the handle," I say. "I saw him touch you, and I lost it."

"Don't apologize," she says. "That's what he wants you to

do. He wants you to think it's your fault when it's not. He gets off on it."

"I don't want to force you to say anything you're not ready to talk about, but—"

"No," Izzy says. "It's time. It's finally time. No more dodging. No more deflecting. It's time I finally come clean to you. And to myself."

Izzy turns to look at me, but stays lying down. I gently brush a piece of hair behind her ear, which she leans into. I can see herself mentally preparing for whatever it is she's about to say. I can't imagine what's about to come out of her mouth. Just hearing the little bit I did tonight from her mother and the fuckhead made me want to fight someone.

"I don't even know where to start."

"Wherever you want."

Izzy inhales slowly and holds it for a few seconds before breathing out. I do the only thing I think I can do right now, which is to take her hands in mine so she knows I'm there for her.

"Matt was my high school sweetheart," she begins. "I started dating him at freshman homecoming, and that was that."

"Really? Never dated anyone else?"

"Nope." Izzy shakes her head. "He was my first everything. I was told after we started dating that our parents actually betrothed us when we were babies. I thought it was a joke. Apparently it was true. Yes, we helped it along by actually having a crush on each other, but thinking back, I think I only did because we were together so much growing up. Which was our parents' doing. Birthday parties, outings to the fair, anything they could think of to put us together, they did."

"Why did they care so much?"

"At first it was because they were family friends. My dad

went to school with Matt's dad, and they grew up together. Our moms were in the church choir together. So from the outside looking in, it was just two families who had children the same age and going on playdates together. The McCalls and the Karrs. We were like a package deal. Seems harmless, right?"

"I'm guessing that answer is no..."

Izzy taps her finger to her nose. "Bingo. One day I was working at the furniture store, and I went into the safe to get change. I wasn't supposed to know the combination, but I figured it out over the years. When I was in there I accidentally saw bank statements. I was sixteen, so of course I looked. I might not have understood everything, but I sure know a zero when I see one."

"The store was broke?"

"Completely. I remember asking my parents about it, and they screamed at me so loud I think people in the next town heard it. Jessie thought Dad was going to get the belt that night. It was bad."

"Fuck," I growl.

"If that makes you mad, then just wait for the rest."

I breathe in and out, doing my best to calm myself down. "Sorry, go on."

"So, the store is broke. The only chance of saving it, at least according to my father, was to have Matt's family invest and hope that led to an eventual expansion. However, Dad was scared that Matt's family might take it over once they bought in, and they couldn't bear for that to happen. As you've heard, this store is *everything* to my family. So they made a deal. The Karrs would be partial owners, and it would be a joint family store, which meant we had to become an actual family. They told us Matt and I would get married the day we were both eighteen. Once our families were officially joined in marriage, the families would have a fifty-fifty stake in the store, and everyone would be happy."

"I know there's a 'but' to this story, and I'm almost scared to ask what it is."

"You'd be right." Izzy breaks for a second, which I don't blame her. What she's told me is a lot in itself, and I know the worst is yet to come. "What my parents didn't know at the time was that Matt and I were having problems. It was great at first. It always is. By this point we were into our senior year. I didn't love the fact we had to get married to save the store, but I did love him. Or so I thought. I mean, he was my first boyfriend. My first kiss. He told me he loved me before he took my virginity in his pickup truck. So I didn't know that it was wrong of him to tell me I shouldn't talk to a guy in class because people might think I'm a whore. I didn't know it was out of the ordinary for your boyfriend to tell you how to dress because he didn't want you looking like a slut. Or that when he told you not to wear heels because it made him look short that it was a him problem and not a me problem. I thought boyfriends told you who you could hang out with and who you could be around. He isolated me. He cut me off from the friends I had—well, everyone except Riley. Every time we fought, I thought it was my fault. And every time I called him out for being in the wrong—the few times I had the courage to do so—somehow it was still my fault. To this day I don't know how he did it. But I know from the ages of fourteen to eighteen, all I knew was that what Matt said went, because I loved him and I was going to marry him."

The restraint I'm showing right now from going back to her mother's house and punching this guy in the fucking face is through the roof. I knew she was hurt badly. I knew it was deep. But fuck...no wonder she doesn't believe in love. Between her family and him, she was trained not to.

The tears have started falling from her eyes, and I don't blame her. I'd be crying too if I was carrying all of this for sixteen years.

"I know what you must be thinking. How could I stay with him? How did I still want to marry him?"

I shake my head. "No. I would never think that. I wasn't in your shoes. I can't imagine what those felt like. No one can judge a person in that situation unless they were there."

She shrugs. "Honestly, I judge me. I don't know why I stayed. Maybe because I thought this was what love was. Maybe because I was told and taught my entire life that marriage and families weren't love based, only for the business side of things. I'm not sure. I only knew that despite everything, I was still ready to marry him."

"God I hope the next 'but' of the story is coming."

"It is. We had turned eighteen, just graduated, and it was the morning of the wedding. It was small. Jessie and Riley were my bridesmaids, and a few of Matt's friends were standing up for him. I was getting ready in one of the rooms in the church and went to use the restroom. The one in the bridal suite wasn't working, so I just used one in the hallway. That's when I walked in on my almost husband having sex with my bridesmaid on the bathroom counter."

"Are you fucking kidding me?"

"Nope," she shakes her head. "Right there for me to see. Dress hiked up. Pants on the ground. Dick going in and out."

That's it. If I see him tomorrow, he's dead. I will kill him, and I won't apologize.

"What did you do?"

"I ran," I say. "That was part of his dig today about me running away. I ran back to the room, tears flowing down my cheeks. At that moment, I realized everything I'd been ignoring. I didn't know what gaslighting was back then, but that's what he was doing. Every emotion and every denial and excuse I made for him started hitting me. I couldn't even get out the words to my mom or Jessie about what I saw or what I was feeling. The only thing I could say was that I was done. I wasn't marrying him."

"Good. That's what you should have said."

Izzy pauses for a second to sit up in the bed, but doesn't let go of my hand. Even if she tried, I wouldn't let her.

"Jessie finally calmed me down and I told her what I saw. She knew a little of how he treated me, and she always tried to tell me it wasn't right. But of course I didn't believe her. She never wanted me to marry him, but she also knew why I was and understood the family obligation. But this was the last straw for her. My mother, however, didn't agree to that."

"I'm going to go on record saying that my mother-in-law is a cold-hearted bitch."

This gets her to laugh a little through the tears. "That's putting it lightly. She told me I shouldn't overreact. That boys will be boys. And that if I knew what was good for me, I'd still walk down the aisle and marry Matt."

"Excuse me? She wanted her daughter to marry someone who was cheating on her?"

"Indeed she did." Izzy pauses for a second, and I can't imagine what else she has to gear up to tell me. "When I told her that I wouldn't, that I was sorry I was messing up the store deal, but I couldn't be around him anymore, she told me that if that was the decision I was making, that I had to go and tell everyone. I cried, begging her not to make me, but she wouldn't hear of it. So there I stood, in my wedding dress, in front of the entire town with gawking eyes, to tell them that I had called off the wedding. I wasn't allowed to say why. I was told to say that I was ending things, it was my decision and not Matt's, and that I apologized for ruining their day."

"Motherfucker...Fuck, Izzy...is that why..."

Izzy nods. "I hate people looking at me in a crowd? Yeah. Every time I'm in a room of people, I immediately go back to being that eighteen-year-old girl again, having to tell the town that I called off my wedding. The worst part? I know I was in the right to do it. But because of what I was forced to say, and how I was forced to embarrass myself like that, I look back at that moment and I instantly freeze in anxiety. That somehow I was in the wrong."

"But you weren't, you know that right?"

"I do. But not according to my parents. Or Matt's. If you ask them, I was—and still am—the selfish brat who didn't know her place in the family."

"I can't believe they seriously wanted you to still marry him? Also, how long were they together? When did she get pregnant? What did they say when they found out she was pregnant? How is he getting off scot free in all this?"

"I'll go in order: Yes, they wanted me to still marry him. They said it would be for the greater good of the families and the businesses. Found out later they had been together for about five months before the wedding. And when everyone found out about Riley being pregnant, I believe the company line was he was sowing his wild oats, but that he was doing the right thing by marrying her because he's a good man."

"You've got to be fucking kidding me."

"I couldn't make it up if I tried."

"Wow," I say, trying to wrap my head around all of this. Everything now makes so much sense. Why Izzy is hesitant to receive love, or to give it. Her fear of crowds. Why she thinks marriage is nothing short of hell. I don't blame her at all. Not one single bit. "I don't know what to say."

"There's nothing to say," she says. "The day I canceled the wedding was the first day of my life. Somehow the light bulb came on that I was more than some girl who was going to be used and abused by the people in her life that were supposed to love her. That night I packed my stuff and Jessie drove me to the train station. I was in Los Angeles two days later."

"Good for you," I say. "I'm so damn proud of you."

"I don't know if proud is the right word. Yes, I got myself out of there. Yes, I got the hell out of a situation that no one should ever be in. I put myself through school and struggled before landing on my feet. But I let that dictate my life. The strength didn't stay. Hell, the only other relationship I tried ended with him cheating on me as well. After that I just decided that it was easier to not try then deal with it at all."

"Come here," I say, bringing her closer so she's now on my lap. I need to make sure she's listening loud and clear for this. "You, Izzy McCall, are the strongest woman I've ever known. And I thought that before today. Now? You're a fucking goddess. Of course your past is going to come into play. That's how life works. Past traumas will always come back. But now you have to make a decision. Do you keep letting them have a say so, or do you tell them to go fuck themselves and send them to the curb?"

This makes her laugh through the tears. "I want to tell them to go fuck themselves, but I might need some help. I don't know if I can do it on my own."

I take her chin in my fingers, holding her to make sure she's looking directly at me. "I told you before and I'll tell you again. I'm here. I'm always going to be here. Tell me what you need, and I'll move a mountain to do it."

Izzy takes her hands that are already around my neck and pulls me in closer. We're inches apart. I can feel her breath. I can feel her pain. I can feel her emotions pouring out of her.

"Help me move on, Oliver. I don't want to hurt anymore."

Chapter 32
Izzy

I ALWAYS WONDERED WHAT IT WOULD BE LIKE ON THE DAY that I finally let that all out. That I let every word, every emotion, every memory leave my body. I wondered if I would feel free. Or maybe empty? That the only thing I've been filled with for the last sixteen years was this trauma.

The answer is none of those things. I feel gutted, but somehow in a good way. Like the only way I'm going to heal is if I bleed completely out, only to be put back together again.

And Oliver's the only one who can help me do that.

I bring him in closer, kissing him like I've wanted to kiss him for weeks now but wouldn't let myself do. He responds at first, wrapping his arms tighter around waist, before pulling away.

"What?"

"Are you sure?" he asks. "You just told me something I know couldn't have been easy for you to do. I just don't want you to regret anything because you did something out of emotion and feeling raw."

I turn, straddling Oliver so I can look him dead in the eye.

"I haven't felt real emotion in years. I couldn't handle it. But I want to. I need to. I want to feel again, Oliver. You're the only one who can help me do that. You're the one I need."

That's all I have to say. His lips are back on me in a heartbeat, his tongue invading my mouth in the most welcomed way. I don't know if someone can actually breathe life back into a person, but I think that's what Oliver's trying to do. And if anyone can, it would be him.

Without breaking our kiss, Oliver picks me up slightly, repositioning us on the bed. His mouth slowly starts kissing across my cheek, down my jaw, and back across my neck. His kisses are so soft and sweet I immediately feel goosebumps all over my body. Especially now as he's kissing his way down my breast bone as he gently, one by one, unclasps each button on my shirt.

"So beautiful," he says as he pushes the blouse off my shoulders and down my arms. His mouth immediately starts kissing each of my breasts as he unhinges the clasp and tosses it to the side. No. This isn't kissing. This is worshipping. The way Oliver's mouth is taking its time, yet also savoring each moment, is making me feel a way I never have before. Is this what feeling is like? Or is this just what truly being with Oliver is like?

I have a feeling it's the second.

"Oliver," I moan, letting my head fall back as he continues to suck, kiss, and massage my breasts. "More. Please give me more."

He lifts me up slightly to lay me down, slowly and methodically bringing my pants and panties down, leaving me naked and exposed on the bed. Oliver doesn't follow. Instead he stands over me, looking over me with the most...I don't know what this look is. I know for a fact I've never been looked at that way before.

Is it reverence? Adoration? Love?

No. It can't be. Could it?

Is it? Would I know it if I saw it?

No, I don't think I would. How do you know something if you've never seen it? If you've never truly felt it. Or what you thought was love was nothing of the sort.

Or maybe I do know it, but I've been denying its existence...

What I'm feeling right now as Oliver looks down on me, his hand slowly stroking himself as he's looking at me in a way that makes me feel every cell in my body. Any man I've been with since Matt, I never let them see me like this. The lights were always off. Sometimes all the clothes didn't even come off. It was quick and transactional.

But it's never been like that with Oliver. Even our first time there was something different. I knew it, but I didn't want to believe it.

Now? I don't know if I believe it yet, but for the first time in over a decade, I'm thinking there might be a chance.

"I'm ready," I say, the words having multiple meanings. Judging by the change in Oliver's expression as he comes down next to me on the bed, he knows it too.

"Then you have one job tonight. Lay back and feel. Let me take care of you."

I don't argue. I don't think I have it in me, even if I wanted to. I do as he says, letting him take both of my arms above my head, his fingers slowly tracing back down as he lowers himself between my legs.

I'd be a liar if I said I didn't think about Oliver's mouth and the wicked, wicked things it could do. Every once in a while, I let my mind drift back to that first night. It was animalistic. Carnal. Two people who might combust if they didn't have each other right then.

This is different. With the first stroke of his tongue, I can feel it already. Don't get me wrong, it still feels incredible. Instead of diving in like I'm his last meal, he's savoring. Taking his time, making sure he hits every nerve ending he possibly can.

Which he is. Holy shit, he is...

"Yes," I moan, my body writhing on the bed with every movement of his magnificent mouth. But as much as I love this, and holy fuck do I love this, I need him. I need him inside me. I need him more than I've ever needed anything in my entire life.

"Oliver," I whisper as my hands run through his golden hair. "Make love to me."

My words stop him immediately. I don't blame him. If I didn't just say it, I would wonder if I actually said those four words. But I did. And I mean it. I truly do.

Oliver leaves one last kiss on my pubic bone before kissing his way up my body, not stopping until he reaches my lips. We wrap each other in our arms, holding on tightly as we pour every emotion we have into each other. We stop as I'm on top, and just as I'm about to position him at my center, he stops me.

"Izzy, I'm not wearing a condom."

I shake my head. "I have an IUD. And I don't want anything between us. Not anymore."

He takes my face in his hands, bringing me down to his lips for another kiss. You'd think I'd be tired of kissing this man, but I'm not. And that doesn't even freak me out.

"Thank you for trusting me."

I don't know how those words are a turn on, but fuck if they aren't.

"I've never trusted anyone more," I say.

With that, I slowly sink down, feeling him fill me inch by inch. I slowly start to move, but not fast. Not yet. I don't think I've ever let myself feel this. To feel the connection. This bond. This emotion. In fact, I know I never have.

When I was young and dumb and thought a narcissistic man was my world, sex wasn't for pleasure. It was because that's what I thought I was supposed to do. After Matt it was transactional. A way to scratch an itch. Yes, I might have had some good times, but there was nothing of substance.

But with Oliver, it's so much more. This is so much more. It's pleasure. It's bliss. It's emotional. It's real. It's everything.

Fuck is it everything...

"Take what you want, Izzy," Oliver says as I start to rock on him, my hands gripping his chest. "Take whatever you need."

And I do. I let myself feel every movement, every pulse, every touch. I throw my head back and grip Oliver's legs, holding on for dear life as I let myself, for the first time in my life, be truly in the moment.

"That's it, Izzy. Take it all."

Holy shit...I don't know why those words just lit a fire under me, but they did. I let go of his legs, returning them to his chest. He takes hold of each of my wrists, helping me steady myself as I let go of every memory, every scar, every wound.

"Oliver..."

I don't know how in one word this man knew exactly what I needed, but he did. He wraps me in his arms and rolls me over, taking real control for the first time. And I let him, I want him to. I want him to kiss away the pain. I want him to fuck away the fear. I want him to make me the woman I want to be.

I said earlier that I wanted him to make love to me. I always thought that meant polite, nice, sweet sex with minimal orgasms. But it's not. It's likely different for every person. For Oliver and me, it's give and take. It's pleasure and sometimes some pain. But the good kind. The ones that make us want more and have us ripping each other's clothes off every chance we get. It's knowing your partner so thoroughly that you can just say his name and he knows what you need.

Holy shit...I think I'm in love with my husband.

"Oliver, I'm so close," I say, suddenly realizing I'm about to orgasm like I never have before. If this is what love makes you do, then I've been missing out.

"I got you, beautiful. I always got you."

And he does. Oliver gets his fingers involved, rubbing my clit as he thrusts into me, which apparently is the detonator switch.

I come apart in a way I never have before. I shout Oliver's name so loud the whole town can hear me. My whole body is alive in a way that I don't think it's ever been in my lifetime.

This is the moment where I know I'm going to start healing.

And it's all because of Oliver.

Chapter 33
Oliver

"You ready?"

When I asked that question to Izzy yesterday, it was more of a check-in. I knew she wasn't ready. Or at least, as ready as she was going to be. But today as we pull into the church for her father's funeral? Today there's something different about her. There's a spark in her eye. A confidence in her demeanor that wasn't there yesterday. Yes, to the passerby it might seem like this demeanor is inappropriate for a funeral, but those people can suck it. Because my girl has a spark in her eye I've never seen before, and it needs to stay there.

Izzy finishes checking her makeup before leaning over to kiss me on the cheek. "I am. Let's go."

Without hesitation, I get out of the driver's seat and walk over to open the door for Izzy. When she steps out of the car she shocks me by putting her arms on my chest, leaning in for another kiss.

"What's that for?"

"Everything," she says as she straightens my tie. I don't know if it needs fixed, but I'm not going to stop her. "I'm here today because of you. I'm going to get stronger every day because of you. I don't know if I'll ever be able to thank you for that."

"You know you don't need to thank me."

She shakes her head. "I do. Every day. You stuck by me. You didn't give up on me. You didn't even know what was going on with me because I was a stubborn ass who would rather be miserable than tell someone my trauma. Most people would run from that. Hell, I made sure they all did. But not you. You wouldn't budge. You saw something I didn't even see. And for that, Oliver Price, I will never, ever, be able to repay you."

I take her hand and kiss her knuckles, because for once in my life, I'm speechless. I didn't mean to take the left one, but I did. And I can't stop staring at the gold band on her finger that my lips just touched.

"I'm going to miss this," I say rubbing it with my thumb. "I kind of liked being married to you."

She smiles and takes a step closer to me. "Who says I'm going to take it off?"

I was speechless before, but now I might pass out. I know I'm not blinking. My jaw might be on the ground. I'm pretty sure breathing has stopped.

"Oliver?"

I still don't move. Did she really just say she's not going to take it off?

"Oh, shit, I broke you," she says, lightly patting my face to bring me back to the present. "We'll talk about this later."

I stare at her for a few seconds, letting all of that process as she laces her fingers through mine as we walk hand-in-hand to the church for the service. Yes, I'm going to need time to let that sink in. Out of all the outcomes of this weekend, having my wife want to be married to me was not on my bingo card.

We get to the door of the church, where a small line has formed to get in.

"I know I asked if you were ready, and I know you are, but I want to remind you one more time that you don't have to do this."

She shakes her head and rights her shoulders. "That's what they want. They want me to run again. They want to still be able to have the narrative that I'm a runner and I leave when things get hard. I won't give them that satisfaction."

I bring her hand up, kissing it one more time as we take the last step inside the church. It's somber and quiet, which is why everyone in town can hear as Benji comes racing over.

"Aunt Izzy! Oliver!" Benji runs over and, to my surprise, jumps into my arms over Izzy's.

"Hey, little man," I say as all eyeballs turn to give me a disapproving look. Wow, this town really does have a stick up its ass.

"Mommy said we can sit together."

"That's great," I say as I put him down but make sure to keep his hand in mine. We don't need a runner today.

On cue, Jessie comes walking over with who I'm assuming is her husband, Jimmy. He's carrying what looks to be a very tired little girl.

"Hey," she says to Izzy, giving her a long hug. "I'm so sorry about yesterday. I wanted to call you after I heard what happened with you and Matt."

Izzy waves her off. "Don't worry about it. Actually, it was the best thing that could have happened."

She looks up at me as she says that, and memories of last night run through me. Holding her as she told me her past. Doing my best to take her pain away. Letting her find her power. It was probably the most emotional night of my life, so I can't even begin to fathom what it must have been like for Izzy.

"Girls. Come here."

We all turn to see Constance standing in a side hallway of the church. Everyone here is in black, as is customary. But something about my mother-in-law's outfit seems even gloomier than everyone else's. Probably because she comes with her own cloud over her head.

Izzy and Jessie walk in front of us as Jimmy and I hang back with the kids.

"Is she always like this?" I whisper.

He shakes his head. "She's usually worse. We're getting the tame version because we're in front of people."

"Lovely."

"Here's how things are going to go," Constance says. "You're going to sit in the front pews with me. Jimmy, you're to sit on the end with the kids in case they start crying. We can't have the funeral ruined with crying kids. If they do, immediately take them outside."

"Mom, they're three and six," Jessie says. "They aren't newborns."

"Watch your tone and just do as I say," Constance says. "I swear, you always get like this when Izzy's involved."

"You mean like having a voice and actually speaking up? Yeah, I can see how you'd hate that."

Oh shit, my girl isn't fucking around today. And I know it's not the correct or appropriate response, but I can't help but let out a laugh.

"And you." Constance points to me. "You will sit in the back. No one knows you. You aren't family."

"Like hell he will," Izzy says as she steps in front of her mother. I don't know what's about to happen, but I quickly pass Benji to Jimmy, who was ready for the hand off. "That's my husband. He's shown me more love in the few months I've known him than you have my entire life. So he's either sitting up front with me, or I'm sitting in the back. Take your pick, Mom. It's one of the two."

Constance narrows her eyes at Izzy and me. Izzy has stepped to my side, taking my hand in solidarity. I make sure to be right next to her, showing we're a team. I know Jessie has tried to help and defend Izzy over the years, but I really don't think she's ever had a unified front when it comes to her family.

Well, that's the past. This is now. And right now, Team McCall-Price is here to stay.

"Fine. He can sit with you. One less thing for you to cause a scene about." Constance looks over to Jimmy. "Now Jimmy, you leave the kids with Jessie, since you'll be a pallbearer. They're gathered in the back."

"Who are the others?" Jessie asks.

"Your cousin and uncle. A friend from the Rotary Club. Mr. Karr and Matthew."

You can hear a pin drop after Constance drops that last name. It's also why everyone in the church can hear Izzy's response.

"Oh, for fuck's sake!"

Constance whips her head at the outburst. "Elizabeth! You watch your language!"

I always love to see those moments where people just snap. You don't get to see them often, but when you do, it's fascinating to watch. It's the moment when they've absolutely had it. Where the cord has broken, and whoever is around to see the carnage has a front row seat.

I just wish I had popcorn, because I have a feeling this is about to be epic.

Izzy starts hysterically laughing. I'm talking can't breathe, bent over, I think she let out a snort, laughter.

"Elizabeth, you're acting like a crazy person. Pull yourself together!"

She stands up, shaking her head but still laughing. "I absolutely will not."

"What is your problem?" Constance asks, pulling Izzy more to the side. "Why are you acting like this?"

"My problem? I don't have a problem. I'm fine. For the first time in sixteen years, I'm fine, despite everything you continue to do. You have *all* the audacity, and I'm out of fucks to give when it comes to you and your bullshit."

I watch Constance actively roll her eyes at her daughter. I grab hold of Izzy's hand a little tighter. Not just because I want to show her that I'm here for her, but to also make sure she doesn't end up in jail for assault. "Elizabeth. You need to let this go. He slept with another woman. Big deal."

"It is a big deal, Mom, and the fact that you don't see that says more about you than it does me." Izzy gives my hand a squeeze and takes a breath. "You only knew half of it. Which was my choice. Out of respect for you and dad back then, I kept you in the dark about a lot of things. I'll take that. That was on me. But sadly, I don't think that would have changed things then, and it won't change anything now. You should have supported my decision, no matter what. I'm your fucking daughter. You put money, a business, and an image that you thought you portrayed over me. That's the big deal."

If I were to have said half of those things to my mother, she'd be sobbing and apologizing. She'd ask what we could do to make it right. But not Constance. Nope. I don't think she's blinked. Her face has gotten a little red, but there isn't an ounce of remorse in her.

I don't know what Izzy's plans are for Christmas, but I'm going to make sure it's not here.

"Are you done yet? Is your little tirade over? We need to get started soon, and I'd hate for you to keep things from starting on time."

"What are you going to do? Make me go out there and tell them why? I don't think you'll want to do that, Mom. I played nice last time. This time I won't stick to your script."

Oh shit…my wife is unhinged, and I'm fucking here for it.

Constance steps closer to Izzy, rage in her eyes. I see Izzy square her shoulders, and as much as I want to fight this fight for her, she needs to. She needs this more than anything in the world. I always said I'd slay the dragons for her. But this time the sword's in her hands.

"You've always been a problem," Constance says.

"The fact that you think that I'm the problem and not you is fucking hilarious."

"If you're going to talk to me like that, you can leave."

"Oh I am," Izzy says. "I'd say I'm mad that I tried to come back, but I'm not. This was actually a very eye-opening trip."

Constance looks at me, her eyes begging for help. Did she just realize that her daughter wasn't going to call her bluff? "Are you going to let your wife talk to me like that?"

Now it's my turn to laugh. "I don't know if you've actually met my wife, but no one tells her what to say. Ever. It's one of the reasons I love her."

I think Constance might explode at this moment. "Fine. Leave. Tell everyone on the way out that once again you're ruining things."

Izzy shrugs. "Bye, Mom. I won't say that, and I won't tell anyone I'll see them soon." She turns to Jessie. No idea where Jimmy went, but I'm guessing somewhere with the kids after Izzy's fifth F-bomb. "You and the family can come visit us for Christmas. We'd be happy to have you. But you, Mom? We're done."

With that, Izzy turns and we start walking to the exit.

"You okay?" I whisper, not wanting to stop her stride, but also wanting to make sure she's not about to crash and fall.

"Never better," she says as we walk out the church doors.

"Running again, I see?"

Izzy stops, but doesn't turn around, at the sound of Matt's voice.

"You or me?" I ask. I am looking for a chance to take this motherfucker down, but I'm not about to take something away from Izzy that she might need to help her heal.

"I know you want this one," she says. "Consider it a belated wedding present."

We slowly turn around to see his smug look. I really want to punch him. If I were in Rolling Hills, I absolutely would. Shane would make sure I wasn't arrested. Simon would make sure Matt never spoke of the situation again. Wes would drive the getaway car.

But it's just me here. Though I must say, Izzy is quite the tag team partner.

"Matt? What was it like to peak in high school? 'Cause you strike me as the kind of guy who still wears his letterman's jacket, talking about that game back in 2005."

"Fuck you," he says, walking down the church steps to meet us on the sidewalk. "I know this marriage between you two isn't real. I heard over the years that Izzy couldn't even get a boyfriend, let alone a husband. But kudos to you for playing the part. She suck your dick for that? I taught her well, so you can thank me later."

I don't even think. I don't even take a second to question whether or not this is a good idea. I just punch him. I cock my arm back and put my fist into his nose. I hit exactly where I want to, causing him to fall down and his nose to start bleeding everywhere.

And I don't have one single regret.

I step over him, giving him my hand to help him up. He thinks I'm being apologetic, which I'm not. Because as soon as he's standing, I pull him in close. He needs to hear every word I'm about to say.

"I didn't know Izzy when she was a teenager, but I can guarantee you didn't deserve her then. You sure as shit don't deserve her now. I have the woman of my dreams, and what do you have? A wife you probably cheat on and a child who's one day going to be in therapy with daddy issues? Or worse, he turns out like you. But I should say thank you. Thank you for cheating on Izzy. It made her see what kind of man you truly were. And I'll make sure that there isn't a day that goes by that she doesn't know how loved she is and how much better off she is without you."

I shove Matt away. He stumbles a bit and is holding his nose. I look up to see that the whole funeral has gathered at the door, probably witnessing everything that just happened.

"Sorry," I say, waving to the crowd. "Nice meeting you all."

Izzy pulls my arm, and we quickly make it to our car. I turn it on and I'm about ready to pull out when Izzy all but jumps straddles me in the driver's seat, kissing me harder than she ever has before.

"Wow," I say with a heavy breath.

"Yeah, wow. That was amazing. You're amazing." Her hand slides down and starts rubbing my dick through my pants.

"Izzy. We're at a church. I know we just swore like we weren't in God's house, but having sex in the parking lot might be pushing it."

"Fine," she says, going back to her seat. "But step on it. I didn't realize my husband punching my ex would get me this horny."

I throw the car into reverse before speeding out of the parking lot, kicking rocks and gravel up along the way.

Happy wife, happy life, am I right?

Chapter 34
Oliver

"What's wrong?"

I don't take my eyes off the road as I turn off the highway heading back to Izzy's downtown condo. "Nothing. Do you want to stop anywhere before I drop you off?"

"You're deflecting, and I'd like to be done with that part of our lives," she says. "Seriously, you've been abnormally quiet since we landed. You didn't even comment on the puppy we passed a block back. It's starting to freak me out."

Funny that Izzy uses the phrase "freak out," because that's exactly what I've been doing since I heard the pilot announce we were back in Nashville. Because now we're out of the bubble. We're home. And I'm scared to death that once Izzy's back to reality, she's going to change her mind about us. I mean, I would understand. But also, it would be a punch in the gut. So yeah, freaking out would be an accurate description of what I'm doing right now.

I make the turn toward her building, but I don't pull into the parking garage, instead choosing to find a spot on the street. Because I don't know if she wants me to stay? Go? Move in?

Make a new appointment with the lawyer? I know I need to talk to her, but I'm terrified of the possible outcome of the conversation.

"Are you not coming in?"

I look over to see a confused look on her face. "Do you want me to come in?"

"Why wouldn't I?"

I shrug. "I didn't want to assume."

"Oh, Oliver." She leans over and gives me a kiss on the cheek. "Come upstairs. Let's talk."

I do as she says, grabbing her bags from the trunk.

"Aren't you going to grab yours?"

"I don't know, am I?"

She smiles and tilts her head toward her door. "I figured you might want your things when you spend the night."

With just those few words, I'm immediately relaxed. Granted, I won't be completely relaxed until every little thing is on the table, but for the next few minutes, those words will hold me over.

"Sit," she says once we get inside. "First, I'd like to apologize."

I wasn't expecting that. "For what?"

She takes a seat next to me, and maybe for the first time in our relationship, she grabs my hand first. Wow, it really does give comfort. "I've been on an emotional rollercoaster the last four days. And I've taken you along for the ride."

"But I volunteered."

"You did. But not for everything. And, the fact that I gave you no background before we went was shitty of me. I should have never let you go into that weekend blind. I was scared, plain and simple. And because of that you had to deal with things you weren't prepared for."

"Now knowing what you went through, I get why."

"That's still no excuse for throwing you into the wolves like I did. You came to Smallwood with me to help me through the funeral. In that time, you helped me deal with my heartless mother, told off my narcissistic ex, dealt with my whirlwind of emotions, and, last but of course not least, took in stride the bomb I dropped about not wanting to get divorced. So yes, I apologize. Because I know how I'm feeling, and if you feel half as off-kilter as I do, then an apology is definitely deserved."

"Thank you," I say. "I appreciate that. But you know I would have done it all over again if I needed to, right?"

She nods as she comes closer to me, taking my other hand in hers. "I do. That's one of the reasons I love you."

I think I'm dead.

Yup. Dead. Deceased. Rest in peace to me.

"Oliver? Did I break you again?"

I nod, still not having blinked or said a word. Did she say she loved me? First? She said she loved me first? I heard that, right? Was I hearing things? I mean, I always knew if we'd ever get to this point, she'd have to say it first. I knew that a long time ago. Because if I said it when I was ready, I would have surely scared her away. I never thought this day would happen.

But it did. I think. I'm pretty sure.

"Shit. I don't know if I have any batteries to reboot you," Izzy says, repositioning herself so she's now sitting on my lap. "Oliver?"

"Yeah?"

"I told you I loved you."

"I didn't imagine it?"

She smiles at me. "You didn't."

I move forward and kiss her. I kiss the hell out of her. I kiss the hell out of my wife, who loves me. Who I love more than anyone or anything I've ever loved in my life.

I dip her so low off the couch I'm afraid we might fall. But who cares? If we fall, we're going to do it together. Just as it should be.

I bring her back up, placing my hands around her face. "I love you. I love you so fucking much."

Izzy smiles again before coming back in for another kiss. She wraps her arms around my neck and lets her hands get lost in my hair. She gently scratches my head as our kiss deepens. I'm a sucker for head scratches. If she keeps this up, we're not going to make it to a bedroom.

She starts circling her hips on me, and as much as it kills me, I stop her and pull away.

"Wow," Izzy says, slightly confused. "Honeymoon phase over already?"

I shake my head with a smile. "No. Believe me, it's not. Because you're going to do that headscratch thing later. And often. Which is going to make me a sex-crazed man. However, before we go any further, I feel like we need to figure things out before we just fall into a routine and have never really talked over how this is going to work."

"Ugh," Izzy says, falling off my lap onto her couch. "Why do you have to be practical?"

"Because normally it's you, and since this is apparently the version of Izzy where she got her groove back, I'm going to take the reins for this one. Plus, I am the relationship guy. This part I've got locked down."

"Good call," she says. "Okay, responsible Izzy hat back on."

I laugh as she pretends to put on a cap. "So...we kind of did this backward."

"Yes and no," Izzy says. "You at least took me on a date."

"True," I say. "And we slept together."

"See? We're not completely fucked up. We just have to figure out how to be married."

"The man who never had a successful proposal and the

woman who spent sixteen years in fear of marriage? That should be easy."

"Piece of cake."

"Okay, so does this mean we're going to date?" I ask. "As much as I'd like to say let's start cohabitation tonight, I don't know if that's our most sensible decision."

Izzy lays back and bites her bottom lip. "You make sensible talk sexy."

Fuck, this woman is going to be the death of me in the best way possible. "Focus. Talk now. Sex later."

"Ugh, fine," she says. "But you're right. Baby steps. We're both relatively new to this. We need to crawl before we can walk."

"Exactly," I say, bringing her back to my lap. "We need to actually spend time together as a couple—a real one, not a drunk one or one that is forged because of grief and drama. We need to be real before we make decisions like where we're going to live or if we're going have a real wedding."

I almost internally smack myself for bringing up something like a wedding. Izzy is a different woman right now, but trauma doesn't go away overnight.

But she doesn't make a face. She doesn't flinch or recoil. It's as if I said something as mundane as the sky is blue.

In no way do I think Izzy magically recovered from everything she's experienced, but she's already made huge strides. Because my wife is a fucking badass.

"I agree," she says. "You have to remember, I haven't tried anything like this in years. I might be all in, but you're going to have to walk me through this."

"That I can do," I say before kissing her. And for the first time since, well, ever, when it has come to Izzy, I feel relaxed. That I don't need to worry about scaring her, or that a shoe is going to drop. I feel like this is where we've been meant to be since that fateful April night at Jake and Whitley's wedding. I knew she was special and worth waiting for. I said it all along.

I've never been so glad to be right.

"I know it's early," she says.

"It's two in the afternoon."

"Yes. Like I said. Early. But you know travel makes me tired..."

"Izzy McCall-Price! Are you asking me what I think you're asking me?"

She gives me a sly shrug. "Maybe I am..."

"Wow," I say. "You proposed to me. Said I love you first. Now you're the one to propose our first real, not forced by circumstance, sleepover. You're really making this easy on me."

"Ha!" she laughs, throwing her head back in the most beautiful way. Not because of the act. But I can just tell she's more free than she's ever been in her life. Somehow her shoulders look lighter. Her eyes are brighter. Her smile is bigger. "There was nothing about this that was easy."

I squeeze her in closer and brush my finger down her cheek bone. "The good things never are."

Chapter 35
Izzy

I STEP INTO MY WALK-IN SHOWER, WELCOMING THE scalding hot water and steam as I let the stream hit my back. I tilt my head to the left and right, letting the pulses work out the knots that have been forming into little tiny balls over the last three days.

It feels amazing.

Once the blowup at the funeral happened yesterday, Oliver and I got back in the car, went to get our stuff, and immediately got the hell out of Smallwood. Our flight wasn't scheduled to leave until this morning, and there wasn't another flight to take last night. While I would have loved to leave Nebraska, I was fine getting a room at the airport hotel. I didn't care where I slept last night as long as it wasn't in that town. And slept I did. Well, after I cried in Oliver's arms until I passed out.

I broke the promise I made to myself when I left all those years ago that I'd never go back. But some stupid part of me thought I still needed to be the good daughter and attend. Not anymore. If and when Mom dies, I'll send a card. Maybe. Though I'm not sure to whom. The only people I want to see are Jessie, Jimmy, and the kids. But I'm a pretty well off woman in the financial department, and I'll fly them out here for the holidays. Yup, that's the plan. Gone are the days I sacrifice having a relationship with my sister and her family because my mother is in the running for World's Worst Mother. Hmm, maybe Oliver can get her a shirt?

Just knowing that I'm done with Smallwood gives me so much relief. If I ever see anyone from that hell hole again it will be too soon.

I turn around so I'm facing the shower stream, sighing as the water pours down my face. I've always believed in the healing powers of a hot shower. But this one might be the most healing of all. I can feel the last three days washing off me. I know this shower isn't going to fix the last sixteen years, but one day it might. And if I have Oliver by my side to help me, I have a feeling it will come sooner than I think.

I feel a quick hit of cold air at my back and look back over my shoulder to see Oliver stepping into the shower in all of his naked glory.

Fuck, my husband is hot.

"What are you doing in here?"

Oliver places both hands on my shoulders, starting to work the knots that I'm desperate to make go away. "I thought I'd join my wife in the shower. Because, well, I can."

"Yes, you can," I sigh, tilting my head to the side, giving him the opening that he takes to press his lips on the curve of my neck. He keeps massaging my shoulders, working the tension through his fingers in the most delicious pain.

I lean into Oliver, loving the feel of his lips and hands working me in tandem. I don't know how something can be so relaxing, yet so erotic, at the same time. On one hand, I'm melting into Oliver's touch with every pressure point he hits. On the other hand, his lips, which are starting to explore further than my neck, are making me want Oliver to do some dirty things to me in this shower before we get ourselves clean.

"Oliver..."

His lips stop only for the second that he needs to turn me around, slowly moving me back so I'm now against the cold tile of the shower wall. The contrast of the temperatures is like a pleasure and pain on my senses. That is, until my attention shifts to Oliver kissing his way down my wet body.

"Ol—"

"Shhhh," he says between kisses. "Let me take care of you."

I dare someone to tell me six sexier words in the English language. Okay, maybe "take it like a good girl" is in the mix. But I still say "let me take care of you" is up there. Because I know just a few weeks ago, that sentence would have sent me into a full-blown panic attack. The thought of allowing anyone, let alone a man, say they were going to take care of me, every ounce of trauma would have drowned me. It would have meant that once again someone was trying to control my life under the pretense of love or adoration. Turns out those words can be used to show love, not use the premise of love and security against you.

So I do something in this moment I thought I would never let anyone do.

I let Oliver take care of me.

He starts kissing his way down my wet body until he's on his knees. I can't take my eyes off him. It's like he's trying to heal me one kiss at a time.

I let my hands glide through my now-wet hair as he gently lifts one of my legs and sets it on his shoulders. With the first pass of his magnificent tongue I nearly buckle from pure bliss. I need something to hold onto, but I don't think that the wet shower tile is going to be much help. I dig my hands harder into his hair, holding on to him for dear life as he eats my pussy like it's his last meal.

Oliver has always seemed to have the cheat code when it comes to my orgasms, and this one might be the fastest one to date. I think I rip out a chunk of his hair when he slides two fingers into me, finding my switch instantly as his tongue works circles on my clit.

"Fuck!" I scream. My whole body shakes from the orgasm, and I suddenly wish this shower came with a bench.

My body is still feeling the effects of the orgasm as Oliver sets down my leg and kisses his way up my body. He takes my hands in his, lifting them over my head as his lips dive into mine. I can taste myself on his tongue, and I know that shouldn't be sexy, but somehow it is.

I am at the mercy of this man now. My hands are in his, and frankly, so is my body. And I'm not mad about any of that. I'm not worried that I can't use my hands. I'm not freaking out that I'm not in charge.

In fact, this is kind of nice. A girl could get used to this.

Oliver releases my hands and slowly lets his fingers glide down the wet skin of my arms. He continues tracing down the side of me, grazing over my breasts as he finishes at my hips. My hands slowly fall to his shoulders, and good thing they do, because before I know it, Oliver is picking me up under my ass and pinning me against the shower wall.

"Oliver!" I yell in what comes out as a squeal.

"I got you," he says, taking one hand from under me to hold it up to my lips. "Just feel me. Feel us."

I nod, doing my best to let our connection take over as he enters me. The second my back hits the tile in conjunction with Oliver pumping into me, I nearly lose it. I'm pretty sure I start yelling swear words in an order that doesn't make sense.

Which is fitting, because Oliver and I shouldn't make

sense. Yet, somehow we do in every way. He helps me see the light when I'm convinced there's only darkness. He made me believe in something I thought was the biggest scam in history. I had heard about opposites attracting, but I never saw how that was possible. How could two people with so many differences make it work?

Yet, as Oliver drives into me, holding me up as my head is buried in his shoulder and my arms are clinging around him for dear life, I know that it's true. It has to be. It's the only explanation as to how something that makes zero sense on paper is perfect in real life.

"I love you Izzy," Oliver says, his thrusts becoming faster. "I love you so much."

"I love you," I whisper, trying to find my words between the waves of the building orgasm about to rip through my body.

Oliver grabs onto me tighter as his pace picks up speed. I clutch onto his hair again, needing something tangible to grip as I feel it build inside of me.

"Izzy!"

Oliver's bellow sends us both over the edge. The sound of our breathing mixed in with the water hitting the shower floor is the only thing I hear as Oliver slowly puts me down on the ground, not letting me go as he reaches for my loofa. My legs are barely holding me up, so I wrap an arm behind me to hold onto Oliver. His free arm wraps around my waist as he begins to work the soap all over my body. He starts at my breasts, taking his time before traveling down to my stomach. He kneels down, pressing a kiss to my stomach that's so sweet I nearly start crying. He continues down to my legs, making sure to get each inch of my body before coming back up and doing everything one more time.

His movements are so gentle and tender it only affirms what I've finally figured out. With every brush and swipe, I feel another part of me washing down the drain, and because of Oliver, I know it's going to be okay.

Gone is the unhealthy relationship with my parents.

Gone is the mental abuse Matt put me through.

Gone is the emotional neglect and hurt I felt for years at the hand of people who supposedly loved me.

In their place is now a life I want to live. I have a job I love. A best friend who saved me.

A man who loves me.

And I love him. I love him so fucking much.

Chapter 36
Oliver

Thank goodness Wes owns a huge home with an equally huge driveway. That's the only way all these cars are going to fit when all is said and done.

Today is Magnolia's birthday, which means we were to drop everything we were doing to come out for the celebration. That was a direct order from the about-to-be-seven-year-old, and as Izzy has quickly realized, you don't say no to Magnolia Taylor.

"Is this a kid's party or a concert?" Izzy asks as she carries the birthday present in one hand and holds my hand with the other. "There was less traffic at Coachella."

"Knowing Mags, probably both."

Normally a Taylor child birthday party isn't this big. Wes prefers to do two parties for his kids—one for the child's friends and then the one for adult friends and family. Or as Magnolia likes to call that one, "the money party." We can all thank Godfather Uncle Simon for that one after his gift of crisp, one hundred dollar bills last year.

But the Taylors are about to leave for three weeks for a

family vacation, so for this year, the parties are combined. And by the number of cars parked, I'm going to guess that most of the seven-year-old population of Rolling Hills is in attendance —most of whom will be in my class next year—as well as all of Wes and Betsy's family and friends.

All of the friends who don't know that Izzy and I are a real thing now.

"What's wrong?" Izzy asks as I suddenly stop.

"We forgot to tell everyone."

Izzy's eyes double in size. "Shit, we did, didn't we?"

In our defense, we've been...preoccupied. Yeah, we'll go with preoccupied. It's currently Saturday, and we got back to Nashville on Thursday. Since then we haven't left Izzy's condo. Or talked to anyone. Or been fully clothed. The only contact we've had with the outside world is the messages we've typed to the food delivery drivers.

"Are they going to be mad?" Izzy asks.

"I don't know," I say. "Nah. They'll get over it. I mean, they'll give me shit for sure, but that would have happened no matter what."

"Okay, so what's the plan?"

I look toward the house, where I can see a bounce house peeking from above the fence. I hear the sound of music and laughter from adults and children. All my life I wanted to attend one of these kinds of functions with the person I loved. The few women I was dating when a birthday party or gathering was happening either came with me to these things, and they complained the whole time or had a very important thing to do and couldn't make it. When I told Izzy about this party today and that it would require us entering the outside world again, she wasn't mad. She wasn't upset. She didn't all of a sudden have to wash her hair. Nope, my wife got up, got dressed, and took me to the department store, where we bought Magnolia way too many toys.

She's the one I was always meant to be here with. None of those other women or people I thought I was in love with. So I'm going to enter this party the only way I see fit—with Izzy's hand in mine.

"Together," I say as I clasp our hands together. "We go in together. That's the plan."

We start walking toward the gate at Wes's fence that leads to the back yard. Only this isn't just a yard. It's big enough to be its own piece of property. It has a huge pool, hot tub, and room for today's additions of a bounce house, a station for face painting, and a photo booth where Disney princesses are currently taking pictures. Oh and a patio where all the adults can hang with what looks like an open bar.

This party has Betsy written all over it.

"Uncle Oliver!" Magnolia says as she leaps into my arms. Luckily she's done this plenty of times, so I know to brace for impact.

"Hey, birthday girl."

"Izzy! You came to my party!"

"Like I'd miss it," she says. "Oliver told me it was going to be the party of the year, so of course I had to be here."

Magnolia wiggles out of my hold and grabs Izzy's hand. "I have to show you the photo booth. We need to take a picture."

Izzy turns and hands me the presents, a smile as wide as I've ever seen on her beautiful face. "Care to come?"

I shake my head. "You two have fun."

I watch them for a few seconds before I make my way over to the gift table. Coincidentally, it's close to where my friends are gathered on the patio deck. I make my way over there, though I'm still staring at Izzy. Since Nebraska, it's like she's a new woman. Reborn, even. It's a beautiful thing to be a part of, and every day I'm in awe of how strong this woman is and how with each day she only gets stronger.

"He's alive!" Simon exclaims, handing me a beer. "We thought you went dark again on us."

"Sorry. Just been a little hectic after we got back."

Hectic. Sure. That sounds believable.

"How'd it go?" Shane asks.

"Good," I say. "Well, not good. But good."

"You're going to have to use more words than that," Amelia says. She's standing next to Shane, and, I don't know if I'm imagining things, but I feel like they are standing very close. Like weirdly close.

"Sorry. The bad things that happened: Izzy's mother is a horrible human. Her ex-boyfriend is as much of a shit bag as I suspected, and I might have punched him. I take that back. I did punch him. And I'd do it again."

"Fuck yeah" Simon says. "You make me proud, best friend."

"Do we have to go over the best friend shit again?" Shane says. "Oliver, continue."

"Thank you. Now for the good things. Izzy got to see her sister and her niece and nephew for the first time in a long time. And good in the sense that going back gave her the closure she needed. Maybe not all of it, but it was a hell of a start."

I want to tell them more, but it doesn't feel right without Izzy next to me.

"Well, I'm glad that something good came from the trip," Amelia says as Wes and Betsy come into the circle, looking quite run down. "Are you two okay?"

"No," Wes says. "Kids are exhausting."

Betsy falls into one of the chairs. By the looks of it, she might not get back up. "Be a nanny, they said...it will be fun, they said...They didn't tell you that you might fall in love with your boss and then have to be a bonus mom and plan extravagant birthday parties."

"Hey, you're the one who said we needed face painting. This was after you already convinced me to hire princesses."

Betsy turns to look at Wes, and while she might not look angry, I can tell she's five seconds from blowing. "Wes. I love you. I love the kids. But right now I'm going to need you to stop speaking and using my own actions against me and just support me when I'm ignoring the problem that I created."

This makes all of us laugh, even Shane, as we find seats on the patio, far away from the children. "Oliver, I don't know how you do it," Wes asks. "How do you deal with this age every day?"

I smile, taking a second to look at my about to be students having the times of their lives. "The key is no bounce houses."

Wes lets his head drop back in defeat. "I knew it."

I look up to see Izzy taking Magnolia over to a group of her friends at the face painting station as Wes's oldest daughter and my goddaughter, Emerson, comes slinking over.

"You okay, Em?"

Emerson falls onto the one open chair left. "I just need five minutes. Five minutes away from the kids. I just...I need this."

It might seem to an onlooker that Emerson is being dramatic, but it's the opposite. She's the most mature thirteen-year-old I've ever met. I'd trust her to run this whole party. Hell, she can substitute for me any day of the week.

"Who says you can sit at the big kids table?" Simon teases. By the look she shoots him, she doesn't find it very funny.

"I'm a teenager now. I've earned my place in this circle. Plus I don't see you taking a turn as event coordinator."

Simon holds his hands up in defeat. "I stand corrected. Sit with us."

"Room for another?"

Everyone says hi to Izzy, which she returns before taking a seat on the arm of the patio chair I've chosen.

"Hey," I whisper.

She smiles and gives me a playful shove. "Hey, back."

"Well, since everyone's here, there's some news I want to share," Amelia says. "Actually, it's news Shane and I both want to share."

No one even has a chance to process that before Betsy lets out a scream that stops the entire party.

"OH MY GODDDD!!!!!!!"

Everyone immediately looks at Betsy, who's covering her mouth and pointing to Izzy's hand.

"What?" Wes asks. Betsy doesn't say anything, instead just doubles down on the pointing, her mouth now completely open.

"Dad, I love you. And you're smart. I know this. But for a smart man, sometimes you are very dense," Emerson says as she stands up, pointing over to Izzy. "Izzy's wearing her wedding ring."

Emerson walks away, which no one notices, because all eyes are on Izzy and me.

"So," Simon begins. "When we asked earlier about Nebraska did you ever think to yourself that part of your answer should be that your wife is now wearing a fucking wedding ring?"

I shrug. "I was going to. I just wanted to wait for Izzy to be here."

"Apologies, Simon. I was conducting very important business with my future flower girl. We were talking shades of pink, and she made sure she took your color complexion into account. What do you think of Barbie pink? The brighter the better."

"No, no, no," Simon says. "When you two do this right, and

you will be doing this right, I'm going to be standing next to my best friend as his best man."

"You're not his best man," Shane chimes in with a glare.

"You shut it," Simon points to Shane before looking back at me and Izzy. "I'm at the very least a groomsman. I'm not doing flower man shit."

"Who says you can't do both?" I say. "I feel like you have that capacity."

"I hate you both."

Izzy smiles at him. "No, you don't."

Simon narrows his eyes at Izzy but then soon cracks a smile.

"Hello!" Betsy yells as she snaps her fingers in the air. "Before I have to go back on kid duty because it's almost food time, can you two please tell me how we got here?"

"I wore her down," I say, earning me a playful slap from Izzy.

"That's not the story," she says, as if she's already tired of hearing my jokes.

The real joke's on her. I have *tons* more where these came from. And she's my captive audience.

"But is it kind of the story?" Wes says. "Because I feel like that's part of the story."

Izzy nods in agreement. "Yes, he did wear me down. But more so in the fact that he didn't give up on me. He saw what I didn't see yet and was the most patient man I've ever met. Then when I was back in Nebraska, I had what you'd call a revelation. Somewhere in between fighting with my mother and dodging looks from townspeople, and after he punched my douchebag ex-boyfriend, I realized I loved my husband."

"Did he punch him good?" Simon asks. "Like did he really get back there?"

"That's what you took from that?" Izzy asks.

Simon just shrugs his shoulders. "I feel like that was the most important part."

Betsy slaps him on the arm. "It wasn't. She loves him! That's so sweet."

"So what now?" Wes asks. "Where are you two going to live?"

I shrug as I take Izzy's hand. "We're figuring it out. There's no rush. We're here and happy. The rest will fall into place."

"Well, that's just amazing," Betsy says, standing and walking over to Izzy to give her a hug. "I have to go round up kids. But girls' day, soon."

Wes gives me a pat on the shoulder as he follows Betsy, leaving the rest of us here.

"Wait," I say, looking over to Amelia. "Didn't you want to tell us something?"

Amelia and Shane share a look. They are clearly having a silent conversation, and whatever it's about, it's ending with Shane shaking his head. What the hell is up with them?

"It's okay," Amelia says. "Another time."

"Everyone!" Betsy yells from across the yard. "Food's ready!"

Kids drop everything they're doing and start rushing to Betsy, who is lining them up like a pro. All of the adults start shuffling over, which gives me the chance to hang back and grab Shane.

"You okay?" I ask. "I know I've been gone a lot. But if you need to talk?"

He shakes his head. "I'm good. But thanks."

"You sure?"

Shane doesn't look at me, instead keeping his eyes focused straight ahead. Which is coincidentally in the direction of Amelia.

"Yeah, man. I'm sure."

I look to Amelia, then back to Shane, before looking back to Amelia. "Is there something going on between you two that I should know about?"

Shane gives me a pat on the back. "Soon enough, my friend. Soon enough."

Chapter 37
Izzy

"How much longer do you need?"

Oliver comes out of my en suite bathroom in the midst of tying his tie, giving me a questioning look. "You're asking *me* that? You haven't even gotten dressed yet."

I tilt my head so I can put in my earring. Because yes, I'm still only wearing a bra and panties and am doing everything I can possibly do before I put that dress on. It's a great dress—tight, off the shoulder, and a slit so high it's just barely acceptable—but breathing sometimes is an issue in it. "I just want to know what my time frame is based off your time frame."

"Right..." Oliver says, clearly not buying my explanation. "I'll be done in five minutes then the bathroom is all yours. Then whenever you decide to put your dress on, I'll be ready for zipper duty."

"You're the best!" I yell, clasping in the second earring.

In the past, a night like tonight would fill me with nothing but dread. It's a black-tie event, so Hazel would have had to set a timer telling me that I couldn't leave until it went off. She'd also make me smile and talk to people, which is just the worst.

But tonight I'm not dreading it so much. And it's not because we're hosting the head of the London office for the dinner. It's because of the man who's currently walking out of the bathroom looking like a whole damn snack. Fuck that. He's a meal.

It's at this moment I now know I want to have a real wedding, because the sight of Oliver Price in a tuxedo is enough to melt these barely-there panties right off.

"Are you staring at me?" Oliver asks, slowly walking toward me as he finishes clasping his cuff link.

I lean back on my hands, biting my bottom lip as I take in my husband. "What if I am?"

I'm suddenly transported back to that night in Las Vegas. I know that wasn't "the" night, but in some ways, it might have been more impactful than the night we said "I do." I remember the fire building inside of me when we were near each other. I remember how he made me feel with just a few words. It's the same way I'm feeling right now.

Man, I really was in denial back then, wasn't I...

"I should be the one staring," he says, walking over to me and gently placing his hand at the base of my throat, tilting it up just enough so I'm looking him in the eye. "You in that lingerie? How do you expect me to behave tonight when I know that black lace is under your dress?"

"Would you rather me take it off?"

He shakes his head, his thumb stroking back and forth along my neck. "No. Because I want the pleasure of taking it off later."

Fuck me.

I spent years priding myself on being an independent woman who, as the kids say these days, didn't need no man. Vibrators did the trick, and when I wanted the real thing, the itch was scratched in a timely and sufficient manner.

But when my husband says things like that, looking the way he does... I'm sorry, but things are going to happen to make me a wanton, feral woman.

And those things might cause us to be a little late to this event.

I sit up, Oliver's hand still at my throat, as I start undoing the belt on his pants.

"What are you doing?"

I look up at him as I work his zipper down. "Something to hold us over until we can come back and you can fuck me right out of this dress."

I push down his pants and boxer briefs, releasing his dick into my hand. I lick my lips as I start to stroke him, which is getting him harder and harder by the second.

"Izzy," he says as his head falls back and he sucks in a breath.

"Do you want me to stop?"

Considering I'm licking his cock from base to tip as soon as I'm done asking that question, I doubt he's going to say no. When he looks back down at me, his eyes fully on me as I tease him, I know for a fact he's not.

"Take it all," he says as he gathers my hair away from my face. "Take everything."

He doesn't have to ask me twice. I give him two more strokes before opening my mouth and slowly taking him in. Part of me is mad I finished my makeup already. Part of me doesn't care. Not when I know my mouth is driving him crazy, which is making me unabashedly wet.

"You're so fucking beautiful," Oliver says as he gives my hair a slight pull as I go in and out on him. "That pretty little mouth taking my cock..."

God, his voice still gets me every damn time. That low tone reverberates through every cell, which only further ignites the heat I feel every time I'm with Oliver. I speed up my efforts, making sure to work my tongue around him just how I know he likes it.

"Eyes on me, Izzy."

I do as he says, though I wasn't prepared for the pure fire I see in them. Shit, I was just planning on giving him a little tease tonight, but if he keeps looking at me like that, we're going to be very, very late.

"Oh fuck!" Oliver's hands suddenly grab the back of my head, controlling it as my speed picks up. "I can't hold back."

I don't want him to, which is why I double down. In just a few more seconds, I take all of Oliver. Every last drop. I know some women don't like that, and I say to each their own. But for me? Seeing the look of satisfaction in his eyes? Worth every second.

And worth being ridiculously late to this event.

Oliver falls onto the bed next to me. "Remember when you asked me if I was ready yet? I'm going to need a few minutes."

I smile and lean down to kiss his cheek. "Then my work here is done."

~

"Where have you been?"

Oliver and I share a smile as Hazel tries to scold me. "We got...held up."

Knox holds up his drink to us. "Yeah you did."

The three of us laugh, because, well, it's funny. But apparently my boss doesn't find it as amusing as we do. "You know Edwin from the London office is here, and he's been asking all night when you're getting here."

"Why's he asking for me?" I ask as we all walk into the ballroom of the downtown Nashville Hyatt. "Is Bridget here?"

"Nope. Just Edwin. And his lackey," Hazel says.

Huh. That's odd. Bridget is the me in London. Also known as, all things communications. I was actually looking forward to meeting her. We've been talking for so long over email and Zoom I feel like I know her already. Then again, we haven't talked in a while because of me having to suddenly take off for the funeral.

"All right then, let's go find him. No sense in his boxers getting in a bunch."

"How about I go get us a drink," Oliver says. "You two go conquer the world like you always do. Knox and I will be your personal waiters and arm candy."

I smile and kiss Oliver on the cheek. "You're the best husband ever."

"That's what the T-shirt says."

He returns the kiss as he and Knox walk toward the bar. When I turn back to face Hazel, there is a big-ass smile on her face.

"Go ahead," I say. "Say what you want to say."

She smugly shrugs. "I don't know what you mean?"

"Don't play dumb. It's not a good look on you."

"I don't have anything to say. Except that I was right all along on so many things that we don't have time to get into tonight. But, to highlight a few, I was right about Oliver. I was right about him being different from the jump. And I was right about love looking good on you."

"For someone who didn't have anything to say, you just said a whole lot."

"I know," she says, giving me a side hug as we make our way to where the members of the London team are sitting. "But it's all out of love."

"I know. And thank you."

"For what?"

"Seeing what I didn't see."

Hazel smiles and gives me one last squeeze as the three members of the London division stand up to shake our hands.

"Sorry to keep you waiting," I say. "Had a little bit of a hold up this evening."

"Things happen," says Edwin. He's what I expected him to look like in person. Mid to late 50s, the air about him that he's been in the corporate world his entire life. Hazel hired him to oversee the London branch once we decided to expand. He came highly recommended and knew the London tech scene. We both felt like we were lucky to snag him.

"Ladies, I needed to talk to you about something. Now, before I begin, I want you to know that I've dealt with the situation, but I felt you needed to know."

Hazel and I give each other a concerned look as we take a seat.

"As you know, the launch for Left for Love: London, is in two months."

"We do," Hazel says. "Everything is right on track. Right?"

"Of course it is," Edwin says, but judging by the way he's squirming in his chair, something is definitely not right. "Though we did have a personnel issue that I needed to take care of."

Oh, shit. What the hell is going on?

"Edwin, you have five seconds to tell me what's going on or you might not make a plane back to London," Hazel says.

"Again, it's nothing we haven't taken care of," he says. "I just wanted you both to be informed of the situation. Our communications director has decided to no longer continue working with us."

My eyes grow wide. "Bridget quit?"

"Yes, she decided to no longer work with us," Edwin says.

I can't believe she didn't tell me. Then again, I was MIA for a bit. Though why is he phrasing it like that? Something is definitely up.

"Did she say why?" I ask.

"She didn't," Edwin says, though he looks guilty as fuck.

"Edwin, spill it," Hazel says. "Now."

Edwin visibly swallows down the lump in his throat. The more Hazel and I push back, the more nervous it seems to make him. "There was an...incident."

"What kind of incident?" How Hazel is staying remotely calm right now is beyond me.

"There was a misunderstanding that led to Bridget not wanting to work at Left for Love anymore."

Oh, this smells like straight up cow shit. "What kind of incident?"

Edwin goes silent, which only makes the stench grow stronger. And only makes Hazel angrier. "Edwin? I'm going to need you to talk. Now."

"Well, my son..."

"Your son?" Hazel says, her voice growing louder. "Since when did your son come on board?"

"I hired him a few months ago. He has a marketing degree and is very capable of running the social media department."

"Interesting," I say. "I never heard about this hire. I feel like that's something I would have been informed about since I've been training every communications department head."

"It doesn't matter," Edwin deflects. "My son and Bridget had a...miscommunication. She felt it was best that she didn't work at Left for Love any longer."

Hazel and I look at each other in sheer bewilderment. This is bad. This is really bad.

"What kind of miscommunication?" I ask.

Edwin doesn't say anything, which turns Hazel's attention to Edwin's assistant. "What happened? You have five seconds to tell me or you can consider yourself no longer employed."

The assistant looks to Edwin before looking back at Hazel, straight fear in his eyes. "He asked her out. She said no. He then started spreading rumors about her in the office. There might have even been pictures, but I didn't see them."

Oh for fuck's sake...

"Oh, okay then. That's easy," Hazel says in a calm voice. Edwin apparently is a dumbass because he's falling into a false sense of security. I just sit back and cross my arms with a knowing smirk. Because I know that hell's about to come down on him, and he's too fucking dumb to see it coming. "Here's what's going to happen. Edwin, you're fired. Your son is fired. Any staff you specifically hired from any previous employment is fired. Anyone who spread the rumors or pictures are fired. Except you." Hazel points to the assistant. "You can stay because you spoke up and didn't cower to this prick."

"Hazel, with all due respect, you're overreacting," Edwin says, the panicked look back in his eyes. "Yes, it was a minor blip, but no one needs to be fired."

"No one needs to be fired? Bridget has every right to file a sexual harassment suit against us. Hell, at this point, I'll hire her attorney."

"But she no longer works for us."

"God, you're a fucking idiot," I say. I need to go back and see who recommended this man because he's a goddamn moron. "Your son is a little dick energy prick who couldn't take no for an answer. You're an enabler who I'm guessing has already bailed him out of jail once or twice, which is why you had to hire him without telling anyone because then people would ask questions. There's a special place for you two in hell. So, as Hazel said, you're no longer employed. Get out of here, leave quietly, or the lawyers are going to come after *you* as well."

Edwin stands up, doing his best to not seem phased as he buttons his jacket. "Hazel, if you reconsider—"

"I won't. Goodbye, Edwin."

Edwin and his assistant walk away from the table as Hazel and I turn to look at each other.

"What the fuck was that?" I ask.

"I'm baffled. And slightly panicked," Hazel says. "We're two months away from a launch. We can't cancel it now. The investors will freak. We've already started the ad and marketing campaigns."

"We need damage control," I say. "We need to make sure this is all taken care of in the right way while also cleaning house."

Hazel looks at me, a sad look in her eye. "I hate to ask you to do this."

I nod, knowing what's coming. "I got this."

Hazel covers my hands with hers. "This has the potential to be a public relations nightmare. You're the only one I trust to take care of this correctly. Plus, we're going to need to hire all new senior management. All new vice presidents. All of those people were Edwin's hires. I want them all gone. And with the launch in two months, you're going to have to stay there and handle it until we know we're up, running, and in good hands."

"Done and done."

It's at that moment Oliver and Knox come to our table, setting our drinks down before taking seats next to us.

Shit...Oliver.

The tears immediately threaten to come spilling out as I think about being away from him for two months. This is more than just living forty minutes apart and deciding some nights not to stay over. I know I need to do this for Hazel and the company. Hell, at one point I begged Hazel to go over to London. Funny that it's happening, but at the sake of me falling in love.

Karma is a fickle bitch sometimes.

"Why don't you head home," Hazel says. "Think it over. Talk it out. Let me know in the morning."

"Huh?" Oliver says, which I get. I'd be confused too. Hell, I *am* confused, and I know what's going on.

I stand up, nodding at Hazel as a thank you. "I will. Come on, let's go."

Oliver stands up, still clearly confused about what's happening.

"Everything okay?"

I shake my head as I wrap my arms around Oliver's. "I don't know."

Chapter 38
Oliver

I'M STARTING TO GET WORRIED.

Izzy didn't say anything from the few minutes it took us to get from the dinner to her condo. She didn't say anything in the ride up the elevator. The second we entered her condo she kicked off her shoes, threw her purse to the side, and laid on her couch.

She didn't even act like this when she found out her dad died. Or anytime when we were in Nebraska. I don't know what's going on, but she better tell me soon because my mind is going in a thousand directions at once. And none of them are good.

"Come here," I say as I sit down on the couch, lifting her head so it's now resting on my leg. I begin brushing her hair with my fingers, wanting to give her some kind of comfort. "I don't know what happened, but I'm sure it's nothing we can't figure out."

It's then I hear tell-tale sign of Izzy's tears. Fuck, this has to be bad. "Babe. Please. You're starting to scare me."

She sits up, and I hate to see the little bit of makeup running down her face from the tears. "I have to go to London."

"Oh," I say, wondering why that's a big deal. "For the launch?"

Izzy shakes her head. "Yes. No. It's complicated. And messy as fuck."

I sit back and listen as Izzy tells me everything about what went on when Knox and I were getting drinks. Here we were talking about football season and wondering whether or not the Fury could repeat as champions when just across the room hell was breaking loose. Though it's probably good we weren't there. I have a feeling this Edwin guy wouldn't have taken kindly to Knox and I personally escorting him out of the building.

"Okay, so you have to go to London to clean up this guy's mess. If anyone can do it, you can."

"That's what Hazel said."

I tip her chin up. "So what's the problem? You go to London for a few weeks. Fix this guy's mess. Bring me back a Buckingham Palace T-shirt and a British flag to hang up in my classroom. Easy peasy."

Izzy shakes her head. "It's not just three weeks. This will take literal months. Two, minimum, because of the launch. Not only do I need to make sure the sexual harassment is dealt with properly and make sure every person who was a part of that is gone, I need to help coordinate the new hires for the London branch. The first round took us almost a year to find who we wanted. Then again, we apparently picked a shitty person, so who knows how long it will take."

I try to hide my shock, but I don't think I do a very good job.

"Say something," Izzy says. "I know you're freaking out. I'm freaking out. And if we're going to freak out, we need to do it together."

"Okay," I say, trying to gather myself. "Two months..."

"At least."

I shake my head. "Let's think positively."

"Positively, Oliver? Really? I might believe in love now, but that doesn't mean all of a sudden I think every glass is half full."

"I'm not saying the glass is half full."

"Well, then, what are you saying?" Izzy's voice is getting louder as she stands up to start pacing. "Because from where I'm sitting, you're trying to be sunshine and rainbows over a situation that fucking sucks."

"Isn't that what I do? That's kind of my role in this relationship."

"That's not what I'm saying!" Izzy yells.

"Then what are you saying!"

"I'm saying that for once I want you to say that something fucking sucks when it does. Because if this doesn't, then I don't know what does."

"Fine!" I yell back. "It fucking sucks. But what do you want me to do about it? Rewind time so the asshole son doesn't harass an employee? Maybe I can go a little farther back and not hire Edwin. Oh wait, I can't."

"I don't know!" Izzy yells, falling back down to the couch, sobs immediately coming from her. "I don't know..."

"Izzy..."

I take two steps to get to her, holding her in my arms and letting her cry. She's right, this does suck. There is no silver lining. At least, not one that I can see.

"We're just getting started," she says between the cries. "I feel like this is being ripped away from us just as we're getting going. We didn't even decide who's taking whose name or where we're going to live. I don't even have a drawer at your place yet."

"I told you, I'll take yours. And you're right, we are just

getting started. But we're not getting ripped away," I say as I rub her back. "Not even an ocean can come between us."

"Oliver. The ocean will literally be between us."

I can't help but laugh. "There she is. Captain Literal checking in for duty."

"Don't make me laugh. This isn't a laughing situation."

I bring her back to my lap, where indeed I see a few chuckles coming in between the tears.

"Yes, there is going to be an ocean between us. Yes, a few time zones will make things difficult."

"Do you not remember my moods when I had morning calls with London?" she asks. "I was the worst."

"Which is why I'll be the one on the six in the morning side of things while you're a few coffees in your day."

"Fine, but two months, Oliver. Two months. And again, that's the best case scenario. What if two turns into six. Six turns into a year. Next thing we know we're sending each other random emails when we think of it and we have to be reminded we're married!"

"Oh no," I say. "That is not going to happen."

"How do you know? We're going to be busy. Life happens, Oliver. I'm going to be cleaning up the clusterfuck that Edwin left. You're going to be in football mode, and it's going to be the start of the school year. Next thing we know it's going to be our anniversary, which neither of us will remember."

"Nope," I say. "Never going to happen. That is a date I'll remember forever."

Izzy gives me a head tilt that clearly says she's not buying what I'm trying to sell. "Oliver, we barely remembered doing it. Cut the crap."

"We now remember because we finally got the video," I say. Though judging by the look she's shooting me right now, I need to stop trying to alleviate this situation with humor.

"Fine, is this going to suck? Yes. Am I going to miss you every day? Also yes. There, happy?"

Izzy looks so defeated right now. I hate I can't make this go away.

"No," she says. "I'm not happy. On one hand, working in London is something I've always thought about doing. Until you, I had nothing keeping me here, so why not go work in a different country, travel, and live life? Hell, I even joked with Hazel a few times she should have sent me out there to do exactly what I'm about to go do. Well, without the whole possible lawsuit and harassment thing."

"Working in London could be great," I say.

"But you won't be there."

I didn't know when your heart broke that you could actually feel it. But I can, because Izzy's words just hit me harder than anything ever has in my life.

"I know," I say, bringing her back close to me. "I wish I could come with you, but football is starting soon, and I'm covering for Wes the first few weeks."

"I've always hated football."

"Well, then, it's probably good you won't be here for the season. Things get a little intense."

She doesn't laugh at my joke. I mean, it wasn't that funny, but I thought it could lighten the situation. I take a second to look down at Izzy, who's now aimlessly drawing circles on my chest.

"Are we going to be okay?" she asks with a sniffle.

I kiss the top of her head. "Of course we will. You're going to go live your dream of working in London, fix up the shit that an idiot caused. You're going to take five of my T-shirts to sleep in and I'm going to keep a bottle of your perfume because I'm weird like that. We're going to FaceTime and talk and text every day. If it lasts longer than planned, I'll come visit during fall break. Either way, before you know it, we'll be back here trying to figure out what's next."

Izzy sits back up, but doesn't let go of my shirt. "I'm sorry this is happening."

"Oh no. We're not doing this," I say, tipping her chin up. "I told you when we first met to not apologize for who you are or what you wanted, and that doesn't change here. Does it suck? Yes. But also you should be proud that out of all the people at Hazel's disposal, you're the one she trusts. You're the one to get the job done. And you're going to kick ass. So don't apologize because we're going to miss a few months. We still have many ahead of us."

Izzy cups my face with her hands, bringing me in for a slow, yet emotional, kiss. I feel a tear of hers hit my skin, which sends me over the edge as well. I've been holding it in, figuring I could let it all out once she got on the plane, but what's the use?

I need to keep reminding myself that this isn't forever, it's just for now. Because it can't be forever. Izzy and I fought through too much for this to be the end of the story. And like hell I'm going to let it end like this.

Chapter 39
Izzy

"Juliet! Confirm the interviews for tomorrow! And please can someone get me a coffee and a sandwich and a water!"

"Got it boss!"

I sit back in the chair that should be occupied with the head of the London division. But in the meantime, that title belongs to me. I've been out here for a month now and we're no closer to finding people to run this ship than we were when I got on the plane in Nashville.

"Here's your water, ma'am."

I look up to my assistant, who's coincidently named Juliet. She's my British Jules. "What did I say about ma'am? Izzy is fine."

She nods, still not sure if I'm serious about that or not. "Yes, apologies."

"No need to be sorry," I take a sip of the water when I get an idea. I grab my phone and take a selfie with me holding up my water bottle. Look at me growing, I'm taking selfies to send to my man and staying hydrated.

"Your lunch will be here soon, ma—Izzy."

"Thanks. Go get yourself something to eat. We have an advertising meeting in an hour, and I'll need you with me."

Her eyes grow wide. "You will?"

"Of course," I say. "I forget to take notes, which means I'll remember nothing. So I'll need you to be my memory."

"Got it, boss." She turns and leaves my office, a little skip to her step.

I smile as I take my phone out to send the selfie to Oliver. It's seven in the morning in Rolling Hills, and I'm guessing he's awake. It is football season, after all.

Oliver: Look at my wife, hydrating all on her own.

Izzy: You taught me well. How'd you sleep?

Oliver: Do you want the truth, or do you want me to lie?

Izzy: Depends what you want me to do when you ask me the question right back.

Oliver: Truth it is. Slept like shit. I didn't realize how quickly I got used to your snores.

Izzy: Oliver Michael Price! I do not snore, and you know it.

Oliver: No. But I figured it was a less pathetic thing to say than I miss waking up with my arms around you.

Izzy: Not pathetic. At all. I miss those arms. And other things...

Oliver: How many more days?

Izzy: Too many to count.

Oliver: FaceTime date tonight?

Izzy: You know it.

Oliver: Wear the T-shirt. Just the T-shirt.

Izzy: Aye aye captain.

"I know what that smile means. Someone just got a message from her husband."

I look up and smile at Bridget as she comes and has a seat in front of my desk. Yes, I got Bridget back. It was my first order of business.

Well, it was my first hire. Or re-hire. Not sure how we're classifying it. Either way, she was the first person I officially put on board for Left for Love: London 2.0. My first actual act of business was officially firing Edwin, his dickweed son, and anyone who I found out spread rumors or pictures of Bridget. It's good having friends in the IT department.

"You would be correct," I say, setting my phone down.

"Juliet looks excited," Bridget says. "Did she finally not call you ma'am?"

"Only once."

"She's getting there."

"She's a good girl," I say. "I'm glad she agreed to stay on."

Juliet was Edwin's assistant. Though from what I've heard from her, Bridget, and a few others who were thankful that I was coming in and cleaning house, Edwin treated her like crap. Yes, I might have her get me food and coffee from time to time, but I need her to help me be successful. I need her in meetings and knowing the ins-and-outs. I learned long ago you can be good on your own, but a good assistant makes you elite. Apparently Edwin never got that memo. Turns out he didn't get a lot of them.

"She's just one example of the difference in morale," Bridget says. "It's amazing the shift in energy in this place."

"I'm so sorry," I say, probably for the hundredth time since I showed up on Bridget's doorstep asking her to come back. "I wish Hazel and I knew. Or that we didn't get faked out by him. On paper, and in every meeting, he seemed like the right guy."

"You have nothing to apologize for," Bridget said. "Turns out he's fooled a lot of people over the years. Or so we're coming to learn."

Turns out Edwin, his son, and really his whole family, had some skeletons in their closet. That's at least what's been uncovered so far after an anonymous call to a media contact got the ball rolling. Turns out sexual harassment wasn't the only thing Nepotism Boy was into. And Daddy was covering up every instance. We're talking cocaine, gambling debts, and other sexual harassment claims.

I don't know who made that call, but I hear she's a fucking badass.

Officially as the head of communications, I knew I needed to get out in front of Edwin being let go, especially if dirt did come out. And we did. We issued a statement that he was being let go, and we thanked him for his work leading up to the launch. It left him without a move. What was he going to do, say he was wrongfully terminated? If he played that card, my move was to spill about his idiot son.

Game. Set. Match, motherfucker.

He might have been scared of Hazel the night she fired him, but he didn't realize he'd have to face me after. And I'm always playing chess. He's lucky if he's playing checkers.

"Well, good riddance to bad rubbish," Bridget says.

"If I had a drink besides water, I'd toast you."

"Speaking of toasting..." Bridget says, giving me a look she has given me every day for the past week.

"Really? That's your transition today?"

She shrugs. "I'm having to get creative."

"I appreciate the effort, but no. While I'm flattered you think I could run the London office, I'm only here to get through the launch and hire the people to make sure we're smooth sailing going forward."

"I know that's what you say. But you do realize we already are, as you say, smooth sailing? You have all the right people in the right places. The launch is going to go off without a hitch, and it's all because of you."

"Quit buttering me up," I say.

"Is it working?"

"Kinda. But my weakness is being courted and flattered on a consistent basis. It's how I ended up going out with Oliver."

She laughs. "I'll remember that. Maybe I'll throw in some booze and make you promise me while under the influence."

"That's how I ended up married."

We share a laugh as my phone rings with Oliver's name and his picture flashing on the screen. "That's weird. I just talked to him. Why's he calling so early?"

"I'll leave you be," Bridget says. "Tell your husband we love you and we're going to need to discuss shared custody."

"Ha ha," I say, shooing her out of my office before answering. "Hey, babe. Everything okay?"

Yes, I called him babe. Yes, I hate that I'm a woman who now uses nicknames. I also secretly love it.

"Can't a man just want to call and hear the sound of his wife's voice?"

I kick my shoes off, already needing the relief, and it's barely the afternoon. "He can, but usually it means something else is up."

"Nothing is up," he says. "I'm up and I figured I'd like to hear your voice before you're exhausted and falling asleep."

"I'm sorry," I say. "I know this time zone stuff is hard, and by the time you're free I'm on the verge of crashing."

"You're fine," he says. "It's just nice to hear you while your caffeine is still working."

"And I have another on the way," I say.

"Some things will never change."

Oliver and I start chatting about everything and anything. Juliet slides into my office and drops off my sandwich, so I eat while Oliver talks to me about football things I barely understand. But it's okay. Hearing his voice gives me comfort. It reminds me every day that I have to say no to Bridget, because this isn't where I'm supposed to be.

Though if I'm being honest, I love this. I love being in charge. I love seeing the teams succeed. The only thing making it not perfect is that Oliver isn't here. Plus, Hazel still wants me back in Nashville after the launch, and she's still the boss. So I'm letting myself have fun now, but remembering this is temporary. Oliver and Tennessee are my end game.

"Oh, and I got my class list," Oliver says as Juliet signals it's time for my next meeting. "And Magnolia has gotten her wish—she's in my class."

"That's awesome, and I hate to cut this short..."

"No, I get it," he says, though I hear a tinge of sadness in his voice. "Go be your badass self."

"Thanks. I love you."

"Love you more."

I quickly hang up and gather my files and laptop.

"Ready?" I ask Juliet as I exit my office.

"Absolutely, boss."

Boss...I hate how much I like the sound of that.

Chapter 40
Oliver

Oliver: How was your day?

~

Izzy: Hey, sorry I missed your text yesterday. Things got crazy. Call you later tonight?

~

Oliver: We have to stop missing each other. Call me whenever you can. I don't care what time it is. I just want to hear your voice.

~

Hi. You've reached the voicemail of Oliver Price. Leave a message....

Oliver: I'm so sorry, babe. I don't know how I didn't hear your call. I'm done with practice today at noon.

Izzy: Shit, we scheduled a late night tonight to go over last minute launch things. But I'll duck out for a second.

Oliver: Don't worry about it. Maybe tomorrow.

Izzy: I hate this.

Oliver: Me too.

Izzy: I miss you.

Oliver: Miss you more.

This is the voicemail of Izzy McCall. You know the drill...

"This is Izzy."

"Holy shit, is that you?"

I shouldn't be this excited to hear my wife's voice, but I am. It's sad that I don't remember the last time I heard it.

"Hey babe," she says, though she doesn't sound like she's sharing my excitement.

"Everything okay?"

"Yeah." She trails off to yell something at someone. "Sorry. Today was the deadline to approve the graphics. It's nuts. And I thought you were going to be Hazel calling and asking me why I haven't sent over the social media language yet."

"Well then, don't let me keep you," I say. "Call me later?"

"Yup."

"I—" I start to tell her I love her, but the line goes silent before I can.

~

Izzy: You up?

Oliver: Mmhmm.

Izzy: You don't have to pretend. I know it's the middle of the night for you.

Oliver: But you're up. Give me a second and I'll call you.

Izzy: It's okay. I just miss you. I know I've been crazy and things have been weird, but please know I love you. And I miss you. Get some sleep.

Oliver: Love you more.

~

Oliver: How was your day?

I THROW my phone on the couch, not expecting a response from Izzy anytime soon. It's already seven o'clock here, which means it's one in the morning for her. Sometimes I catch her still up, but she's been putting in such long hours she crashes as soon as she gets home. I usually try to message her at the end of her day, which is around noon for me, but today we started two-a-day practices, and it was break time. And frankly, I needed a nap after staying up last night hoping I could catch her, which I didn't.

I remember the days when I'd text her to ask how her day was, and I'd shoot up a prayer that she'd even respond. I remember every time she answered me back a warm feeling ran through me. I was so excited we were talking, even if it was just in a friendship sense. Now I just want her to answer so I know we're still okay.

Because the more and more this separation lasts, the more and more I'm worried we're not.

A knock on my front door saves me from going down the dark rabbit hole of outcomes. I'm about to stand up to open it when Shane comes walking around the corner into my living room.

"Hey," I say as I turn down the television. "What brings you by?"

He holds up a six-pack of beer. "Figured we could just hang out. Catch up. Make sure everything is okay."

I take one of the beers from the six-pack and twist off the top. "My wife is in London. I'm here. I've talked to her twice in the past two weeks, and that's being generous. I'm miserable. The worst part is that I'm letting it show. Today I told a freshman to run a gasser because he only called me "Coach" instead of "Coach Price." I had the kid in my class back in the day. He used to draw me pictures. I felt like shit."

"It's understandable," Shane says. "This is the first time you've been in love."

"I've been in love before." I say defensively.

Shane raises an eyebrow. "Really? I know you thought you were. But honest to God, think back to every proposal. Is there anyone out of that group that, now that you have Izzy, you wish would have said yes? That they were the ones who got away?"

I think long and hard about my numerous failed attempts. At the time, I was devastated after each one. Some more than others. Some I knew immediately I dodged a bullet. Some I was truly heartbroken. But this? This feeling of every night like the knife is digging more and more into my chest? I've never felt like that before.

"You're right. I love her. I love her so fucking much it hurts."

"I get that," Shane says. "Which is why it hurts so much that she's away. I remember guys I served with in Iraq talking about how they went days without speaking to their wives or girlfriends. It takes a toll. Not only on you but on the relationship."

Well now I feel even more like shit. I'm not out there risking my life. I'm just a sad sap who misses his wife.

"Was I stupid to think that we could survive this?" I ask. "Because I thought this was going to be easy. Well, not easy. But I thought we could make it easy. Turns out, this is hard as fuck."

"I don't know," he says, sitting back in the recliner. "I mean, two months doesn't seem like that long of a time when you're hopeful. And maybe it would be different if you weren't playing the most epic game of phone tag I've ever witnessed. So I can see why you thought you could navigate the waters. But in reality, that's a long ass time, especially when you two were just getting going."

He's right. We had just gotten on the same page. Things were great. We were happy. Yes, we were still getting our bearings, but we knew it would come. I loved her and she loved me, and that should have been enough.

Then Edwin and his son fucked everything up. I think I now hate him more than Matt the ex, and that's saying something.

"I love her," I say. "I love her and I miss her, and I'm fucking miserable without her."

I let the emotion pour out of me, tears and all. Fuck it. I'm not too proud. I've cried in front of Shane before. Granted, that time was because I thought my world was over because the first girl I ever proposed to said no.

Those tears were from a kid who thought he knew what he wanted. These ones are from the man I've become who knows more than ever what he wants with his life.

"How much longer is she out there?"

I wipe the stray tears away and take a sip of my beer before answering. "We've hit the two month mark. The launch is tomorrow."

"That's good. Light at the end of the tunnel."

I shake my head. "No. The launch wasn't nearly as ready as they were led to believe it was, so they haven't even started to try and find a replacement for Izzy to run London. Until that happens, she's across the pond."

"Fuck..."

"I'll second that."

We sit in silence for a few minutes, and I truly think about how much time there's still left on this. No way is she coming home anytime soon. Not without a miracle. And I feel like I used up all my miracles when it comes to Izzy.

Unless I create my own miracle...

A thought hits me out of nowhere, but it sounds crazy, even in my head. I don't know if I can say it out loud, but man, it sounds good...

"What would you do?" I ask Shane, seeing if he's going to even come close to saying what I'm thinking. "If you were in my shoes, what would you do?"

"You want to know what I would do?"

"Yes."

"Shouldn't this be something you ask Wes about?"

"No," I say. "Wes used to be the practical friend. He still is, but now he's in love and that would cloud his judgment. I want to know what you would do."

In all the years I've known Shane, he's never even hinted at dating a woman. He's never brought one around or introduced us to one. I'm sure he does his thing when he needs to, but like most things about his life, he keeps it to himself as much as possible. So yes, I want to know what he would do.

"I'd go be with her."

Good thing I'm sitting down. I wasn't expecting that direct of an answer.

"Really?"

Shane sets his beer down on the coffee table and rests his elbows on his knees. "Listen, love isn't something you can find everywhere. And even when you do find it, shit tends to get in the way. It's never easy. Sometimes the timing is off, sometimes the person is with someone else, or maybe you are. Maybe it's like you and the location is the hard part. Some things you can't control. But some you can. Location? That's one. You can change that. You can be with her. You could book a flight right now and be in London tomorrow. Maybe she says she wants to come home, or maybe she says she wants to stay. Then guess what, you stay. They have teachers in London. So as far as I see it, the answer is easy. But I guess the question is, would you go?"

I don't even have to think. "In a heartbeat."

"Do it. I know what it's like to live with regret and thinking that it just wasn't the time. I know that pain when you don't act on things you could have controlled then have to sit back and watch the things you couldn't change. Don't live with regret, Oliver. There's not a worse feeling than knowing you let the one you want get away."

"Damn," I say, standing up from the couch. "I wasn't expecting that."

"What were you expecting?"

"For you to have a sensible way to deal with this and end up having to talk me out of heading to the airport right now so I could catch a plane to London."

Shane laughs and stands with me. "Go get your girl. I'll drive."

I give him a man-hug, complete with three back pats, as I head to my bedroom to start packing when something he said hits me.

"Wait!" I turn around and point at him. "What did you mean you know what it's like to live with regret? Who do you regret? When did you ever regret things? Are you hiding something from me? Who got away? Wait! Did Amelia get away? Is that why you've been acting weird? You were standing close to her. Like a weird close. What's going on? Why don't I know any of this? Am I even your best friend?"

Shane laughs and shakes his head. "I'll fill you in later."

Chapter 41
Izzy

"And last, but certainly not least, we could not be here today without Izzy McCall." The office each holds up their glasses of champagne to me as Hazel continues to make her speech. "Not only did she fill in when things were looking, well, bleak, to say the least. But she also created a culture here that not only gave this company the energy it needed to push through during crunch time, but will continue for years to come. Everyone, raise their glasses to Izzy!"

I give a small wave as a round of applause comes from the room full of employees as we celebrate the official launch of Left for Love: London. And it's a well-deserved celebration. We became the most downloaded app on the first day in United Kingdom history, we had a record number of new users, and, even better, we got it done when things looked like it wasn't going to happen.

These two months have been literal blood, sweat, and tears. It's been sleepless nights and early mornings. But it's done, and I should feel proud. I take that back; I am proud. I'm proud as hell of every single person in this room who did what they needed to do to get this ready. What I'm not proud of is how I treated Oliver over the past few months.

I've ignored him. I didn't mean to. And I didn't do it on purpose. It just felt like every time he called, or I had a second to call him, something came up here and I'd have to go. Or I'd fall asleep before we could talk. Or I'd already be in the office and busy when he got home from his day.

For years I didn't care about love or relationships, so pulling these kinds of days excited me. I'd basically ask Hazel for projects that would keep me so busy I could ignore the loneliness in my life.

I don't think I can do that anymore.

"Why aren't you excited?" Hazel asks as she finds me hiding in the back of the room. "You should be in the center of the floor, receiving every bit of praise and congratulations you've earned."

I shrug it off. "It was a team effort."

"Bullshit," Hazel says, giving me a head nod as I follow her away from the crowd. "I mean, it's not bullshit. You had a hell of a team here, and once they knew what to do, they were solid. But they only knew what to do because of you."

"Thank you," I say. "We got it done."

"Now I need to ask you the important questions, how are you doing? And if you say you're fine, I'm going to smack you."

I let out a small laugh. "I'm fucking exhausted."

"As you should be. But I meant personally. I hate what I had to ask you to do. Ask Knox, I spent nights feeling guilty."

"Why did you feel guilty?"

"Hiring Edwin for one," she begins. "I can't believe I missed so badly on that one."

"Don't beat yourself up. He had us all fooled."

"I guess," she says. "But then that blunder required you coming out here and fucking up everything with your life. I saw

Oliver at the grocery store one day and he looked so sad. I wanted to go up and give him a hug but I didn't because I was afraid he was going to be mad at me for sending you away."

We both take a seat on a couch in the hallway. "Don't beat yourself up. Remember, I volunteered as well. This was a mutual decision. But you were right, I was the logical choice. Did it suck having to leave Oliver? It did. But you know what? I'd do it again. I'd do it again every time you asked."

This clearly surprises Hazel. "Really? Why?"

I grab both of her hands, cupping them in mine. "Do you remember all those years ago when a random red head inserted herself into a conversation you were having at a bar and hired herself to come work for your company."

"Vaguely," Hazel says with a chuckle.

"I never really told you this, but you saved me that night. And for that, I will forever be grateful."

"Saved you? I mean, you were going through a breakup, but I don't know how that constituted saving you?"

"For years I told you that I had been dumped that night and that's why I was at the bar. And that's the truth. What you don't know is that the guy who dumped me that night was the first guy I had tried to date since I had moved to Los Angeles three years before that."

"Really? Why did you not date in that time?"

"Because my ex from back home was...he was bad. Narcissistic. Emotionally and mentally abusive. And, even though he was my high school boyfriend, our families were pushing us to get married for a business situation. When I caught him cheating on me the day of our wedding—"

"Excuse me, what!" Hazel yells, drawing a few looks from the crowd.

"Yup. Walked in on him and my maid of honor fucking on the bathroom counter."

"Holy shit," Hazel says. "I thought they only made movies with that plot line."

"Nope, that was my life," I say. "I immediately left Nebraska and headed to Los Angeles. I barely had a penny to my name, my family had all but disowned me, and I was dealing with trauma that I was about to push down for the next decade."

"Izzy," Hazel says. "I had no idea."

"Of course you didn't. I made sure of that. But eventually, I thought I got better. I was working full time and going to college because I was determined to make it on my own. And I started dating a guy from one of my classes. He seemed nice. We were in a few study groups. He had asked me out for months, but I told him I was focusing on school. The night of graduation he asked me out again. I thought it was cute, so I said yes."

"Please tell me you didn't catch him in the bathroom."

"Not a bathroom," I say. "This one was in his car."

"Fucking men..."

"That's what I said, and that's what I was saying all the way to the bar that night. I got drunk and convinced myself that men cheated. That's just what they did. That was my experience, so why keep going after something that you knew the outcome of?"

"Oh, Izzy," Hazel says.

"It's okay," I say. "That night you gave me light. This job kept me sane, functioning, and let me find myself. When I left Nebraska, I promised myself I was going to make it on my own. You helped me do that. I always said that you saved me that night, and I mean it. So, when you say 'Hey Izzy, go to London,' or 'Hey Izzy, fix this unfixable thing,' I will do it without thinking twice. Because that's the only way I can think of repaying you for what you did for me all those years ago."

Hazel is in tears as she reaches out to me for a hug. We wrap each other in a tight embrace as years of friendship and emotion flow through us. I don't know if there are soulmates, or if there is someone above pulling the strings, but I truly believe that Hazel and I were meant to be in each other's lives. Because this kind of friendship is once in a lifetime.

"I'm so proud of you," she says into my shoulder, still holding on to me. "You've come so far. From what started as managing a few influencers has turned into being my number two. And not only that, you are running this whole damn branch. I don't know anyone else who could do what you did these past two months. You're amazing, and I want you to make sure I tell you that every day."

"Will do, boss. Though I'm guessing for a little while longer it will have to be over Zoom."

We break the hug, the mood now lower since I changed the subject. "Actually, that's something I wanted to talk to you about."

Shit. Why did my stomach all of a sudden drop to my feet?

"I'm going to do this in two parts. Because for all these years you've been the most valuable employee and work partner I could have ever asked for. But on the other hand, you're my best friend in the entire world. And for what I'm about to say, boss Hazel and friend Hazel are very, very separate people and mindsets."

"Okay..."

Hazel sits up a little straighter and gives her blazer a little tug. Clearly she's getting into CEO Boss Bitch Hazel mode.

"Izzy, you have been a valued and exemplary employee for thirteen years. There hasn't been a single situation you haven't been able to handle or project you haven't been able to conquer. What you've done with this London overhaul and launch has been truly miraculous. And while I know the plan was for you to come out here and interview the next head of the London division, there would be no other person better suited for the job than you. That is, if you want it."

"Wow." I pause for a second, making sure what she said was for real. "Wait, did Bridget put you up to this?"

Hazel laughs. "No, though she did send me multiple emails on the subject. But I didn't need her emails. You're the logical choice, and I've known that for a long time. I was just too selfish to let you leave Nashville."

"I...I'm flattered," I say. "I don't know what to say."

"Don't say anything yet. Because I haven't told you what friend Hazel wants to say."

I smile, having a feeling I know where this is going. "Then please, continue."

"You would be amazing over here. Hell, you'd probably lap us back in Nashville in no time. But as your friend, I want you to come back home. But unfortunately, friend Hazel has to take a back seat. Because if I didn't offer you this job and let you make this decision, then I'd not only be a horrible boss, I'd be a horrible friend as well."

Shit, I really don't know what to say. On one hand, I did enjoy this work. I enjoyed being the leader. And in fact, I kind of kicked ass at it. That feeling isn't something you can replicate easily.

Yet, as soon as I start thinking about that, Oliver's face comes to the forefront of my mind. His smile, his eyes...the way he always knows what to say to make things seem okay. How he puts corny music on my phone to make me smile at random times. How he always knows what I need before I do.

Hazel saved my life at one time. But Oliver brought me back to life. And yes, I could ask him to come over here and do this with me, but that's not where I see us. I see us in a house with a yard. Maybe a pool and an area to have everyone over. I want his summer vacations to be filled with travel and adventures. I want our days and nights to be filled with more love than I ever thought I was capable of having. Hell, I'll even learn about football and go to his games. I bet sitting next to Betsy would make it really fun.

I want the real wedding. I want to walk down the aisle and see Oliver, after Magnolia and Simon paved the way with flower petals. I want to laugh and drink and celebrate our life together. I want to love him. I want him to love me. I want to show him all of the love that I know I have to give, that at one point I didn't think I had.

And I want to do it where we first fell in love.

I never thought in a million years my decision would be this easy. In another life, I would have killed for this kind of job. I would have been on a plane before Hazel could officially transfer me. But I've had this experience. I got to say I did it, and I'm proud of what I did.

Now I want the chance to see where love can take me. Because I bet it's farther than any ocean.

"Thank you for the offer, I'm truly flattered," I begin. "But, if you don't mind, I think I'm going to come back to Nashville. Maybe even move a little closer to you. I kind of miss my husband."

Hazel literally jumps on top of me for a hug. "Wow. What would you have done if I would have said I'm staying here?"

She lets me go and reaches for something in her pocket. "I would have been happy. And I would have given you the note that's in my left pocket."

I give her a questioning look, because I don't know if the time change is messing with her, but I'm downright confused. "What's this?"

Hazel just smiles at me. "Open it."

I do as she says, and as soon as I read the first word, I burst into tears.

"True love is your soul's recognition of its counterpoint in another."
– John Beckwith, Wedding Crashers

I shoot up from the couch and look around. "Where is he?"

Hazel tilts her head toward the offices. "I think if you head that way you'll find him soon enough."

I don't even say goodbye. I just start running. I'm sure everyone is looking at me funny, but I don't care. I need to see my husband.

I turn the corner, and as soon as I do, there he is. Every office light is off except for mine. That's how I can see Oliver in the middle of my office, down on one knee.

Chapter 42
Oliver

THE PLAN WAS SIMPLE.

If she wanted to stay and take the job in London, Hazel would text me her answer. Then I'd come out to where she and Izzy were sitting, and I'd surprise her that way.

But if she said she's coming back home, then the text was telling me to stay put in the office.

It was my idea to add the part where I got down on one knee.

"Oliver?" she says as she walks into her office. "What are you doing here?"

"Something that I've been wanting to do for months now."

Izzy walks up to me as I open the ring box. "Elizabeth McCall..."

"Wait!" she says, pulling me up to my feet.

"I swear to goodness, woman, if you're going to say no after we're already married then I was never meant to propose."

She shakes her head and brings me over to her couch. "I'm just...I'm a little all over the place right now. Where did you come from? How did you get here? When did you see Hazel to give her a note? Why are you wearing a T-shirt with Paddington Bear on it?"

I set the ring down on the table in front of me. "I had time to kill so I walked around. Found this at a cool T-shirt shop."

"Time to kill? How long have you been here?"

I smile as I pull her closer. "I'll tell you all of that, but first, there's something I'm going to need to do."

I place my hand on each of her cheeks, my body immediately rushing with the warmth I've been missing from the touch of her skin. I bring our mouths together in what I'd classify the absolute best kiss of my life. She's grabbing my shirt, trying to bring me closer, or maybe not let me go. I don't know which one, but I'll take either.

As much as I want to keep kissing her, and I plan on doing that for the rest of the night, there's a lot I need to say. And a lot she needed to catch up on.

"Okay, where would you like me to start?"

Izzy shakes her head in confusion. "Let's go with how you got out here. Or maybe why you're here? I feel like both of those are safe places to start."

"Fair enough," I say. "It started yesterday when I was talking to Shane. I was miserable and grouchy. Pretty much how I've been since you left."

"Same."

"I know, but I think I hit a breaking point. I just felt like this time was never going to end, and you were going to forget about me. I was a mess."

"Oh Oliver," she says, bringing me in for another kiss. "I'd never."

"I know. Anyway, Shane came over, and I asked him what he'd do. He said he'd go get the girl. So that's what I did."

This takes her back. "Shane said that? Shane said go do a crazy romantic gesture?"

"Right? I was shocked too. Oh! And I think he has a girlfriend. It might be Amelia. He wouldn't tell me, and I have a lot of feelings on the subject."

"Oliver," Izzy snaps her fingers in front of my face. "Focus."

"Oh, sorry. Where was I?"

"Never-been-in-love-Shane told you to come get me."

"Yes, that's right. So, I called Hazel, because all I knew was to fly to London. I didn't know this secretary, so I couldn't charm her into helping. I figured at least Hazel could get me here and then I'd figure out the rest. So I gave her a call, and I'm glad I did."

Izzy's eyes double in size. "Did she bring you here?"

"Yup," I say. "I got to fly in her new private jet before you did."

Her eyes narrow, but the smirk she's wearing tells me she's not too mad. "I want to be mad at you right now but you're here so I can't."

"You should be. I never want to fly commercial again."

She shakes her head. "I'll hate you later. Continue with the story."

"Anyway, Hazel was coming here anyway for the launch, so that wouldn't have tripped off any alarm bells for you. So I hopped on the flight, and over the course of eight hours we talked. I talked about how much I missed you, but how proud I was of you at the same time. She told me how great of a job you were doing, which I of course knew. And she added that she missed having you around."

"Wait," Izzy says. "The job offer to stay here...was that part of the plan?"

"Yes and no," I say. "Hazel was always going to offer you the job. She knew it was the right thing to do, but that you needed to make the decision on whether to take it or not. When she told me that, I told her I had a similar mind frame. That you needed to pick where you went. Because I knew no matter your decision, that's what I was doing, too."

It takes Izzy a second to process what I just said, and when she does she almost falls off the couch.

"Whoa. Hold the fucking phone. You came all the way out here on the chance that I wasn't coming back with you? Were you ready to move here?"

"I did. And I was," I say, bringing her closer to me. "If there's one thing I've learned these past few months, it's that I need to be where you are. Would I have missed my friends and Mom? Yes. I'd have missed my kids and the team. I've never lived anywhere other than Rolling Hills. But where you are is where I want to be. That's my home. So if that was in London, I'd be here. I figured I could be a real-life Ted Lasso."

Izzy starts laughing. Fuck I've missed that sound. "I don't think you could have pulled off the mustache."

"That's fair."

"Thank you," she says, giving me a quick kiss on the cheek. "The fact that you were going to pick up your life—your entire life—and move here with me means the world to me. But this isn't home."

Even though I know she's already made her decision, I still want to hear this. "It's not?"

"It's not," Izzy says as she laces her fingers with mine. "This was a once-in-a-lifetime experience. While I missed you every day, and Hazel—hell, I even missed Simon a few times—I'm glad I did it. I can say I did this major thing. This really amazing thing that I never dreamed in a million years I'd ever do. Sixteen years ago I thought I was going to be working at a furniture store for the rest of my life, in between popping out children. I thought that's all I had to offer the world. But I did this. I helped launch a major project with a company I love."

"You did. And I'm so damn proud of you."

"Thank you. But while this was fun and exciting, this isn't what I want for the rest of my life. I want you to love me like only you know how to. I want to get a greasy meal at Mona's on Saturday mornings before you drag me to a farmers' market. I want to see you in action while you mold the young lives of Rolling Hills. I want to argue with you about why you don't need another drawer for your socks. I want to have a family. Maybe we'll have biological kids. Maybe we'll be the ones to receive a precious gift from another mother, like your Mom did. Who knows? We have so much time to do this, but we can't do it here."

Holy shit, I know I was here to make the grand gesture, but she's kind of stealing my thunder right now. I don't care though. She can have it all if everything she just said one day happens.

"You want to move to Rolling Hills?"

She nods. "Despite years of saying I'd never go back to small-town life, yes, I want to move to Rolling Hills."

I have so much more I want to say to her, but none of it seems to matter right now. All that matters is kissing the living daylights out of her.

And I do. My force sends her down to the couch, which causes her to laugh. Or maybe it's me peppering her cheek, lips, neck, and everywhere else I can find, with kisses.

"I love you," I say, hating that I have to keep her clothes on for at least a little while longer.

"I love you, too. And I've missed you."

"I've missed you."

Our kisses turn from playful to passionate. I wonder if anyone will be walking by or if they're going to stay occupied at the party in the conference room. But just as I'm trying to figure out how far I need to take off my pants to be able to have sex with my wife, I remember that I forgot one very important thing.

"Wait!" I yell, popping up off Izzy. "Hold on."

"What?"

I take Izzy's hands and sit her back up as I move to the floor and go down on one knee.

"Oliver..."

I grab the ring box from the table and open it. Izzy immediately gasps when she sees the oval-cut diamond.

"Elizabeth McCall, I bought—"

"Wait! Wait for me!"

Izzy and I turn our heads to see Hazel running into the room, phone in hand. "I need to get this on video. I was given strict instructions by Betsy."

We both laugh as we turn back to face each other. She gives me a reassuring smile as I take her left hand in mine.

"Elizabeth McCall, I bought this ring days after we got back from Vegas. You had just told me you wanted a divorce and were going to start a countdown of our sixty days to singledom. But just like I had a feeling about us when I first met you, I had a feeling about us then. What we have is too special to ignore. Most things about us don't make sense. I think the only thing we have in common is each other. But that's all we need. Because what we have is special. What we have is for life."

I need to take a breath, because even though I've done this thirty-four other times, it never gets easier. Even if you're already married.

"Izzy, I want to love you forever. I already know I'm going to, because I don't think I know how to *not* love you. I've done this part a lot, but it's never felt like this. But that's because I've never had a love like yours."

I pause to take the ring out of the box and take Izzy's left hand.

"Izzy, will you marry me? Again?"

Usually this is the part where the silence goes awkward,

which means a no is coming. This time there's silence. Well, except for Hazel crying in the doorway.

"Izzy?"

I look up at her, that devilish smirk gracing her beautiful face.

"I figured I'd make you wait a few before I said yes."

I smile as we both stand up. "All I heard in that was yes."

Izzy wraps her arms around my neck as I do the same around her waist. "Good. That's all you needed to hear."

Home. That's what this feels like. This kiss feels like home and forever.

Exactly how it's supposed to feel.

I break away, giving her one more kiss on the nose before I turn to look at Hazel.

"She said yes!"

Hazel laughs as I go back to kissing my fiancée. Wife. Whatever I want to call her, I know this for certain.

She's mine. Forever.

And I'm hers. For even longer.

Chapter 43
Izzy
~~One month later~~

"Ladies and gentlemen! For the first time, well, technically...not really...is again a better word? Oh, fuck it... ladies and gentlemen, put your hands together for Mr. and Mrs. Oliver McCall!"

"That your doing?" Oliver says to me as we walk hand-in-hand into our reception with the song about being crazy in love playing over the speakers. I can't help but look at Simon—who requested to all of a sudden decided last week he wanted to DJ our reception—as we make our way to the head table. I think he thought it would get him out of flower man duty. It didn't. I can't hold back my laugh as we walk past him in his DJ booth. His tuxedo makes him look like the Easter bunny is going to prom.

"I believe you once said that if I agreed to stay married to you, you'd take my name. Are you going back on your word?"

Oliver twirls me around once we hit the dance floor. "Never."

The applause gets louder as Oliver dips me low, following

me for a kiss that is the perfect amount of seductive, and wedding appropriate.

"You ready to do this, Mrs. Price?"

"After you, Mr. McCall."

Oliver brings me back up and lifts our joined hands as we find our place in the center of the dance floor. We wanted to get the first dance done soon. Well, I did. You know, just in case the panic got a little too real. But now that I'm here, in Oliver's arms, my head resting on his shoulder as we sway back and forth to the first song we danced to all those months ago, I don't want this to end.

Today was surreal, to say the least. And a roller coaster of emotions. All day, leading up to the vow renewal ceremony, I was admittedly nervous. Just the thought of wearing a white dress and going in front of a few hundred people sent me for a mental tailspin. Poor Whitley. She might have served as the event planner, but I don't know if she was ready for my sudden breakdown.

But Hazel knew what to do. She went and got Oliver. Like always, he knew what I needed. Him. He's the only one I need. When the time came to walk down the aisle toward him, there wasn't a drop of anxiety. There wasn't a hint of fear. I was walking toward Oliver; how could I be scared?

It helped that my mother was nowhere near this wedding. She wasn't invited. She knew about it. My sister made sure to tell her where she was going. Her, Jimmy, and the kids all came out. My niece and nephew were both in it, with Magnolia, of course. My sister stood up with me, as did Hazel. Of course, the entire crew was flanking Oliver, including Amelia, who looked quite fashionable in her suit. Simon even wore his pink tuxedo.

He looked quite dapper.

"I finally got my dance."

"You did that night too!"

"Technically, yes. But I wanted one where everyone could see I was dancing with the most beautiful woman in the room."

I smile as I look up to Oliver, who has our joined hands against his heart. "You're persistent, has anyone ever told you that?"

"It's part of my charm."

Oliver pushes me out before spinning me back in, earning him some cheers from our guests. I take a second to look around the room. I see Oliver's mom, holding her heart as the tears fall down her face. I know I broke my promise to her by saying I'd make sure her son didn't get married in Las Vegas, but at least now we were able to give her the wedding she asked for. Then there's all of Oliver's friends, watching us with nothing but love in their eyes. My family might be screwed up in sixteen different ways, but I know I'll never feel like I'm not part of a family. Not while I'm here with Oliver in Rolling Hills.

We're in the same venue that Jake and Whitley used for their wedding. Or, as we like to call it, the scene of the original crime. Before this started, we even got a few pictures of us standing at the bar. The same bartender was even working. And yes, he gave us shit for stealing the champagne.

We made sure to leave him a healthy tip.

After Oliver came out to see me in London, he stayed a few days before he had to go back. Unfortunately, I couldn't go with him. I might not have been staying permanently, but I still had the task of finding the person to lead the team.

Turns out she was right in front of my nose the whole time.

When I approached Bridget about taking the job, she thought I was joking. She spent five minutes making cracks about how she was now technically going to be my boss, and if I was drinking a different kind of English tea. When I didn't reply, she realized I was serious.

When she woke up after fainting, she said yes.

Juliet is going to be her assistant. The London office is in good hands.

As soon as Bridget was settled in, I took the first flight back to Nashville I could find. I thought it was rude that I didn't get to fly back on the private plane, but I didn't say anything when Hazel told me that her gift to Oliver and I was the use of said plane when we finally go on a real honeymoon.

Which, of course, has to happen after football season. Hell, this vow renewal either had to happen today, which fell on a bye week, or we had to wait until January. Oliver and I agreed that we had waited long enough, so Whitley pulled some magic out of her event planner ass and got us in at the place where it all started. We even requested Oliver's room at the hotel instead of the honeymoon suite. I wonder if the old guy's going to be next door to us again.

"Ladies and gentlemen, please come out to the dance floor and join our newly re-married couple for the first official dance of the night."

"When did Simon all of a sudden become a decent DJ?" I ask as couples begin to come out around us.

"I quit trying to figure out Simon years ago. He's a mystery wrapped in a conceited riddle."

We look over to Simon, who's currently having words with the caterer, Charlie. What the hell is he doing?

"Hey, you two," Wes says as he brings Betsy into his arms for a dance. "This is great."

"It is," Betsy adds. "And thank you again for letting Magnolia be in it. I know you didn't have to but it really took the pressure off us."

"Anytime," I say. "Though, just to let you know, I did hear her talking today when we were getting ready about the next time she did this, which was going to be your wedding, she maybe wanted a blue dress. So just be mindful."

"Thanks," Betsy says, but she turns her attention to our right. "Though I don't know if we're going to be next."

The four of us look over to Shane, who's currently sitting at a table, his eyes never leaving Amelia. She's on the dance floor with her son, Luke, who looks like he'd rather be anywhere else.

"Oliver? Izzy?" Whitley says, tapping me on the shoulder. "I'm sorry to interrupt, but how about you head back to the table so Oliver can do the toast. Then we'll cut the cake and get back to the dancing."

"Sounds good."

We do as Whitley says and head back to our table. It's just the two of us since we had such an unbalanced bridal party. But I like it. I also can't believe I like a setup where literally every eye is going to be on me.

Oh, how far I've come.

"Everyone, if I could have your attention," Oliver says as the guests head back to their seats. "I want to thank everyone for coming out tonight. I don't know if everyone knows this, but this place, right here, is where I first met the woman who turned out to be the love of my life..."

I smile up at Oliver as he tells the tale of how we met. Well, the PG-rated version. I can feel the smile on my face as I listen to him talk. I told him I didn't want to make a speech tonight, but if I did, this is what I'd say:

I'd like to take the time to thank all thirty-three other women who said no to this man. I'd actually like to interview them and ask what was wrong with him. Too nice? Too sweet? Too caring? Too handsome? Too good in bed? Too patient? Yes, I can see where all of those things must just be horrible to have to deal with in a partner.

Even when I was stuck in my ways, I knew Oliver was a catch. I was stubborn, not an idiot.

I'd also like to thank my shithead ex and my horrible

excuses for parents. I hate to talk ill of the dead, but my dad had just as much to do with what happened sixteen years ago, so he gets lumped in. Without them, strangely enough, I wouldn't be here. And here is the only place I want to be.

I've thanked Hazel a million times, but I'd thank her again. I'd thank her for the years of support and friendship. And for seeing what was in front of me before I knew it.

I'd thank Wes, Betsy, Shane, Amelia, and Simon. I remember being intimidated when Oliver told me about the close knit friend group he had, but since day one, these people made me feel like family. Oliver once told me about the family you choose, and now I know what he means. And I'm so grateful they chose me.

And speaking of choosing me...my husband. Though, now that I think of it, and as the applause resonates through the banquet room, I want to thank him in person.

"Whitley?" I flag her over to our table. "Is it okay if Oliver and I go take a minute outside to ourselves?"

"Of course," she says. "It's your day. Take all the time you need."

Oliver looks at me, slightly confused, as we walk out to the patio.

"Why do I immediately smell whiskey and champagne when I step out here?"

I laugh as I hold each of his hands. "Every time I smell either I think of us."

"How romantic."

We both laugh as I bring our joined hands up between us. "You've always said that you knew from the moment you asked me to dance that I was different."

He nods. "I have."

"Well, this is the spot I realized that about you."

His eyes grow wide at my confession. "Really?"

"Yeah," I say, taking a few steps closer to where we sat that night. "This is where we first danced. This is where I told you something about me no one knew. I'd never done that before. I remember it scaring the shit out of me. And I didn't know what was happening. Turns out, I was just falling in love."

Oliver leans down as our lips meet. Love. That's all I feel when I kiss Oliver. Love and forever.

From the sound of the music inside, Whitley has let the guests back on the dance floor, but they can go without us for another minute.

"I know I said I didn't want to make a speech, but I did want to tell you something. I've loved you since day one. I didn't know it. In fact, it took me months to know I did. I'm sorry it took me so long, but thank you for loving me back. Thank you for seeing what I didn't see. And thank you for waiting. Thank you for coming to get me. Just...thank you."

Oliver lifts me up, making it a little easier for our lips to meet one more time. This kiss is a little more intense than the last one. I have to remember we're in front of a glass wall and that every guest can see us.

They're really cramping our style.

"Guys?" Whitley says, interrupting us. "I'm sorry, but Simon is going rogue, so we need to cut the cake soon."

We both laugh as Oliver puts me down. "We'll be right in."

I start walking toward the reception, but Oliver pulls me back. "We've been told to go in."

He shakes his head. "I have something I want to say."

"Well, then, by all means..."

"Thank you," he says. "Thank you for not giving up on love, even when you thought you did. Thank you for letting me into your life. Thank you for giving me what I'd always dreamed of but never thought was going to happen. Thank you for being you. And thank you for loving me."

Oh for fuck's sake...he's going to make me cry. Or jump him. One of the two. Maybe both.

"Come on," I say, pulling him toward the door. "Let's go."

"What? No kiss? I give you that whole romantic speech, and I don't get anything?"

"Nope," I say as we approach the door. "If I kiss you after that, I'm going to be having sex with you on this patio, and I'm pretty sure we'd traumatize our guests. Especially if you let a 'good girl' fly."

Oliver opens the door for me, but not before a playful smack to my ass as I enter. "Remember that for later, Mrs. Price."

"Oh I will, Mr. McCall. I absolutely will."

Epilogue

Shane

~Jake and Whitley's wedding, six months ago ~

"Shane?"

"Yeah?"

"I need to fix this."

I take a sip of my drink before telling Wes that yes, in fact, he is a dumbass. "No shit, Sherlock."

He slams his hands on the table at the wedding reception before walking off, thankfully not toward the dance floor where Betsy is dancing with one of the Nashville Fury players. It's nothing suggestive or sexual. Just two people having a good time.

They aren't the only ones. Tons of people are on the dance floor as the song changes from a fast, upbeat one to a slower ballad. I'm not one of those people. I don't dance. I never have. I'm a proponent of not doing things you don't want to do. Like now, I don't want to dance with the few women who have made eyes at me tonight. I don't want to follow Wes as he tries not to punch a hole in the wall. I don't even want to go and stand at the bar and drink with Oliver. No, I'd rather sit at this table, sip my whiskey, and stew as I watch husbands and wives, couples, and even strangers, make their way to the dance floor.

Especially one couple.

Like she knows I'm thinking about her, I see Amelia walk onto the dance floor, hand-in-hand with the guy who has been hitting on her all day. He's about my height, at six-foot-two, and well built, likely one of the many professional football players or coaches in attendance tonight. I wanted to put my fist through his face at the ceremony when I saw him kiss her hand. I almost flipped a table watching them dance earlier.

And now, as I watch him pull her so close there's barely enough room for air between them, I might kill a man.

What is Amelia doing? She doesn't do this. She doesn't dance or date or hang out with men. And why is she laughing like he just told her the world's best joke?

Wait...is he pulling her closer? How can that happen? Wait...is he about to kiss her?

Fuck this shit...

I feel my hand tighten around my rocks glass as I watch this play out. He doesn't kiss her, but their foreheads are touching, and that's just as bad.

I'm shocked I don't break the glass. But holding onto this is the only thing keeping me from racing to the dance floor and pulling her away from him. I know I need to look away, but I can't stop staring at her. It's been like this all day. It's like my eyes are searching for her every second.

I've always thought Amelia was beautiful in her understated way. Her curves are subtle, and she rarely shows them, but today, in her fitted pink dress, every single one is highlighted. My mouth has been watering since the second I saw her walk into the ceremony. She's wearing makeup, which is another rarity, but it's not what makes her beautiful. It's highlighting her already perfect features. Like her eyes. Her brown eyes seem to be sparkling. Her long brown hair is styled in a way I've never seen before, with soft curls hitting at her shoulder.

All those things are different about Amelia, but that's not what I'm being drawn to tonight. No, it's that for the first time in a long time, she looks happy. Free. Like she doesn't have the weight of the world on her shoulders as a single mom to two kids. Or a demanding career. She just looks like a woman who's enjoying her night.

And I'm the bastard who's about to ruin it.

I look around, hoping that one of my friends is here to stop me from doing the stupid thing I'm about to do. Not that they would know what they're stopping me from. None of them know I've been in love with Amelia for decades. That I once kissed her. That since I can remember, I've pushed down feelings for her because I couldn't risk ruining our friendship. Or risk ruining the dynamic of our friend group.

All of those reasons are feeling flimsy as hell right now.

I remember years ago when I decided I was going to kiss her. It was a split-second decision. Like the wire had snapped, and it would be the biggest regret of my life if I didn't kiss her.

That's what I'm feeling right now. I know I need to be stopped. But I also don't want to be.

I look around to see if any are near me. Wes is gone, hopefully trying to figure out how to get Betsy back. Oliver's at the bar hitting on a leggy redhead. My guess is he's three drinks away from proposing. I have no idea where Simon is after he randomly got up from the table and stomped away.

I need to let this go. Or if I'm going to stay, I need to ignore Amelia and the Fury asshole. It's not my place. I'm her friend. That's it. I'm Uncle Shane to her kids. The guy who mows her lawn and shovels her driveway because that's the kind of friend I am.

I kissed her once and it could've ruined everything. The only reason it didn't is because I left for the Army the next day and was gone for the better part of the following eight years. If I do something stupid again, I'll have to face the consequences. And I don't know if I'm ready for that.

Sit still Shane. Breathe. Take another drink of whiskey. Don't look at her. Ignore that her lips are now dangerously close to that fucker's mouth.

Fuck! How can I ignore that? I can't.

I won't.

I'm about to do something stupid again, aren't I?

Fuck…I am.

I can't hold back any longer. Maybe it's the whiskey talking. Maybe it's knowing that Amelia has only dated—or been married to—losers and assholes. Maybe it's still thinking about that kiss from seventeen years ago way too often. But I can't sit by and watch this happen.

Especially now that his hands are starting to drift down lower and lower on her back.

Fuck. That. Shit.

I nearly knock my chair over as I stand up and march to the dance floor. The song ends as soon as I get to Amelia, giving me the perfect opportunity to grab her hand and pull her off the dance floor. I hear her say a quick "Sorry!" as I all but drag her outside.

"Shane?" Amelia asks, clearly confused about what's going on. "What are you doing?"

My hand tightens on hers as I take us to the terrace. There seems to be a dark corner out of sight from the ballroom. I don't know if it's truly private, but it must be better than being in front of every wedding guest who just watched me drag Amelia away like a caveman.

"What the hell, Shane?" she says, pulling her hand away and shaking her arm.

"What were you doing in there?"

Amelia looks at me like I'm crazy, which I might be. "You're going to have to be more specific."

"In there." I point back toward the reception. "Who were you with?"

"Anthony?"

Why is she asking me like I should know?

"I don't know. That fucker who was all over you?"

She rolls her eyes at me, which is warranted. "Oh, my God. Yes, his name is Anthony. And he wasn't all over me."

"Who is he?"

"Why do you care?"

"Humor me."

Amelia lets out a frustrated groan. "Anthony is a Fury coach. We met before the ceremony. He's nice. And polite. And funny. And I thought, you know, because I'm a grown woman, I could dance with a man without being tarred and feathered for it."

"That was dancing?" I say with a bite. "I didn't realize you needed to be that close to dance. Who knew?"

Amelia's eyes are beginning to bulge out of her head. And, because I know her so well, I realize she's five seconds away from ripping me a new asshole. Fine. I'll take it. As long as it means she's away from Coach Grab Ass.

"You're fucking unbelievable!" She starts pacing back and forth, throwing her hands in the air. "Why do you care? Why can't you let me live my life? Are you my keeper tonight? Is that why you've been staring at me all day? If so, I apologize; I didn't know I needed to ask permission to dance with a man who I find nice and attractive. Oh, and have I mentioned that what I do in my private life is none of your business?"

"Nice? Attractive? Really, Amelia? Don't act like you're interested in this guy. You barely know him."

"Are you kidding me?" she screams. "I can't with you. This is always how it is."

"How what is?"

"This! You. Me. The rest of the idiots we call friends. Ever since my divorce—which was *seven years ago*, by the way—whenever I show interest in someone, one of you idiots gets involved and ruins it. Either I get the third degree, or worse, they do. Or you run them off. The others have cooled off over the years, but you? You seem to have made it your personal mission to make sure I die alone."

I take a few slow breaths as I do my best to push down the words that are threatening to come out. "I'm just trying to protect you."

"Protect me? From what? Dating? The outside world? What is it, Shane? Tell me." She takes a few deep breaths to calm down, but it doesn't lower the sound of her voice. "I know you've saved me before. And I'll always be grateful for that. But what are you saving me from now? I'd love to know. Because all I see here is a man, who claims to be my best friend, treating me like I'm a dumb woman who can't make her own choices."

I don't say anything. I can't. She's right. I do all those things. I'm doing them right now. But I can't tell her why I do them, so I don't say anything.

"Of course, the trademark Shane Cunningham silence," she says, her voice growing louder. "Well, since you have nothing to say, let me tell you this: I'm a divorced, single mom of two exhausting teenagers. I rarely get nights to truly let my hair down and forget about my responsibilities. And you know what? I did. I was having fun. I didn't feel guilty for living a little. I was having a lovely evening with a lovely man until you pounded your chest and dragged me away because apparently, fun isn't allowed where you're concerned."

"You can have fun."

This makes her laugh, though I doubt she's finding it very funny. "You really don't get it, do you? You're supposed to be my best friend. Same with Wes and Oliver and Simon, but you more than anyone. You know everything I've been through. Everything *we've* been through. So why? Why can't you let me have this? Why do you insist on being my unofficial bodyguard? Why for one night can't you let me be a single woman who wants to have a good time at a wedding and not worry about work, or my kids, or—"

She doesn't see it coming. She didn't see it coming seventeen years ago, either.

I just grab her and kiss her. I kiss *the hell* out of her. I kiss her the way I've wanted to kiss her for years.

And in that moment, I know that now everything is about to change...

Hold up! Did you think we were done with Oliver and Izzy? Well we aren't. For the first time ever, I have a deleted scene to share. It's the wedding. The day that Oliver has wanted his entire life. The one Izzy never thought would happen. Scan the QR code to get the deleted scene!

As you could judge by the epilogue, Shane and Amelia are next in The One I Love. Did I put in that kiss to tease everyone? Maybe. Is their story going to be a friends-to-lovers story with a fake engagement thrown in? Also maybe.

Fine, the answer is yes to both.

Also by Chelle Sloan

All titles available with Kindle Unlimited

THE NASHVILLE FURY, PRO FOOTBALL SERIES

Off the Record (A secret relationship, office romance)

Off Track (A surprise pregnancy romance)

Off Season (A second chance romance)

Off Limits (A sibling's best friend, close proximity romance)

NASHVILLE FURY WORLD

Off the Market at Christmas (A childhood friends-to-lovers, opposites attract romance

LOVE ONLINE SERIES

Thirst Trap (A one-night-stand turned more, social media romance)

Match Maker (A female billionaire/blue collar mechanic, fake dating romance)

Run Run Rudolph (A celebrity on the run, one bed romance)

ROLLING HILLS

The One I Want (A single dad/nanny, age gap romance)

The One I Need (An opposites attract, accidental marriage romance)

The One I Love (A friends-to-lovers, secret relationship romance)

The One I Hate (An enemies-to-lovers romance - Coming April 2024)

THE SALVATION SOCIETY

Reformation: A Salvation Society Novel (A friend's-to-lovers, redemption romance)

Acknowledgments

This book was unlike anything I've ever written. I've never written a hero like Oliver. Izzy I knew was going to be a force of a heroine when I introduced her in Match Maker, but I never knew *how* much of a force she was.

Then I realized somewhere along the way that this was my therapy book. I'm a little like Oliver. I'm single, and though I've never been proposed to, I have caught the bouquet at 15 weddings in my lifetime. And then there's Izzy, who had an ex who made her think she wasn't capable of love. I had one of those. And yes, the man who got punched by Oliver was his name.

Somehow, without me even knowing, I put a little of me into each of these characters. Before I knew it, this book was healing me in a way I never imagined.

So thank you Oliver and Izzy. You have no idea how much this book has helped me. And I hope everyone loves it as much as I do.

Now to the things that won't make me cry when I write them...

First and foremost, my parents. As always, you are my biggest cheerleaders even if you still have no idea what I'm doing. You've allowed me to follow my dreams and my path, and for that I am forever grateful.

To my family and friends: Your support has been amazing.

Many of you have no clue how I ended up here, but that doesn't mean the support hasn't been there. I love you all.

Kelly, you've been with me on this book journey since day one. Not only are you an amazing alpha reader, but you are an amazing friend.

Amanda, who would have thought when we met seven years ago that one day we'd be here together? Thank you for keeping my life in order. Thank you for reminding me to drink water. And thank you for being my best friend.

Julia, Georgia, Mae and Claire: How did I write a book before I met you ladies? All I know is I don't ever want to write one without y'all again.

Kiezha, thank you for correcting my bad grammar habits and being an amazing editor.

Michele: Thank you for dotting the Is and crossing the Ts.

Corinne, I'm here because of you. If you wouldn't have given me a chance I wouldn't have started writing. You forever changed my life.

Adriana, thanks for always picking up the phone and procrastinating with me. And special shout out for our first crossover. That was fun. We should do it again sometime.

Last but not least: Readers. I love you all. Whether this was your first book by me, or you've been here since Reformation, I'm truly thankful for all of you. There are so many amazing authors you could be reading. I'm humbled that you chose me.

About the Author

Known for her witty sense of humor, Chelle Sloan is a former sports editor who recently completed her Masters in Journalism. She's now putting that to good use—one happily ever after at a time.

An Ohio native, she's fiercely loyal to Cleveland sports, is the owner of way too many — yet not enough — tumblers and will be a New Kids on the Block fan until the day she dies. She does her best writing at Starbucks, or anywhere that's not her house. Oh, and yes, you probably saw her on TikTok.

As for her own happily every after? Maybe one day...

Stay up to date with all things Chelle & join the VIP Squad!

Made in United States
Troutdale, OR
01/20/2024